"A deeply sensitive book!"

—CLIFFORD D. SIMAK

THE TWO OF THEM
JOANNA RUSS

"... is frightening because of the power of its portrait of a future sexist society and because of its heroine, the rebellious product of an American '50s upbringing and savior of a little girl being driven mad on her own planet. It would be nice if this were a comedy, but it isn't."

—*Louisville Courier-Journal*

"Beyond questions of genre or gender, Joanna Russ is one of the best prose writers working in the English language today. *The Two of Them* is informed throughout by her intelligence, wit and imagination ... by *her vision of the pertinence and necessity of speculative fiction to feminists.*"

—MARILYN HACKER

THE TWO OF THEM

Joanna Russ

A BERKLEY BOOK
published by
BERKLEY PUBLISHING CORPORATION

Berkley Publishing Corporation
200 Madison Avenue
New York, New York 10016

SBN 425-04106-9

BERKLEY BOOKS are published by
Berkley Publishing Corporation
BERKLEY BOOK ® TM 757,375

Printed in the United States of America

Berkley Edition, JUNE, 1979

This book is dedicated to Suzette Hayden Elgin, who has generously allowed me to use the characters and setting of her short story, "For the Sake of Grace," as a springboard to a very different story of my own.

THE TWO
OF THEM

HERE THEY ARE. They're entirely in black, with belted tabards over something like long underwear that make them look like the cards in *Alice*, though nobody here has heard about that. They're not—at the moment—wearing guns. Both are tall; the elder (grey-haired, clean-shaven, approaching fifty) has the beaked nose, high cheekbones, and deep-set dark eyes of a desert prophet; the younger (by twenty years) is a stockier sort with the flat dish-face of a Slav peasant: dab of a nose, washed-out eyes, and that no-color, fine hair the Russians go in for when they forget to be blond. They're white, but this must be understood conventionally; it excludes snow-color and paper-color. Around them is the cave of Ala-ed-Deen, a little tacky perhaps and too much early Manet in the moveables; there are embroidered pillows, filigreed screens, inlaid tables, little tabourets, figured hangings, heaps of rugs, everything fretted and pierced and decorated with endlessly repeated geometrical motifs; but there are no plants anywhere, living or in pictures, and there are no pictures of anyone or anything.

1

The Jewish prophet stands, leaning against a wall hanging, his arms folded except that now and again one strays free and he taps his thumb thoughtfully against his teeth; the other sits cross-legged on cushions, reading aloud from a large book, which is illuminated like a medieval manuscript. This is how the book goes:

And the maiden Enees-el-Jelees was the daughter of the Wezeer Abd-el-Hassan, who served in that time Sultan Haroon-er-Rasheed may his name be exalted forever—thought they'd miss that—*and he had given him Budr-el-Badr to wife. And this was the manner of the appearance of Enees-el-Jelees, she was like unto the letter Aleph, her gait was as the Oriental willow, her eyebrows met across her forehead, her face appeared shining as the full moon, and upon her cheek was a mole like ambergris. Three days after, as she went with her maidens into the bath*—tittering like mad, I suppose—*there appeared to them a Jinneeyeh of the most frightful and hideous aspect, having upon each shoulder three arms and upon each arm three hands, and long black nails of surpassing filthiness and blackness*—like every other Jinn in the book—*and thick lips and a black face*—racists—*and tangled hair like a cloud of smoke, and this Jinneeyeh spake unto Enees-el-Jelees,* spake for God's sake, spake, *saying 'Fear not, thou temptation to God's creatures, I am Muslimeh, that is to say, of the believing Jinn,' and snatching up the maiden Enees-el-Jelees, carried her swiftly through the air*—

Snapping the book shut. "They're cracked," and if you yourself had been there you would have noticed that the

2

book's cover—which resembled embossed leather a little and embossed paper a little and cloth not at all—was really quilted polyethylene bonded to some sort of fill. As is the surface of the tabouret on which it now lies. (Both are intricately and elaborately figured in red, blue, and gold.)

The younger adds with venom, "Racists!"

The elder points out mildly that the culture is third generation and undoubtedly won't last. "Once they get over the excommunication—"

"Did Islam do that? I'd no idea they were so sensible. Throw them out on their ear, right."

"Isn't there anything...?" (pointing to the book).

"No," she says, getting to her feet in one motion, her dead-colored Polish eyes most nasty, no thick lips, no black hair, no nine hands; "There is a prince, see, and he's graceful as the Oriental willow, his face is as the full moon, he has a mole like ambergris, and his brows meet. He is addressed as 'thou temptation to God's creatures.' His name is Mes'ood. Everybody's got a name, even the Jinn. What's-her-name, no, not this one" (stabbing the air in the direction of the book) "sees him through the lattice of the window of the *hareem* as he's playing *goff*. That's not what you think; it's a kind of polo. She throws him a note composed of sixteen classical verses, quoted in full. Her gait is like the Oriental willow, her face like the full moon, her brows meet, and she has a mole, et cetera. He sends her a note composed of twenty-four classical verses. They meet. Then it's 'Efreets again. To say that you spit. Guess what color 'Efreets. Twelve hundred pages. I told you they were cracked."

He says, "But *The Thousand and One Nights* is that long, Irene." (Saying it the British way, I-ree-nee.)

She says, "*The Arabian Nights* is genuine. It wasn't published last week."

3

He says, "Ah! so much?" meaning not the book's date of publication but her own dislike, and she adds, "Mind your business, Conscience Neumann. No advice now. You report later, that's your business."

She says then, "I know what it is, Ernst; you're fretting because you can't sit down properly. It's a damned imposition, but they do have benches or something; they're mentioned in the book. I'll find one."

He produces from his barrel chest a sound like a rumble: "I can stand." He adds, "I didn't ask you here, Sklodowska, don't blame me."

Irenee Waskiewicz throws back her head, laughing, and slides delightedly down the wall and onto a heap of rugs. She puts her head on one bent knee, hair falling around her face. He has an immense power to please her and is himself vastly pleased by it; this name—Maria Sklodowska Curie, her Nobel prize-winning daughters Eve and Irene, all three countrywomen of hers, all three famous; she's hardly ever so pleased, not even when he calls her Mikolaj Kopernik. Sklodowska means: *I know your anger is only put on*, Kopernik is for admiring surprise, and the name of Augusta, Lady Lovelace, Byron's daughter, whose mother was a mathematician, who bred racehorses, and (for the eccentric genius Babbage, who invented and built the first computer, out of wood) created binary numbers . . . well, Lady Lovelace means something else.

Some things to know: that she was his pupil for seven years before she became one of The Gang. That there are people who like titles and so call The Gang something else; these two just call it The Gang. That earlier he had got her out of a very bad place, which was something like this place, though not to look at. That she's been assigned here and didn't want to come, though it's supposed to be some sort of vacation, an Honor Guard to a diplomatic

4

mission. That upon learning his name, she said, "Yes, of course, you are the most earnest-looking person I ever saw in my life; of course, your name is Ernst" (and later, "It has always been my ambition to love someone of the name of Ernst; that name inspires absolute confidence.". He had answered, dazzled, "Kopernik!" for they shared a culture—if not quite the same world). That this dignified Jewish refugee, who had been tormented by the other schoolboys in England, had chosen—when his deep, dark, beautiful eyes were set in a face very much younger than it is now—or had been given (it was a long time ago) his new name: the earnest new man. That Waskiewicz was given her at birth, likewise Irene, but that she saved herself in adolescence by thinking of herself as Irenee Adler, *the* woman. A sample:

He: Who owns, names.

She (curiously): Don't you mean "He who?"

He: I do not.

He says, "Do you know, Irenee, I think we were sent here because we look so unlike the people here. To be impressive. You know?"

"Impressive, my eye," she says. "In long black underwear? We're as impressive as hatstands. If The Gang ever wore dress uniforms, we'd all drop dead of the shock."

He thinks: *You'd complain in Heaven, just to keep your credit up*. Ernst does not ordinarily attend to the form of words other people use, perhaps because of his childhood (five countries in six years), and having been able to translate Irene as soon as he met her—though no one else can, or she talks that way to no one else—says only:

"Oh sure, there is the contrast." As usual, his "sure" is attended by the ghost of a polite, a European "surely."

She says, "Seriously, Ernst, for myself I can see it but

5

you're Semitic enough. Damn it, you look Semitic. Have they changed themselves that much?"

He nods. "I've seen them. Got here yesterday, you know. With the gravity set a fifth lower, they can do anything they like, I suppose. Within reason. But they stay small. So we—"

"Are Neanderthals," she says. "Yes, of course, great ugly beasts. Only bigger. And how we stand out in all this clutter!" He can't read her voice now. When Irene is really thinking she becomes opaque to him and he automatically switches to her words.

He says, "Well, there's nothing to do. Nobody expects a row. Unless you start one. I am worried about you, Irene."

"Me?" she says. "Oh, I'll try, but I won't get to first base." There's a moment's gap. He doesn't know what *first base* is. They look for a moment at each other and register—momentarily—that they've again hit one of those minute differences between the United States of America and the North American Commonwealth. Both of them know about Hitler, about Stalin, about the two World Wars, about Mao, but now they can't (for the life of them) remember which world is which. One reason they're so often paired for work in The Gang.

She says, "I told you about bezbol."

"No, *I* told *you*."

"Ah, yes. Different rules."

"Lady Lovelace!" he says, shaking his head in admiration.

She says, closing her eyes patiently, "Ernst, again tonight? At your age?"

So now you know what "Lady Lovelace" means.

● ● ●

6

At night, half-asleep, two shadows, her breath warm on his bare shoulder, that poky ridge his lust or his hipbone, which?

One sleepy voice says, "Alabama."

"Arkansas," says the other.

"Spain."

"Nebraska."

"*Another* A? Armenia."

"Aruns."

"What?"

"It's real."

"The dickens it is."

"Yes it is."

She says, sleepy and exasperated, "What I have to put up with."

"But Irenee," (pedantically) "it is really true in my world. So it's all right."

She sits up in bed with a hoarse ultimatum: "Common names only!"

There is an earthquake among the shadows, someone's arms, his or hers, a dark arm, a light arm, cross-barred in moonlight, impossible to see clearly.

A loud "Ow!"

"Oh my." Concern and movings about.

"Huh! Aruns." She adds, "The Seychelles."

"What?"

"Seychelles, the. The Seychelles. S at the beginning to hook up with Aruns, which has an S at the end."

"Are you sure—"

She sits up, desperate, in the moonlight: "My living God, why do we always go on like five-year-olds?"

"Everyone does." He means: *lovers always do.*

She's silent for a moment, and—not moving or speaking in the darkness—vanishes. Then she says, "All right, let's stop. Let's fuck."

He laughs helplessly in the dark: "You're so graceful."

A flurry, a lot more moving around.

"I *said* the Seychelles. Listen, next time let's stick to names we both know, right?"

A long silence. The two of them as isolated in unseeing as a raft on the sea, a raft, holding one or two survivors, which slides about on the watery element effectively enough but is so small that it's impossible to spot from the air or from a ship, and therefore it's alone.

She says bitterly, "Playing games—!"

That was two nights ago.

The old, familiar misery, the unmistakable flavor of it: involuted, impossible, self-caused. Lying awake when he's not, exiled to some awful promontory of consciousness, shadows, and wishing. Wishing what. She turns, stretches carefully (for something to do), and stares into the dark. Tears in her eyes. Maybe count until morning, see what large aggregations you can come up with.

He gasps. Over and over again. Standing neatly on a desert island, like the one in the cartoons, carrying the valise he carried so long ago from country to country, the sand always on the point of giving out under his feet, soon he'll be standing on water. He can't move, switched off from the neck down. Anyway, there's nowhere to go.

He's having a nightmare.

Tears of self-pity in her eyes, she shakes the sleeper awake; she looks impatient (if anyone had been awake to see her), brow furrowed and underlip caught between her teeth. She shakes him urgently, quite selfishly.

"What? What?" He comes up a bit wildly, not with the full force of the dream but disjointed, alarmed, not quite awake. She draws back more gently, better now that he's really there, and since she's happier, suddenly more considerate.

She says softly, "What's the matter?"

He groans, protesting at being pulled out of sleep, "Ahhh, no, no!"

"Ernst?"

He says, "I was on this damn island with this damn suitcase. Going to drown, you know."

She says, "I don't think either of us wants to go tomorrow." She scratches the end of her nose. Almost conversationally she adds, "Why on earth were you carrying a suitcase? What was in it?"

"A Jew," he says. She looks imperceptibly at him, then down at her knees. "Oh my." She adds, "Oh, I don't think you look as Jewish as all that."

After a silence he says: "I don't want to go, either."

Ernst Neumann wants to retire.

He's been playing with the idea for several years now, that is, for some time after he trained Irenee Waskiewicz, of whom he thinks often as a kind of junior partner or an heir, sometimes (with sophisticated surprise) as his daughter, sometimes (with genuine simplicity) as his son. He's proud of her; he's beginning to be tired. It'll be some time before his mental field becomes so massively or so completely reversed from what it was, but he likes to play games with the idea. He knows that Irenee still thinks she will live forever and this amuses him and touches him, although he's careful not to let her know it. (She would deny it.) At times—to himself—he thinks, "When I stop working, I'll—" or simply "When I retire," and the words are sweet in themselves, quite apart from any clear idea. He doesn't think of it seriously yet. He thinks of keeping bees or raising roses. Outwardly he has never been better; he knows that. He also knows that his childhood deformed him or scarred him in some way he'll never get over, or rather he believes that everyone's childhood does so, though he's not aware of making a certain distinction between his own childhood and his pupil's, that he is *scarred* but she is *deformed*. The new place poses similar dangers for both kinds of mental process, he knows that. His nightmare, sometimes disguised, sometimes not, has accompanied him most of his life like the famous Examination Dream, across four worldly continents, across more worlds than continents, more years than worlds. Foreign service families, army brats, and people like that have this common quality, the ability to get along anywhere and be at home nowhere.

It occurs to him that Irenee is not like that; you can see the strain that new places put on her, she has no detachment and insists on being truly at home everywhere, she doubles up and groans with frustrated exhortation at every change.

Scarred, he thinks. *Deformed*, he thinks.

He says, "You can't sleep?"

There's a third party to this triangle on Ka'abah, a little man who's a bit fussy but quite harmless, really, and next to our heroes, although not unnaturally small for his own race and certainly not thin, he is of such a different appearance, such different bearing, of such a manner and such sidelong, self-important, busy... but you've already ended the sentence. He's working at a computer outlet, attending to family business. His name is Wezeer (this is a common title now) 'Alee Shems-er-Nehar, also 'Alee the grandson of Bekkar, and if you want to know which it is, it's both. These people stand upon newly invented ceremonies, which are their lights, and they do the best they can by their lights.

But what color, what shape, what pattern, and of what intensity are the lights of the son of Bekkar (also his name)? Have they shone steadily all his life? Do they occasionally go out? What is their function, their operation, their significance, and their flicker (or pulsation) in the matrices of his mind?

Don't shoot the player piano; it's doing the best it can.

Ka'abah has almost nothing in the way of public accommodation, and what there is (they don't encourage strangers) has been severely taxed by the diplomatic-economic meeting now in progress. So 'Alee Shems-er-Nehar is playing host. As he enters his mock-Arabian cozy-corner between the curtains (the right height for him, but they keep hitting Irene in the eye) both strangers have the same flash of memory: that Richard halved an iron bar with his sword and Sala-ed-deen a feather. This much they have in common, probably from the same novel.

He offers them tel-o-tales so that they may never get lost but always be found, and both—seeing instantly that the things can be turned off—accept without bothering to consult one another.

'Alee says, "Welcome, thou. Welcome, thou." So far,

11

routine. This is Ka'abah's idea of a first greeting, and he won't use it again. People starting a new society often do things like this, not because the details matter but because they impart the ritual feeling of being inside a play or story. So with him. There's a little flash of pleasure inside his lights. He bows (Indian-style, but he doesn't know that).

Ernst Neumann bows.

Irenee Waskiewicz bows.

The grandson of Bekkar is in scale with his surroundings but not so these Impossibles; for the first time he's able to get a good look at them. They terrify him, so he darts up at them the fiery glance the poet hath named Moonbow.

"Mash' Allah!"

He bows (again).

The elder brother bows.

The younger brother bows, rather sourly.

The young one, the ill-looking one, the evil one! He knows he's being superstitious. If there were a Wife-stealer, this is what It would look like. (He sees the unhappy woman being carried away, separated from him by the pane of glass of the television screen, her arms held out beseechingly, terror in her eyes.) No, he's not fond of that young man. The standards of beauty on Ka'abah are finicky and though Shems-er-Nehar is prepared to accept into the medieval canon foreigners with gap-brows, one cannot after all tolerate people with brows of no color at all. There is a saying that no man is truly fine-looking who could not play the role of female impersonator in the theatre, and this great, pale, lounging brute with the death-colored eyes and the disappearing hair could never be mistaken for a woman; he has no grace and no virile beauty. He is unhealthily fat. The son of Bekkar decides that in the absence of the female principle, the male

12

principle has overbloomed and is tending towards its own extinction, that is, cunning, shapelessness, and pure matter. He has seen eunuchs impersonated in plays; he knows what he is looking at. The balancing of male and female is a great matter on Ka'abah, for each alone tends to become a caricature of its opposite. Thus one must marry, however formally, and thus the Wife-stealer and the unmarried woman.

Bleach-face (fish-face) compounds his host's prejudices by actually sitting down in his host's presence, lowering himself to the carpet on great, ungainly muscles.

'Alee decides to show them that he can be impolite, too; *he* sits down.

Elder Brother smiles graciously and sits.

Perhaps the point has not been taken. Abandoning it (for their rudeness may have been accidental) he bows again, from the waist, and keeping his eyes on the unpleasant phenomenon that has walked into his house, ventures a remark on the impending economic treaty, that trade between worlds (he says "nations") is a desirable thing, and that Ka'abah has great natural resources (he doesn't specify), its people's ingenuity, and their long history.

"We are glad to be here," says Elder Brother.

Younger Brother says, "Thanks for putting us up."

'Alee cannot mention—not yet, anyway—the possibility of wrangling over the treaty; this precludes asking how long the visitors will be staying and that means you can't ask them what would make them most comfortable. Manners narrow possibilities. He looks dubious and pulls at his beard, thus signifying his concern; he asks them if they would like refreshment.

He says, wondering what sort of ghastly behaviors they may bring forth to complicate his life, "This son can punch the computer terminal for food. One can do that.

This son's son can do that. Or drink. Or set the household machines to do so. One can do that." (Having your robots order anything is an expensive game in other nations; here they are very serious about robots' possessing "shadow-life." They have to be; otherwise they'd run into the same prohibition as the one against representative art.)

"You are very kind," says Elder Brother. That's quite human. Younger Brother smiles, transforming his face into something almost manly.

"I believe we would like something to drink," says Younger Brother.

"Oh, good!" says 'Alee, forgetting his manners. It is, truly, heartfelt gratitude to Younger Brother for assuming the position of guest—the arrogant one who says *I*. The host must be self-forgetful. Rising, the son of Bekkar claps his hands twice (you can get a surprisingly loud sound out of this and they've had three generations in which to practice) whereupon part of the tabouret near the elbow of Younger Brother lights up, revealing itself to be another computer terminal. Something like a large humming top enters the room, using the same gap in the curtains their host had, but the barbarians show no special interest in it. It's an allover Household Gadget, economy model, and several years obsolete.

"This is a true person," says 'Alee absently; "It has shadow-life," unaware of Younger Brother looking at Elder Brother and Elder looking at Younger. "Order drink," he says to the machine, specifying *nebeedh*, and the machine spins to the tabouret (brushing against Younger Brother's skirt), extends a metal finger, and turning from side to side, pushes the proper terminals. Household Alls have imitation faces which serve as codes for what they can do; this one has, shallowly molded in a plate set on the top, shut eyes, a squidge of a nose, and a perpetual, simple smile. It spins out. Having demonstrated that he is a man of substance, 'Alee now takes the *nebeedh* from a cupboard in the wall, where the household computer has just placed it, and serves it to the guests, bowing. They take it. It is mere politeness for the householder not to drink himself, but to attend with much feeling the guests' drinking.

They sip at their ruby-and-gold glasses. He would swear that Younger Brother has just made a face at the computer terminal.

"Are you well?" says 'Alee.

They admit that they are well.

"And yourself?" says Elder Brother.

"And your family?" says Younger Brother. Before the son of Bekkar can overcome his shock (and his suspicion) there is a flurry at the bottom of the curtains and the women's pet red squirrel, Yasemeen, runs up the neighboring drape and clings to the top, her tail a question mark. Her harness-bells shake. Voices outside are giggling and calling "Yasemeen! Yasemeen!" but 'Alee, quickly pulling himself together, draws himself up and shouts "Go away!" There's silence. Yasemeen turns her head to him, thus causing her harness-bells to shake again. If 'Alee were not still suffering from the effects of Younger Brother's frightening impropriety, this would be a pleasant accident, for chance has just demonstrated, without any wish on 'Alee's part, that he has many secret female lives dependent on him and that he is rich enough to bring a live animal from Outside to be their pet. But Younger Brother—perhaps without meaning to—has just now spoken into the air that most ominous and pregnant line of all in the Play of the Wife-stealer, in which the sexless demon breaks the rules of propriety, thus half revealing Its sinister nature.

And then, in the play, the wife runs mistakenly into the room.

15

(He recalls his daughter, Zubeydeh, watching the play on the women's television, her mouth open in the concentration of the very young. So young was she that she hadn't understood that she was seeing a play and had openly declared her wish to be the woman in the play when she grew older. For a long time nobody could make her understand that a real female could not impersonate a female-impersonator. That would unbalance everything.)

'Alee approaches the drape to the top of which Yasemeen clings, but this unusual ornament blinks once and dashes down to the floor, round about the room, and out the other side. More giggling from beyond and little spurts of high-pitched sound from Yasemeen's bells. The son of Bekkar ambles back to his cushion, smiling politely. Many years ago, during his adolescence, he used to bite his nails; he wishes now that he could do so again. Younger Brother yawns, stretching fat arms over his head and almost dislodging some of the room's hangings; he says, "Excuse me" and his shoulders writhe. Is this a hint? What is it a hint of? 'Alee shrugs modestly, to match his guest's action. He knows that the women are still behind the curtain, watching everything, and this nerves him to better behavior; he inquires conscientiously, "You wish perhaps to rest?"

"In a few minutes, thank you," says Younger Brother. Elder Brother nods.

Younger Brother adds, "You're polite. You're taking this very well, you know," and some complicated signal passes between the two strangers which 'Alee can't interpret; the younger says, "Tell me—" and the other interrupts, causing the first to raise his nonexistent eyebrows.

"You are related?" 'Alee says patiently, wanting to know about the sleeping arrangements. Men are as public on Ka'abah as women are private, men's genealogies are

16

the subject of absorbing general interest (he is not committing any impropriety in asking this), and brothers are usually close enough to wish to remain together. Also, one displays one's position by offering separate apartments. He comes out of his reckoning trying to look as expectant as possible. Elder Brother is smiling.

"We are teacher and pupil," says Elder Brother, "but we are close friends, and if it does not offend you, we would like to stay together, yes."

'Alee bows. He likes Elder Brother, although that too-deep voice still puts him off. Elder Brother adds:

"The teacher's great joy is to see the pupil exceed him."

(Well, if Elder Brother likes Younger Brother, Elder is either misled or Younger is not so bad as he looks. Maybe the acquaintance improves with time.)

"We switch a lot now," continues Elder Brother, looking with odd intensity at the son of Bekkar. "This trip Irenee is the doer and I am the conscience. Next trip it will be the other way around. We like this arrangement."

"You mean the authorities like it," says Younger Brother, in that idle, offhand, vicious way of his, tossing the words over his shoulder.

"I mean that I am not in charge," says the elder. "I want to make that clear to Shems-er-Nehar."

'Alee bows. Admirable, he thinks. It occurs to him that they may be lovers and he reminds himself not to mention this possibility in front of the women; it would not be right. They can watch such things on the television, if they like. (His eldest son is already writing poems to another boy; he has often sighed and shaken his head with other householders over the age at which they get started nowadays. One really cannot, though, right in front of one's female family, rub their noses in the competition, and in plays such things always end with a proper marriage, leaving everyone happy.)

17

"This way," says 'Alee, indicating the curtain.

The teacher and the pupil rise to their feet. The pupil's face has composed itself into an alarming expression, that is, the creature is actually smiling at him, and after a moment's uncontrollable shrinking, he decides to trust it, or at least to pretend to trust it because it may be true after all and it's not good to multiply distrust since there is already so much of it in the world.

"I think—" says the Wife-stealer.

"My house is yours," says 'Alee, bowing, aware as he does so that he probably shouldn't have and only God knows what this creature may come out with.

It says, "I want to sleep with the women. Why do you mind, you fool?"

(What Irene has actually said: "I prefer to stay with the women. You fool, do you really—")

"My partner is a woman," says Elder Brother.

The son of Bekkar hides his face in his hands. Then he looks between his fingers. It's true, it's true! Those great maenads who grow enormous, eat horseflesh, have no breasts, and wear men's clothes.

"Where are your children!" he shrieks accusingly, throwing his beard up over his eyes.

"This man is a fool," says Younger Brother. 'Alee subsides. It's worse than a jinneeyeh with six arms and six hands on each arm and six fingers on each hand, with clawed nails and a black face.

They'll think he's not civilized.

"Forgive me," he manages to say, showing his face again, "I am ill." His beard is disarranged and he stares wildly, wisps of hair sticking to the upper part of his face.

"No offense taken, please," says Elder Brother courteously, although Younger Brother (whom 'Alee cannot look at now without a trouble of the eyes and something like dizziness) looks violently angry. If she

18

doesn't want to be mistaken for a man, why has this unnatural woman removed her veils and her beauty spot, her necklaces, the dye on her fingernails? 'Alee puts his hands together and bows several times toward Elder Brother—"Forgive me, forgive me"—humiliating, to be sure, but he's frightened and remembers also that he's a host. Nothing's humiliating if undertaken for the sake of hospitality, as in the Play of Meymooneh whose hero chops wood and draws water for a guest, even descending to the impersonation of a public dung-carrier. Not that any position like that exists any more. But he can do it, too. He bows toward Younger Brother.

"Forgive me."

The woman says nothing. Then she says, "I'll think about it."

'Alee has recovered enough to say, "Don't misunderstand, please. I admire offworld customs. To take a woman for a pupil, that is admirably broad-minded. I admire it."

"I have not been a pupil for ten years," says the thing.

"I mean . . . to have done so," he says lamely. "But you said you were her ruler?" This appeal is to Elder Brother, as the sight of that smooth, hairless face still scandalizes him. Clean-shaven is bad enough.

"He damn well did not!" says the person.

"Well," says 'Alee hopelessly. "Forgive me. Such disharmony! But I do admire, to admit a woman as a pupil."

"Think no more of it," says Elder Brother.

"You will undoubtedly think no more of it," the pupil echoes.

"Indeed, indeed," says 'Alee hastily (because he can think of nothing else); "Well, well, it's reassuring to know, is it not, that our horizons are broadening?" (This is an improper speech, since Ka'abah has no horizons. It is

19

almost completely underground, hollowed out of the rock, and realizing that he has transgressed, he adds a bit wildly), "We must take our rightful place in the comity of nations!"

"You have already done so," says Elder Brother.

The woman pupil adds quietly, "You have done so unmistakably," and 'Alee dives for the door out, forgetting in his haste that his guests are tall and must be protected from curtains in the face; there's a smothered imprecation behind him. He says:

"This way. This way, please. Did I tell you? We also have women students. They are students of poetry. My own child—"

But here he stops. Out of a fresh sadness. He had forgotten.

"No offense," says the man teacher, again.

"Hell, no," says the other. "I'm used to it."

Irene Waskiewicz stops shouting long enough to see that her friend is sitting hunched sadly in the corner of the room with his arms wrapped patiently around his knees; he looks up at her, irresistibly reminiscent of an aged turtle. She's been obscene and she's been funny; she's called the authorities names she thought she'd forgotten years ago. He doesn't even understand some of them.

"Well?" she says.

Ernst sighs.

Irenee kicks the bed viciously. The room looks like any other on Ka'abah: decorated, cluttered, everything made of plastic. An enormous bed takes up most of the floor space, a canopied, looped-up, pom-pommed, beribboned monster that is also too short. The sense of being in a cave is very strong.

Irenee says, "This place smells."

Ernst scratches his head, changing from turtle to monkey.

Walking over to him, hopping over the corner of the bed where it intrudes on her route, she bends down:

"Ernst-God-damn-it!"

He says, "All right, Irenee." There's a moment's silence. She wanders back across the room, toeing the monster again as she goes by, And then sitting on it, testing its firmness with her hands. She says, half-angrily:

"All right, Conscience Neumann, what have I done wrong this time?"

He says, "Wrong? I'm tired."

She says, "I'm tired, too." And then, after a moment's silence, "Ernst, I'm sorry. Really I am. It's unprofessional. It's not objective. It's all that. Why you hired me I'll never know."

He smiles. "For your beautiful eyes."

"Yes, I was young," she says. "And totally graceless. And I still don't know what you see in me. Ernst, this is a mercury bed."

"Eh?" he says, interested.

"Yes. Let's hope it's sealed thoroughly. Do you think they let it leak to poison their guests?"

"Hardly," he says. "The embassy wouldn't like it."

"No. Ah! here. It's standard." (She's been rooting under swags and pom-poms. She turns to him now, very graceful, everything different, the I-don't-know-how-you-stand-me-look.) "Ernst, I am sorry."

He puts his hands over his ears.

She says, "I don't know how you stand me," then shakes herself suddenly as if coming out of something. She adds, "How shabby this stuff is. Years old."

He says, pointing to his lap, "Look what you've done," and she roars. She says:

"You're shabby. You're years old. Don't you ever give

21

up?" and shedding her shift, rolling down her black stockings, she walks across the mercury bed, stilt-up, stilt-down, sinking down cross-legged on the side next to him.

She says, turning red, "Lie down. I want to ride you."

'Alee thinks of his daughter, Zubeydeh, who is growing up to be a woman. Not like the breastless barbarian, whose ribs one can almost see as ridges under her clothes; Zubeydeh will be narrow-shouldered and slender-armed, almost bent over with the treasures of her femininity: soft, smooth, and heavy, with long black hair and heavy brows, and (if business stays good) an amber mole on the right place on her forehead. Surgery will be expensive, but for his dove, his temptation to all God's creatures, nothing is too good. He wishes representations were allowable; he would like (and so would the mother, Zumurrud, for all her craziness) a painting of his daughter, perhaps with the squirrel Yasemeen on her shoulder, a very delicate and elegant touch. He misses things like that. 'Alee's marriage has been unsatisfying and—aside from his three sons, whom he does not usually think of in connection with his wife—he has only one consolation: his daughter. He imagines her with a delicate gait like the Oriental willow, grown-up, veiled, sounding with clashing jewelry, with the fullness of her body swaying under the *izar*. What a marriage she will make! He sighs. He knows that Zubeydeh has not inherited her mother's instability, but there is still the wife's sister, Dunya, who went plain, outright mad years ago, who rushed out of the house unveiled and babbling and had half her clothes off in the marketplace before they could force her back. He has paid the expenses of her illness all these years. And strictly forbidden any reference to the tragedy in front of his daughter.

Passing the guard-robot at the door to the women's apartments, the grandson of Bekkar pauses for a moment, and then—with the sense of virtue reluctantly set into motion—modifies the guardbot to admit the barbarian woman's tel-o-tale. He hopes that she won't come. He hopes she won't frighten Zubeydeh. He hopes she won't corrupt anyone. 'Alee carries a bunch of keys, tape slugs, and cards; every householder has them. At the computer outlet right inside the door he checks on his family: Dunya is in her cell, the boys are at school, Zumurrud's dose of medicine has nearly worn off, and Zubeydeh is jumping about in the courtyard (under the artificial sunlight) with a tiny, dashing spark which must be Yasemeen. For a moment he watches the glowing lines on his daughter's phosphor plate, then checks everything else. Everyone is well. No messages. Nothing to buy. Everything is fine if only Zubeydeh has not taken off her toe-rings again.

"Daddy!" A small cyclone blows in from the court and hurls itself at him. Yasemeen, riding Zubeydeh's shoulder, jumps off, streaks to a cornice, and chatters angrily.

He kisses her and holds her at arm's length. "Look at you!" he cries melodramatically, and then, "Oh, dear, your feet!"

She says, "They make me trip."

He says, "That's because you never leave them on. You're not used to them. Don't you want to be pretty?"

She makes a face and goes into the court to gather up her toe-rings and put them on. She says, poking her head around the arch, "Daddy, Yasemeen is eating too much. She ate part of Jaafar's schoolbook and Jaafar got mad at me, but I can't *discipline* her. After all, she's only a squirrel."

'Alee opines that it is his son's responsibility to put his

schoolbooks in a drawer and that Yasemeen can't be expected to understand the importance of property.

Skinny Zubeydeh says, "That's what I told him. Daddy, can we watch the television? Mother turned it off. Mother's asleep. Daddy—" (here she turns her head away and skins her lips back over her teeth, speaking very quickly) "can we talk about what you said not to until you came back? I've been practicing with Jaafar. I can do everything he can now. I know you said—"

'Alee goes to her and puts his finger on her lips. Zubeydeh's brows are crooked. Probably the squirrel has been climbing all over her. He smooths them out with his forefinger and then (looking to see that nobody sees him, and of course nobody can except the computer, but he looks around anyway) takes his own comb out of his sleeve and combs her hair. He finishes by guiltily kissing the top of her head. He knows he's spoiling her, but she's an unusual child.

Encouraged, Zubeydeh hurls herself forcefully into his embrace again. Slyly she says from the depths of his robe, "Daddy?"

"You're a good girl," he says.

"Daddy, I want to enter the poetry contest. Please? I would bring honor to you. I can do all the forms now."

He exclaims, shocked, "What?"

"But I want to!" she says, exasperated, kicking him in the foot as she used to when she demanded a sweet or a toy, "I want it! I want it so much! Daddy, I'm *good!*"

He says quickly, "That's quite enough," and wonders if he should program the guardbot to keep everyone out; it's true they go through this kind of crisis very often at this age, but it's still unpleasantly reminiscent of Aunt Dunya. To have another—

Artful Zubeydeh says, counterfeiting innocence, wide-eyed, "But there's nothing *wrong* with it, is there?"

"That's quite enough," says the son of Bekkar sharply. "It's impossible. It's not allowed. I've told you many times. Now go and wake your mother." He adds more indulgently, "And then I want to see your new game with Yasemeen."

Zubeydeh flies off. He hears her say excitedly, "—and Yasemeen's *smart!*" and then he is looking into the still confused, still slightly drugged face of the Wezeereh Zumurrud, his wife. It's wrong somehow, it's an admission of failure, to keep the woman medicated all the time, and he refuses to do it; yet when he sees Zumurrud, the ghost of her former self tugs at his heart, the lovely girl he married, whose face has been reproduced in beautiful Zubeydeh, the woman who bore him three sons. (He wonders sometimes if her childhood was as merry and willful as his daughter's but can't believe it. Also her family was never any good. The usual impulse to denounce them, take them to court, and make them pay somehow for the way they have ruined two lives, rises in him and—as usual—dies.)

He says, "Good-day, Wezeereh wife."

She says, "Oh. Good-day, Wezeer husband," and sits down heavily on a bench. She's still sleepy but her eyes are clear. He says:

"Is there anything you wish to buy?" (Let Zubeydeh see how generous husbands are.)

She shakes her head. He sees in her face that wily shrinking, that mad dislike that he so fears to see; Zumurrud conceived her last two children while medicated in the hopes that the pregnancies would bring her back to herself, but later she actually tried to abort the youngest boy. That woman, her maid, had acted as go-between to the female abortionist and had, of course, been dismissed. He has assured himself that the one who attends the family now knows her duty.

"How do you feel?" says 'Alee, dreading the answer.

Zumurrud begins a long, slow recital of her pains, the shadow in her face transferring itself somehow to Zubeydeh's so that 'Alee, frightened, holds up his hand for silence. Zumurrud obediently stops. She remains quiet. After a while, seeing that the effort of conversing on any other subject is too much for her, 'Alee says cheerfully:

"If you are too weak to make conversation, Wezeereh, I will do so for you. Do you know how hard I worked today?"

"How hard, daddy?" says Zubeydeh, eagerly. She always loves to hear about his work.

"Very hard," says 'Alee. "I worked two hours today." He's about to tell them of the visitors, but thinks that he'll do so later. Zumurrud would wake into active life then, and would begin those sly, malicious threats of madness that so unnerve him. He has tried in vain to think where such perverseness can come from. Zumurrud has been pleating and unpleating the material of her robe; now she says:

"I suppose you're afraid I—"

"Quiet!" shouts 'Alee.

"Afraid I will not have the strength to oversee the boys when they come home," says Zumurrud doggedly. She's smiling secretly down at the stuff of her robe.

"I know my duty," says Zumurrud in that slow, obstinate voice. "I may be dying—"

"Go away!" says 'Alee to his daugher. Zubeydeh is shrinking against the wall hanging, turned into herself somehow, her narrow arms folded in her dress, looking down in a horrible way that mimics her mother. When the girl was little, Zumurrud loved to put makeup on her and dress her, loved to play with her and carry her about; the daughter was her favorite. Now she seems to have claimed

Zubeydeh for some other purpose, something draining and parasitic. But he's getting fanciful. He takes his daughter by the shoulders, whispering into her ear, "I have a surprise for you," and turns her into the next room. He comes back to find his wife laughing. She laughs as she smiled, downward and secretly, wringing her hands in her lap.

"Don't you care about your daughter at all?" says 'Alee sternly. Zumurrud begins to cry, this time in earnest. 'Alee talks to her seriously, glad to see her so repentant, driving home his points with unnecessary repetition (but it relieves his feelings) and representing to her that she is neglecting her duties, that she has abandoned every woman's lifelong project of forming a feminine personality and has become unbalanced inside in consequence, that she is failing her daughter (at this Zumurrud sobs painfully), that a madwoman is more rebellious and unclean than a madman because a woman ought to be better than a man, that her sons need her for the feminine component in their personalities, and finally that he may impose social responsibilities on her in the near future and if she can't meet them, what will he do then?

"But there is nothing for me," says Zumurrud, wringing her hands; "there is no way out."

'Alee says she need only make an effort of will.

Zumurrud says, "You don't understand. There is *nothing*. I am no one. Am I to chase after Zubeydeh's squirrel all day?"

'Alee begins—

"Husband, husband," says Zumurrud in a low and rapid voice, "Bedeea-el-Jemal kept a shop. Budr-el-Badr went to seek her husband on foot, disguised as a man. The wife of Haroon-er-Rasheed oversaw a whole manufactory. What am I to do?"

'Alee says this is scandalously silly and he can't think

what's the matter with her. Men would be only too glad to rest if they could. He adds, "Think of our hardships if your mind becomes troubled. Think how lucky you are." He adds sternly, "I don't understand you."

Zumurrud leans back among the cushions; that crazy, plaintive smile comes back into her face. She says, "I couldn't do anything anyway. My back hurts. I'm ill."

"I will send for the diagnostic machines," says he.

"I'm ill all over," says Zumurrud quietly, and then opening her eyes and looking at him with an intense expression he cannot fathom: "I am waiting for the Wife-stealer to come for me."

This is too much for 'Alee. It is just like her spiteful tricks. He claps his hands furiously, summoning into the room one of the family machines, which will carry Zumurrud off to her bed. She will have to be medicated again. He wonders wildly if some of his neighbors are not right; that some women should be medicated from the cradle upwards, because truly there is an epidemic among the women of today. If only he could afford a mistress! Once the daughter is married—

"Zubeydeh! You bad girl!" The little one is holding the curtain and peering around it. Upset and angry though he is, 'Alee notices for the first time that he has a rather plain-faced little girl on his hands, someone oddly pinched and pale; then she's kneeling at his feet, knocking her head absurdly on the floor, a gesture she must have picked up from the television, and crying:

"Is she sick? Is she sick?"

"Yes, dear, but she'll soon be well," says 'Alee, raising her. "I shall make her well with the medicine. Would you like that?"

"Oh, yes, yes!" says Zubeydeh in relief, and then, "Do you mean like the way she was yesterday?"

'Alee nods. "Would you like that?"

"Ye-es," says she doubtfully, the traces of tears still on her face; "it's easier then. I like mother better then. But—"

"But what, dear?"

"She's so *silly*." Zubeydeh has whispered this, as if it's something shameful. She looks at him carefully and adds, "Can you make her really well?"

'Alee embraces his daughter.

From the region of his sternum, he hears:

"Daddy, the poetry—"

"Impossible!" shouts 'Alee, his cup of domestic afflictions running over. He repulses Zubeydeh. "Impossible! Do you want to be publicly stoned? You are a fool, Zubeydeh, and I forbid it. I forbid any mention of it. I forbid you to practice with Jaafar. I forbid everything. Go play!"

And leaving his beloved daughter to the care of his mad wife, he rushes out of the *hareem*, wishing (as he so often has lately) that the leavetaking could be (this time) forever.

Irene Waskiewicz was sixteen in the year one thousand nine hundred and fifty-three. She was a high school student in a respectable, lower middle class family. Her mother alternated periods of loud heartiness, in which she told and retold the romantic episodes of her life (she had eloped with Irene's father and had almost died when Irene was born) with fits of weeping which she tried to hide from her daughter. Rose had been working in a factory when she met Casimir and used to boast that he'd kept his promise; she'd never had to work again. Cas was an accountant, a cold, finicky man who opened up rarely, never when he talked about his work (which he hated) but occasionally when he took Irene to the city park to look for plants. Their nationality as an oppressed people, her father's romantic name, the story of the marriage, all these glamorized the five-room brick house (like all the others in the neighborhood) and the pocket-sized front lawn where Irene would see her father working on weekends and in the evenings. As a child she'd wondered why men were not supposed to like flowers but were supposed to like working in the garden; as a teenager she dismissed her father's quirks as simply not among the things that mattered and spent her free time almost exclusively with boys, not as a mascot or a boy-crazy girl but as one of the gang. Her parents at first worried that she would get "in trouble" and then that she would never "grow up"; what they did not know (and this would have frightened both those highly intelligent and perceptive people) was that Irene's major concern with her friends was either to beat them up or beat them at games, and when that was impossible, to stage-manage subtle and imaginatively vicious revenges, frighteningly complex and long-term efforts for a sixteen-year-old, which worked.

Rose found out about one of these, and being in a good mood, laughed over it; she said it served the boy right. When she asked her daughter about dates, Irene said roughly "Who cares!" About the other girls, "That's the only thing they can do; they're disgusting." She had one girl friend, a high-powered brain whom nobody else liked. Her pleasures were talking with the one friend, baseball, hiking, or hanging around with the men. Her grades were good. She had begun to worry about sex, getting excited over her boy friends, excited over some of her teachers, even her girl friend. When Ernst Neumann arrived in the family she had just completed her sadistic masterpiece; there was a vain, handsome, athletic boy, popular with girls, who disliked Irene and wanted her out of the group.

30

Over a period of months, disguising her own dislike of him, even pretending to fall in love with him, and carefully disseminating bits of false information through the girls' network and through people's parents but never directly to the boys (except once or twice and then ostensibly about someone else), she managed to convince the group that he was a homosexual, and so get him thrown out. Grown-ups might have known better, or at least known that it was serious, but in this period of her life Irene's instinct for the direction and timing of a rumor was diabolic. She could never do it as well again.

The most frightening thing of all: she never daydreamed about her revenges.

Irene Waskiewicz was coming home from the school recreation center one cold winter's evening. The street lamps had just been lit in front of all the brick bungalows. Her own family's had squares of colored glass on either side of the door and some small evergreens set along the base of the house, not quite like those in front of the other houses; not for the first time these details seemed to Irene to shed beauty over the house. The bare tree branches curved speciously around the street lights, and at this blue hour the lights themselves were pure fantasy.

She was being Irenee Adler, *the* woman. She hesitated before going indoors—it would all vanish in there—but she loved her parents and wanted dinner; besides, she had to call her friend Chloe at eight o'clock to make a movie date for the week-end. She could be Irenee with Chloe; Chloe was also Irenee. She pushed open the front door into the hot inside of the house, exchanging worlds, and took off her winter things in the hall. She came into the living room as Irenee, disdaining the china shepherdesses and the mustard-colored carpet, went through the dining alcove as Irenee, and entered the kitchen, trying to incorporate the running, weeping windows into her story.

31

There was a strange man in the kitchen.

Now opera is crucial to the erotic life of the West; for two hundred years we have exalted the highest voices as the most ideal, that is, the coloratura and the tenor, but Irenee was a mezzo, and a mezzo is a throwback. When her intellectual friend played opera for her she liked the heartless, jolly affairs the baritone had, especially when he had them with the mezzo, who got to boast, to show off her hips, to wear fancy earrings, and to associate with robbers. Not for her the high, taut, vibrating, nineteenth-century, electric-knife-voice that sounds as if it's going to cut its owner's throat. Nor the unearthly lunarities of the soprano. She thought the stranger was moderately interesting. Irenee, who had high ideals, didn't approve. Irenee was always going to go off with some beautiful young man or other but somehow she never did. Sometimes she cherished an unrequited passion for Sherlock Holmes.

Rose said, "Mr. Nooman, this is my daughter i-REEN. I-REEN, this is Mr. Nooman."

He was a big, lean, not particularly attractive baritone with a barrel chest. He said reasonably:

"Your daughter?" and his voice made her fix on him automatically. He said, "i-REE-nee?"

She turned pale. At sixteen one's sense of genuine erotic possibility is much restricted and Irene, despite appearances, had been brought up like everyone else. But she liked him. She wanted to put her hands on his chest and have him talk again. She ticketed him as "okay." She had, for a moment, the sense of being about to walk off a cliff.

He said politely, "ee-RAH-nay?"

She gave an adolescent snicker. That was too much. They shook hands. She decided to add him to her imaginary seraglio; he would be a nice one to have fun with. The real pleasure was in not having to fall in love, as in the movies, not having to give one's heart wholly or give in or "fall" or be crazy about someone or submit to love. Not to be overwhelmed. She thought he looked lovely and wanted to shake hands again.

Rose said, "Mr. Nooman is staying to dinner."

"Please: Ernst," said the stranger.

Irene had once enjoyed watching her mother work in the kitchen and although she knew it all by heart now and disliked it (she had long ago put it in the category of things that didn't concern her), Rose was still happier there than anywhere else. It was easier to talk there. Which made it odd when Rose said, "Your program's on the TV," and turned her back on them. Irene wondered if her mother were going into one of her bad moods which nobody was supposed to know about. So she went as far as the dining alcove, her manner such that only obtuseness could have kept anyone from coming with her. He took the cue and followed, although when Irene settled into one of the vinyl-covered dining chairs, he remained standing. She was playing with the lace doily in the middle of the table, which had figurines and an arrangement of artificial flowers on it.

He said, "Your program?"

She said, "It's an old movie series. You know, the famous dancer who looks like a hatrack. Well, I love the dancing but he's always right and she's always wrong."

"She?"

"All of them. His partners." She said this stubbornly, looking at the table. Irene often says whatever comes into her head. Irenee does, too, but Irenee is above getting into trouble. (An uncle had once said, with ferocious jocularity, "Oh, so you want to be right *all* the time, do you!")

Ernst said, "Everyone wants to be right."

33

"Yeah, I know," she said angrily, digging her thumbnail into the plastic of the tabletop. "But it's rationed."

Adolescents flock to him as if he were a beacon and tell him things. She didn't know this and would not have thought of herself as one of them anyway; Irene always exempted herself from regularities. She added in a low voice, "Where you from?"

"Staying nearby," he said.

"Oh." She added, without guile, "You friends with my mother?"

"Friend of a friend," he said.

"I guess you know my Dad?"

He shook his head.

He said, "Don't you want to watch your program?"

"No." She smiled at him. She was wondering what he looked like without his clothes. She was also figuring what to do to him when he tried to put her in her place. As far as she was concerned, this would happen with the inevitability of natural law. She said, "Do *you* want to watch it?"

He shook his head.

She smiled at him extravagantly. She thought perhaps she could shock him. She said, leaning back with her hands in her pockets:

"Oh, you know, I have this friend called Chloe. A couple of months ago some guys were saying we must be—you know—queers because she's not popular and we hang around together a lot, though I don't see what that has to do with it. Anyway I didn't care but everyone else does, so I acted shocked and yelled a lot. I even beat up one guy. So they stopped." She grinned. She said, "What do you think of that?"

He laughed delightedly. "Good for you."

"Well...." Then she said quickly, looking at her lap and smiling, "We're not queer."

34

There was a moment's silence. She said stubbornly, "You didn't tell me where you're from." She wanted to say, "Look, I'm not just a kid." He made no answer, and as if this silence had been the real, reassuring answer, she reached out and daringly took his hand in her own, lifting a hundredweight.

His eyebrows went up; she dropped the hand miserably. "Never mind." She was going to say, "I read palms," but at that moment she heard the front door open and shut; Dad had come home.

Surprisingly, Irenee had had nothing to do with any of it.

Then she forgot about him. She had thought sometimes that her love affairs could only be something even worse than the mezzo's in opera, because she was too big and too athletic and too opinionated. She never talked with Chloe about love, because Chloe, an opera-nut and balletomane, a small, sandy-haired, freckled girl, would stagger at such talk, literally stagger if she were walking, or wince at other times, because she'd had poliomyelitis a few years before and walked badly. (She would go up stairs holding on to the banister with both hands.) Irene also had something going with a boy called David; they never quarreled but didn't talk much either, and Irene was worried about going too far with him. She never told any of this to Chloe. At dinner Irene thought of clowning for the stranger's benefit but did nothing; she turned off, missing the dinner conversation completely, and afterwards called Chloe and talked about music for an hour, provoking her father to his usual cold, helpless, sarcastic comments (she would have said, "Oh, that's just Dad,") which she countered with her usual, automatic, loud yelling ("I have no rights! I don't live in this house!"). She hardly thought about it any more. She went out after dinner, telling her mother she was going to meet Chloe on the corner.

Her mother winked.

There were still places to go in Irene's neighborhood: the corner drugstore, the roofs in summer, the park. Nobody went to the church center, but in a pinch you could sit on the steps. Irene met David at the entrance to the park; she was burning up; she wanted, for some reason, to tell him about the stranger. She would have said, "Listen, can't I tell you everything?" She was grateful to him; when the neighbors talked about "that big Waskiewicz girl," too big, too athletic, too opinionated, she thought of him and something softened inside her. She believed even Chloe would have liked him. She opened the conversation by saying, "You know, you look like—" and then stopped. Of course; they were both Jewish. The big dark eyes, the cheekbones, but David was beautiful. She said shyly, "I wasn't sure I could get away."

He said, "That's all right," and put his arm around her. She thought: I'm going to drown in those eyes. It was a literary thought but it was a true thought. She really couldn't see where she was going. They walked through the park, saying nothing, to a place they'd discovered a few weeks before, and because it was clean and dry he pulled her down on to the dead leaves and they fussed with each other's clothing. David got inside her for a while, as usual, only this time she thought she was going to come; but he got out too soon and had to bring her off by hand. During this last, Irene used to try to imagine that he was stronger, older, bigger, and more masterful, that he was holding her down by force and was going to make her pregnant but she didn't care because the pleasure was so extreme; she knew this fantasy was masochistic and that bothered her. What bothered her even more was the mockery that went on under the fantasy: that she wanted to laugh and say coarse things, bite him, throw him down and sit on him. It occurred to her that she wasn't normal, that what happened to her wasn't real because it was in the wrong place and she always seemed to want more. She had once said to him in a whisper, "I wish you could stay inside me" and he'd explained (turning red) that the real thing ought to be saved for after marriage. Irene had petted his face and said nothing. Irene-apart-from-David made jokes about it that would've stripped him to his bones.

She said, "I adore you." She put her arms around him. Beautiful David, his beauty stabbing her to the heart, guided her hands downwards; she knew this was the real thing for boys, though it wasn't for girls. He groaned on her shoulder and her heart melted; she loved him, it was the way it should be, she wanted to be with him always.

He said a little later, "Irene, will you marry me?"

"What?" She was smoking a cigarette, something that always made her feel bold and distinguished; her thoughts had drifted away.

He turned his big, dark eyes on her. "Let's get engaged."

Silence. Finally she said, "I guess I'm not myself today."

"But will you? You know what my Dad thinks about Gentiles. But I'll work on him."

It didn't seem courteous to say, "Let me think about it." She turned her face away. He started to tell her how beautiful she was—this was something that always vexed her—but tonight she said abruptly, "For goodness' sake, stop it." He fell silent. Then he said:

"What's the matter? Are you mad about something?"

She started to put her clothes back together. She didn't want to hear: Wear eye makeup, wear jewelry, fix your hair.

She said, "I don't know why you assume I'm going to get married. Ever."

He laughed. "But that's foolish."

"Not me." She had a shocking impulse to burn him playfully with the tip of her cigarette, and so stubbed the cigarette out on the ground.

He sat up abruptly. "It's because I'm Jewish!" She shook her head. His attitude softened; putting one hand on hers, he said, "You're not ugly, you know."

"Oh, quit it," said Irene.

"Well, look," said David persuasively, "why, then? I'm not asking you just to get married; I'm asking you to marry *me*, you know. I mean, don't you want children, for example?"

"No," said she.

"But that's neurotic!"

She almost said, What a Jewish word. She had a nagging feeling that she wanted to fuck again, fuck really hard this time; she wished she could tape his mouth and throw him down.

She said, "Look, David, I've told you. I don't want kids. I don't want to be tied down. I'm going to college, you know."

He said pedantically, "A mother who works is neglecting her children. Everybody knows that."

She stared.

She said, "Well, *really*—!"

She said, "Look, we *talked* about it. You said you didn't mind if I had a career. I told you it mattered a lot to me. I didn't lie to you."

He said, "But you've got to stay home when the children are small."

"Hell! *You* stay home!"

He laughed. "Honestly, Irene—"

"Can't you take care of your own kids? Can't you wear an apron and scrub floors? Would it kill you?"

He said quietly, "I didn't think you wanted to castrate me, Irene. I didn't think you hated me that much."

38

He added, relenting, "Of course I don't mind my wife having a career, but the children come first. I couldn't allow anything else, could I? And I feel very sorry for women who don't want children; they're just not normal. I mean, it's all right for a woman to have interests outside the home, but all the books say—"

She hit him. It was a big, sincere haymaker, not thought out at all, and it almost missed him. He rolled over in the leaves; it had surprised the both of them. She rubbed her fist, thinking: What would Irenee Adler do? and realized that never in a million years would Irenee ever get into such a situation, not for all the beautiful Jewish eyes in the world. She noticed that David did not get up; he lay there looking shocked, his pants still open and pushed down around his hips.

She said, "You are a God damned fool. You can get into somebody else's pants from now on."

He pulled his trousers up quickly and got to his feet. "You're not a woman. You're not a real woman at all."

She said suddenly, "It's men like you who killed my mother."

He was zipping his pants and buttoning them. She saw him turn pale. He said, backing away from her, "Irene, that's crazy. I don't think you realize how crazy that is. You know, you may not realize it but you've got a father complex. There's nothing wrong with your mother and she's certainly not dead—I mean, that's insane, she's very much alive and she's had the normal fulfillment of a woman's life, hasn't she? Your parents aren't that different from mine or anybody else's, and what I don't understand is how they managed to bring you up. Irene, you're *crazy*!"

She said belligerently, "Yeah? Well, I'm going to be a city planner and fuck you, David!"

"Look, Irene," he said nervously, "nobody's against your career, but you've got to realize—"

She swung experimentally at him and missed. He still looked amazed rather than scared. Irenee Adler had deserted her; she knew not only that Irenee Adler would never have had to hit anyone but that Irenee had had the deck stacked, and rather badly, too, because no one could ever mistake Irenee Adler for an ordinary woman.

She said, not realizing she was stammering, "Me? Me? You expect me—"

"Well, why not?" he said, thoroughly bewildered, "you're a girl, aren't you?" and then he did look scared; Irene Waskiewicz, her lips compressed intently and one hand pressed to her heart (she was unconscious of this) had, with the other hand, melodramatically picked up a rock. She was stalking David.

She said carefully, "You dirty, stinking little Jew. Come and get it, you filthy little Jew."

He turned and ran.

She dropped the rock, not at all surprised that it had worked. She knew how easy it was to frighten people. She paced automatically, hands in the pockets of her coat, thinking vaguely that she would have to change Irenee's scenario from now on, change it quite a lot. Get rid of the rotten girls in school, for one thing; if they had only behaved like human beings, boys wouldn't try to treat her the way David had. She thought briefly of mothers, but here affection stopped her; Rose would be a famous, retired coloratura, a queen, an English gentlewoman-explorer, somebody. Shithead David would undoubtedly tell, treating the whole school to her nuttiness; she'd have to get some other story circulating fast. She began to think about who could be trusted to spread it. Worst of all, her insides were still shuddering in *that way* and it made her feel furious and vulnerable all at once. Irene sat down. She thought of stretching out in the leaves and masturbating, but that made her madder than ever; she couldn't think of sex or David without beginning to gag. She consoled herself with the thought that she could masturbate in her room at home, but knew that in a mood like this she wouldn't be able to; any fantasy would bring on the same excited, convulsive nausea. She rocked on her heels with her eyes shut; no good. Couldn't either focus it or make it go away. Nobody to fuck. Nobody to put up against the neighbors, she supposed.

She imagined saying in a sort of boast to Rose, about the stranger, "I don't like him; I just want to fuck him. I think I'll rape him," and knew what her earthy mother would say back: Oh, honey, don't say that even as a joke, that's terrible. Rose would explain earnestly (as she had before) that a woman had to have love or some kind of security before she could be happy sexually with a man, but that it wasn't the same for a man.

There were ways, though. By God, she'd find ways.

She got up; time to go home. Cas wouldn't notice an earthquake and she could avoid Rose. Pretend nothing had happened. She thought that it wasn't David, it wasn't even sex; it was some kind of deeper trouble, not only painful but unbearably, exasperatingly boring, something that would've been a lot better if it had been tragic and easier if it'd been sad.

Something unbearably disillusioning.

And old. Very, very old.

In the three months afterwards Irene dropped almost all her friends. She lost weight. She studied a lot, which made Rose say, worried, "Irene's getting serious," and made Cas leave her alone on the presumption that she was behaving as she ought to at last. She even kept up an unassigned program of reading long after school was out, well into the summer, and when Rose would say, "Honey, don't you ever want to have any fun?" she'd answer dryly, "One meets a better class of boy at college, don't you think." She would look up from her book for all the world as if she were looking over reading glasses, quite severely; Rose's depressions had no effect on her any more. She told Rose nothing about David.

Rose said, "Oh, honey, do you have to waste your time in stuffy old museums like that?"

Ernst Neumann came back at the end of July, on his way out of the country, and stopped off for an evening. Irene had been to the movies with Chloe, the only friend she saw now, and the two of them were sitting in the dining alcove. Irene was avoiding Casimir unconsciously and out of habit; the two girls were looking up scenes in an art-film magazine and drinking Pepsi. Irene looked up first at the sound of the door opening, thinking it was her mother coming back, and saw him; she smiled involuntarily. She got up and looked round him to see if her mother weren't with him; then she said to Chloe:

"It's a friend of my father's, Mr. Neumann." Mothers, after all, didn't have male friends separately like that.

She added, "My father's on the back porch, Mr. Neumann. I think he's reading the paper."

But Mr. Neumann made no move to go through the living room to the back porch.

Irene said then, "Chloe, this is Mr. Neumann. Mr. Neumann, this is my mad friend, Chloe." The stranger held out his hand. He was (she noticed) wearing a short-sleeved, printed sports shirt, the kind you didn't see much in the city, flamingoes, she believed. They tweaked her sense of humor. Chloe got up and limped around the table, holding on to the edge with both hands; she said formally, "How do you do? We've been to the art film."

"You know, earthy and adulterous peasants," said Irene, tapping the magazine. "They're in the book. Do you want to see my father?"

Neumann said, "Thank you, in a few minutes," and sat down with them. Chloe got back to her seat and glanced at her friend for advice but Irene had gone back to her magazine. She said, from its depths, "You left early the last time you were here. I expected to find you when I came back. Will you stay for dinner?"

He said, "Oh yes. If it's no trouble. You see, there will probably be a letter for me."

"From my mother?" said Irene, raising her eyes.

He looked embarrassed. "No, no, your mother . . . in-herited me, so to speak. From a relative."

Irene told Chloe calmly, "Mr. Neumann is my mother's cousin." She got up. "I'll tell my father you're here," she said, leaving the stranger to make small talk with Chloe, who immediately pushed her chair backwards as if bracing herself or preparing for flight; Chloe was nervous with people.

It was still light, the sky just darkening above the neighboring roofs and the air damp and fragrant in the back yard; according to whether he thought it light enough, Casimir might be in the garden or in the garage where he made a hobby of fixing things. Irene found him in the garage, working on a neighbor's clock; parts were spread out in front of him and he looked (as she so rarely saw him) thoroughly absorbed and happy. From time to time his lips moved. She watched him for a bit, rather pleased, and then she said:

"Dad, that fellow's here again." Irene had lately adopted a bantering, ironical style of conversation with her father that appeared to both fluster and please him, perhaps because it guaranteed their distance from each other.

He said, "Look here, Irene, do you see this? This is the clock's escapement."

She said, "I can't now. There's somebody inside to see you. You know, the tall man who was here in January. The one who looks like a gorilla."

He came out of his work, disappointed. "Oh," he said. Then he added vaguely, "Your mother's friend."

Irene said, embarrassed, "Yes, ah . . . mother's friend. Look, Dad, I can talk to him for a few minutes. You go on working." She wanted very much to add, "You know Mother's crazy about you."

He said, "I have a responsibility, Irene."

She said, "Look, I can take over as the head of the household for a few minutes." Then she added, she hardly knew why, "Man to man, OK?"

Her father said coldly, looking over his glasses, "I hope you will remember to be polite and ladylike, Irene."

She said nothing. Then she said, drumming her fingers on his work table, "Oh sure, I'm always everything I should be. Hadn't you noticed?"

He retreated immediately behind his glasses and went back to work.

When she got back to the dining alcove, Ernst Neumann was showing Chloe card tricks. The cards were miniatures and hard to handle; the sight of them in his big hands affected her unpleasantly and when he fumbled several tricks in succession—Chloe enjoyed these just as much as the successes—Irene said deliberately: "You'd better give them to me, Mr. Neumann. I'm sure my father wouldn't want you playing with them."

He did and she put them back on the living room mantelpiece, in their box.

She thought: *And I thought you were a superman!*

Chloe said, "Mr. Neumann was telling me what you do with the aces,"

44

Irene said, "May I get you some more Pepsi, Mr. Neumann?"

He declined. Chloe started to talk about the card tricks again, but trailed off after looking at Irene; Irene excused herself and picked up the magazine; Ernst Neumann sat without speaking. When Irene looked at him sharply over the top of the magazine (over a photo of the beautiful and profound Michele Morgan who was not just a star but an art star) their eyes met—he was looking at her, unembarrassed, neither comfortable nor uncomfortable as far as she could tell, but only waiting. She almost said, "Do you have any other tricks?"

But then Rose came home.

Chloe, whose fits of terror lest she fall usually disappeared around Rose, helped Rose with her shopping bags; Irene said she would help, too, in the kitchen; Ernst Neumann took the letter Rose gave him and went to read it in the living room.

Chloe had to leave for dinner at her own house.

Casimir saw the kitchen lights go on and came to the house through the back yard, which was not quite dark.

Rose asked Ernst Neumann to stay for dinner.

Casimir, coldly incurious, made desultory conversation with the visitor and then asked Irene about her reading, giving her with some warmth a list of books she must read: *The Decline of the West, Worlds in Collision,* and *The Power of the Catholic Church.* He didn't appear to like the visitor's flamingo-covered shirt.

Irene said, "Dad doesn't approve of informal dress." She thought: *Well, I am a holy terror!* She went on to make lots of conversation, conversation about books, conversation about the weather, talk about movies that were showing in the neighborhood and whether they were good or not. She said brightly:

"I thought *Anne of the Indies* was a very artistic film.

45

The character of the heroine is very true to life and the actress in the film played Anne admirably. She does everything for love. Her awakening womanhood is poignant and beautiful and the final transformation of Anne from the unhappy, boyish pirate of the first scene to the beautiful, mature woman at the end is very moving. It's tragic that she has to die to save the life of the man she loves and his wife."

She noted with delight that the visitor had almost inhaled his soda pop. Casimir, on the other hand, had heard this sort of thing too often to respond. Besides he approved of it. She went on in an ecstasy of lying, "It's all her father's fault, Mr. Neumann. To bring her up to be a pirate and neglect the things that any woman needs, the things that would make her a normal—" but Rose would hear, Rose would believe it, Rose would say, "Isn't that all true! Doesn't she speak well, Mr. Neumann?"

Irene stopped. She said, "Excuse me, I ought to help my mother."

"What?" said Cas, sensing the ironical mood coming on and made uncomfortable by it.

Irene said, "My mind was wandering. I'll go help Mother."

At dinner Mr. Neumann gave Rose the phone number of the place where he'd be staying the night. Rose wrote it down in the kitchen, on the pad under the telephone, and shortly thereafter Irene excused herself gravely, went into the kitchen for some more Jell-O, and copied it. On her way back in she said:

"Don't you want the number, Dad?"

He told her not to carry her napkin tucked in the band of her skirt when she wasn't at table.

—the tail end of a conversation between Mr. Neumann and her mother: "... if there are any messages."

She said, "Well, Dad, after I go to college we won't be

seeing so much of each other, will we?"

Rose broke in: "Just think of the people you'll meet! Isn't that right, Mr. Neumann?"

Cas said, "I believe that your reading will help you there, and I think you'll find—"

"More Jell-O, Mr. Neumann?" That was Irene. She then said to Cas, "I'll have to look very hard at both of you in the time that's left, so I won't forget you." She added, to their visitor, "I've been accepted by our local junior college, but I'm not going there. There's no future in it. And State in Home Economics, that's another. Mother made me apply to that."

"But, honey," said Rose nervously, "I only suggested—"

Irene said, "That's right, dear. You see, Mr. Neumann, the tuition's free. But I won't go."

At length he pushed back his chair, thanked them, excused himself, and both Cas and Rose saw him to the front door. Irene nodded distantly, standing in the archway to the living room. Not waiting for her parents' return, she went up to her room: cheap books, a maple bedroom set, no record player, no telephone, two reproductions of a single Van Gogh painting in different tones of color. She sat on the bed, looking at nothing, then dressed herself in two layers of clothes and a sweater, put on new shoes, put her savings account book in her shoulder bag, and taking an armful of books with her, went downstairs. Rose was in the kitchen; Irene leaned around the corner of the doorway to say good-bye. She said:

"Mother, I'll be at Chloe's for a little while." She added, "Would you tell Dad?" Casimir would be in the garage, or reading, or washing the car out back. He was resisting getting a television set but would probably do so (she thought) sooner or later. He took evening classes in the winter, usually in something to do with botany. She

47

remembered a conversation with him; he'd said college was important financially and had added, "When I got married—" and then realized that he wasn't talking to a son. He had switched it to, "The man you marry." She went out, and once out in the street, dropped her books in the nearest trash can, looked in her shoulder bag for the piece of paper with Ernst Neumann's number on it, couldn't find it, coolly searched her pockets until she found it, and then put it in her purse. The corner drugstore was open, and Irene spent some time there looking unhurriedly in the phone book; she couldn't find the number itself, which might have been an extension, but found a number which matched the exchange and the first digit; she copied down the name and address of the hotel and tried calling the number.

They had never heard of him.

She had money for a taxi, but prudently took a bus, sitting with the pocketbook on her lap, holding onto it with both hands. It couldn't be an extension number like that in a business office because the first two digits were four-zero and there wasn't a hotel in town with forty floors. Perhaps it was zero-something-something, the first floor. It didn't seem to her that she was doing anything desperate, only taking advantage of a chance that might not come her way again for years, not that you had to run away with someone, but here was someone who obviously knew the real places to run away to. She would settle for advice. She imagined him telling her to go to junior college and laughed. The address was that of an ordinary commercial hotel, not in the downtown but on the edge of another suburb; she went into the lobby and told the man at the desk that she was looking for her father, but they still hadn't heard of him and they had no room number that began with forty.

She called him from a house phone.

"Hello? Mr. Neumann? This is Irene Waskiewicz. You know, Rose's daughter. No, my mother hasn't got a message for you. But somebody came with a package for you and she wants to know where to send it."

Pause.

Irene said, "But I can't. She's gone out."

She said, "Look, Mr. Neumann, I've got the package with me. No, I'm not calling at home. I'm in the lobby of the Bradford. Only they say you're not here. Tell me where you are and I'll bring it over."

She listened. Then she said, sounding sincerely aggrieved, "Well, look, how can I tell who it's from? Rose didn't tell me. Yes, I would like to go home, frankly."

She said, "But how can I leave it here at the desk if it's not the right hotel?"

She said crossly, "They'll *forward* it to you? Oh, Lord!" and finally, in a different tone, "Ernst, I will find you if I have to go through the phone book all night. Yes, of course I know what areas of the city the exchanges represent; I'm very observant. Besides, you must be in this hotel because I'm calling you on a house phone. And I will go through this damn place room by room, if I must, and if I don't find you, I will make sure you never use my mother as a letter drop again. Of course I know what letter drops are, do you think I'm blind."

She said, "No, there's no package! And you might as well get it over with."

She added, "I'm not going to kill you."

Whistling, she took the elevator down to the basement and wedged the elevator door open with a standing ashtray. The basement was full of ashtrays. She thought she might've got sand in the elevator mechanism but that was all right; they could put it on his bill. Then she walked up the proper number of floors to his room, rang the bell, and arranged herself in a grand attitude: a plain teen-ager in clothes too tight for her, with thumbs hooked braggingly in the waistband of her ill-fitting skirt. He came to the door barefoot and wearing only trousers and an undershirt; that was nice. She approved of that.

She said breathlessly, "My parents don't know I'm here."

For the first time in her life someone's eyes followed hers as she looked rapidly around the room, checking it out; this pleased her. She decided he was an astute man. But when he turned and plodded to the chair on the other side of the hotel room (a plain, overstuffed, green chair, a rotten hotel room, she couldn't understand why he wasn't spending more money) she changed her mind; she took the opportunity to zip into the bathroom and out again, collecting not only his razor from the sink, but in addition the room key off the bureau.

He said, from the chair, "So you intend to run away with me, Irenee?"

She smiled brilliantly, aware of the razor and the key. He was not so smart after all. Keeping her hands behind her, she said with immense energy, "Don't flatter yourself, Ernst! I'm just running away, that's all. With you or without you, who cares? I don't need you."

He scratched his chest. He looked tired. He said politely, "Well!" and then, "Yes, of course, the clothes, that's for running away. On your own, as you say.... And you want money? Advice?"

"You're with the C.I.A.!"

He shook his head.

She said hotly, "Yes you are! Or something like, anyway. I'm not blind. Look, you can fuck me if you like," (she thought: I am amusing myself) and swaggered, adding, "I know the price."

He said, "What do you really want from me, Irene?"

She shrugged. She looked away. It was getting depressing after all. She thought: what if I tell you that my mother is crazy, my father is cold and loves nobody, and my best friend falls down on the floor if you try to get her to live outside books or movies.

She said, "You forget. I start rumors. I beat people up. I'm very good at it." She added, "And I just stole your razor!"

She produced it from behind her.

She said, smiling brilliantly, "That's right. Nobody watches you all the time. They think they do but they don't. That's how magicians work. And you turned your back on me. *I* think you're careless."

She added, "I could run downstairs and tell them you raped me, and they'd believe me, you know, but I never say what I'm really planning unless the other person knows all about it. That's a waste. Shall I put the razor back in the bathroom?"

He said, "Be quiet for a moment," and this daunted her. She had assumed that he was nice, trained to be nice; most people were and most people worried endlessly about being nice. It gave you a handle on their behavior.

He said abruptly, "Do you want to eat?"

"What?" She was puzzled.

He said, "You must eat, Irene, if you're not going home."

Dazed. She said joyfully, "Oh, no thanks." Sat on the bed with her shoes off and put her feet up. She said, "I've got money, you know. I can draw it out tomorrow. Three hundred dollars." She smiled freshly. "Ernst, you look just like a zoo gorilla. I think you're beautiful."

He said, "Put your shoes on; I'm getting you another room."

She sat up, alarmed. "You'll skip!"

"God damn it!" (and she saw him catch his breath in anger) "if you slept across the door, I could still get out! Put your shoes on."

She produced the room key. "I'll swallow it."

He said, "By Heavens, I will be followed to my grave by adolescents all swearing that I have mesmerized them or hypnotized them or magnetized them! All right, sleep with your clothes on. Do anything you like. We will be touching bums all night, which ought to reassure you that I'm not going anywhere. I would ring for a cot, but what you might tell the bellboy terrifies me. Put the key on the dresser."

She said, baffled, "Why are you so angry?"

He didn't answer but only pointed to the closet, so she peeled off her extra clothes and hung them up in it, two to a hanger. She got undressed in the bathroom, humming, and then dashed back to the closet in her slip, and then back into the bathroom. She was delighted and alarmed. She felt as if she'd turned into somebody else. When she finally ventured into the room he had wrapped himself in his overcoat, with trousers and all, and was lying feet-to-head on one side of the bed, so she lay down the proper way next to him. In the dark she decided to tell him about Irenee Adler *The* Woman, and so she did, in a dry, self-mocking, grown-up voice that scared her and made her bones ache; here is the little girl (said the voice), here is the trap, here is the little girl in the trap.

"Hey, who are you?" she whispered, suddenly shaken. "Who are you, anyway?"

She found herself whispering into the silence, "If you won't talk to me, then at least give me a good time, you bastard." She sat up in bed and tried to pull his coat off, which wasn't easy because he wasn't cooperating.

Ernst tried to choke her. Then he grabbed her and threw her against the wall. Terrified, she rolled off the bed and on to the floor; suddenly the night-table light came on, a bad connection, evidently, which her weight had accidentally jarred together. Ernst was sitting up in the bed and blinking.

She said, holding her throat, "Are you crazy?" His coat and the blankets were all over the floor. He stared at her stupidly, resembling more than ever the gorilla in the zoo, and it came to her that he was still asleep, that he had done all that in his sleep. He did not look attractive. Her heart pounding, she said sharply, "Get under the sheets and stop being silly." She added, "I won't touch you if it scares you."

He said thickly, "I collect them."

"Huh?"

"Little girls and little boys." His voice was a little clearer; he was probably waking up.

She said, "You know, you actually tried to kill me just now. I suppose it's your training, like the samurai just woken up. It really surprised me, though."

She got back into the bed and studied him in the light of the night-table lamp; it should have been kind to him but he still looked old. Old and dull, though he must know all sorts of exciting things like self-hypnosis and ju-jitsu and how to spot other agents, things like that. Was everything so dull? He appeared to fall asleep almost instantly and Irene felt let down, felt that she didn't want to get tied up with this character, who wasn't beautiful, that she wanted to go home to David. The feeling was very strong. There was an odd motion in the bed and Irene realized that it was herself, the desperate character, rocking back and forth, thoroughly exasperated and almost crying. Then she found herself throwing her arms about him, about his beautiful smell and his comfort in the dark. She was horribly horny. She cried, "Ernst, Ernst, please!"

"Oh come *on*, come on, *please!*"

• • •

It was not so different with Goliath than it had been with David. Though Rose wouldn't have believed that. She really had done it all before, though not in the same order or the same way; Ernst was nicer and had lasted much longer than David, he seemed to know more what she liked (and he talked about it while he was doing it, which embarrassed her), and doing it sideways was infinitely preferable, in her opinion, to being on bottom. She said to her lover:

"My mother would insist that I marry you. God knows, I've listened often enough to the story of her romantic life, but it always seems to end up the same way, there's something wrong with it. I love her, though. But you haven't a chance at seventeen, you haven't a chance as a girl. I've gotten into two bad colleges and the Marines won't take me, and I never did give much of a damn about culture, really; I'm not like Chloe. I'm lucky. I'm glad I found you. So I guess I've got to say 'Take me with you' though I'd rather cut my tongue out. But what I really need is to get right out of this world."

She wondered why he laughed so hard. She could feel his big chest shaking up and down like a steam engine. She wanted to crawl inside him or have him inside her again, not erotically but something else. She put her arms around him. She liked him well enough but was glad the sex was over; it had stirred her up too much and it wasn't brisk enough; if there was anything she did not like, it was Ernst Neumann's way of touching her all over, as if he loved her behind and her calves and the insides of her elbows. Still, she liked her mind being clearer and her senses more settled. Some of the things he'd done delighted her by the very idea of their wickedness, and she was trying to memorize them. She would tell them to . . . not to Chloe.

"Why," said his slow, deep voice in the darkness (and

somehow the voice was more exciting than he was, less material and more suggestive, like an embodied penis with something superhuman attached to it) "pick me? Why, out of all this, trust me?"

She said, "Because you're a good man," and to her own horror—for what would she do, what could she do if it ever proved to be not so? What if David and Goliath turned out to be the same?—she put her head down on his chest and began convulsively and hopelessly to weep.

Countess Lovelace (with her mathematics), Maria Sklodowska, and Mikolaj Kopernik are all on the loose in 'Alee's rock-hewn corridors. While the male visitor takes sherbet with their host, Irene Waskiewicz is performing a part of her job, which is to observe, and also satisfying a personal curiosity, perhaps a grudge. Dropping her tel-o-tale neatly and lightly on the bed, Irene follows with a lightened heart the plan for the particular type of middle-class housing to which the son of Bekkar's apartments belong; he and his family live in Ka'abah's version of tract housing—and this amuses her, but it also occurs to her that, except for freaks of conduction, the rock walls are nearly soundproof and this suggests too strongly what can be perpetrated and hidden behind walls no other family ever penetrates. It is a criminal privacy. Irene has much in the way of a glass-and-ceramics technology hidden about her and she passes the guardbot ready to use it, but the 'bot (a large, rectangular solid with a locked plate at stomach height) has apparently been programmed not to bother her. Nothing happens. The family control console shows four separate lights; she can't read the personnel codes but suspects that one—in a room about six feet by six feet—must be the maid, as 'Alee is listed for a domestic. There is a family member in the courtyard, moving rather fast, and two together in the large central room. From beyond the curtains, music is coming, as tacky and tinny as 'Alee's furniture, and stepping noiselessly through the curtains, she prepares to see And-His-Family at home.

Her first impression is that she has stepped into a store window at Christmas. The room is a mass of dancing, glittering specks of light. A false ceiling admits rays of artificial sunlight around its edge as if through a clerestory; someone in the middle of the room (Irene always checks exits and entrances before she bothers to individualize or distinguish people) is throwing handfuls of glitter into the air, and the room itself is draped in swag after swag of glittering white gauze. There is a door behind the two inhabitants through which Irene can see the beginnings of another room, and to her left (on their right as they're facing her) is a broad archway through which solid sunshine falls, more artificial light. It gives the feeling of light coming from miles above into a cave. Water is falling somewhere in the courtyard and the squirrel is out there, too; Irene has heard that characteristic bell noise before. She knows that the door behind the two women leads to a series of apartments nested around the two larger rooms like satellites, each opening into the other like a railroad flat. The confusion of light and dark is painful to the eye, but now the standing woman ceases to throw glitter-dust into the air and instead begins to wave up and down an odd sort of toy, something like a butterfly on a leash.

The standing woman is the maid. Her mistress—without the face-veil but as heavily laden with dress as Elizabeth the First—looks not regal but affected or ill; she's lying back on a cushioned bench. In *The Thousand*

and One Nights the lady Zubeydeh, wife of Haroon-er-Rasheed (after whom 'Alee's daughter has been named), is so ornamented and heavily dressed that she can't stand up; the old book is delighted at this and elaborates on it with medieval pride. To Irene's eyes all these people are as eerily narrow-boned as a Mannerist drawing, but it's clear that the maid is not only younger than the lady but a good deal healthier and handsomer.

It is also clear that the maid is sober and the lady either drunk or pretending to be.

As they catch sight of Irene it is the maid who collapses melodramatically, bending to the floor with a piercing scream: "Mistress! Mistress! Veil yourself!" The Wezeereh merely says, "Oh, shut up," and then adds in a slurred voice, "Look, I rend my veil," which she then does, at least symbolically, by pulling at her *izar* negligently with her two hands. The other woman, after having done her bit of proprietary playacting, seems more vexed than afraid, and as she prepares something very sharp—her handsome black brow corrugates with the intention—Zumurrud cries out in a loud voice, "El-Ward fi-l-Akmam! See to the visitor!"

Irene steps into the light.

"Oh, yes," says the Wezeereh, "look, El-Ward fi-l-Akmam, It's the stranger lady. The one who goes about with her face unveiled. Go on!"

El-Ward fi-l-Akmam comes forward, kneels, bows, and knocks her head against the floor. 'Alee would be very angry if he saw this; he doesn't want his child exposed to servile behavior. The maid says sulkily: "Welcome thou, O moon of stars, O dawn of day—"

"Yes, yes, sit down," says Zumurrud. "Don't be all day at it, El-Ward fi-l-Akmam!"

Behavior in the *hareem*, it seems, is not so formal as elsewhere; El-Ward fi-l-Akmam retreats behind her mistress's couch and Zumurrud simply waits for news from the outside. Irene waits, too. She remains in an unintimidating posture, insofar as this is possible when you weigh twice what your hostesses do and are two heads taller than the maid, who is the taller of them.

Zumurrud giggles. "Oh, you are such a big person! This little person must serve the big person." (She tries to climb out of her couch, overbalances, grabs at a bench's ornamental gilt, and subsides back into her languor, gasping and laughing.) "Tell me, dear visitor, are all the people so big in your country?"

El-Ward fi-l-Akmam say something spiteful under her breath.

"Shut up," says Zumurrud casually. "No. *I* will tell *you*. Only the women are so big. The women serve in the army and keep the men in *hareems*. El-Ward fi-l-Akmam, get our visitor *nebeedh*."

The maid skitters away in a servile, half-bent-over gait that in no way accords with her other actions; Irene is aware of El-Ward fi-l-Akmam's penetrating eyes and stubborn face. Therefore Irene does not teach the Wezeereh Zumurrud to shake hands; she returns her hostess's sloppy bow with one like the son of Bekkar's: hands joined palm to palm and back bent.

The Wezeereh screeches with laughter.

Then she says, confidentially, "Have you bought anything?" and launches into an account of her own latest purchase, a device to throw shining dust all over the room. There are remnants of sparkling stuff here and there on the floor. Zumurrud wants to amuse her guest by a demonstration but Irene demurs, the lady insists, her voice growing shriller and more careless, and Irene—for a moment—becomes a bit sharp.

The Wezeereh Zumurrud stops, with her hand on her heart. She looks as if she might weep. Slipping quickly to the floor, she bows in front of the foreign giantess and then climbs back on her bench, clasping her hands in front of her and staring blankly ahead. Tears run down her cheeks. From behind Irene a voice says with contempt, "Oh, don't mind her." This is El-Ward fi-l-Akmam. The maid slaps her mistress's cheeks lightly, cries, "Think of your children, Wezeereh! Think of the honor of your house!" and then, "Do you want your embroidery, Wezeereh?" Zumurrud nods. From behind one of the artificial waterfalls of white-silk-shot-with-silver, El-Ward fi-l-Akmam brings a piece of brilliant embroidery and a pair of reading glasses; Zumurrud continues to weep effortlessly and meaninglessly as the material is pushed into her hands and the glasses clapped on her nose; then she notices what has happened and slowly stops crying. She loosens the needle from an uncompleted place and begins to stitch.

El-Ward fi-l-Akmam moves away behind the couch and motions with her head that Irene should follow. She says loudly, "When the Wezeereh has finished that piece of embroidery, she will sell it for a large sum." She adds positively, "No, no! My employer trusts me. My employer knows I would do nothing dishonest," and then, with her forefinger over her lips, she reaches into the curtained wall and does something invisible to something invisible. She offers one hand to Irene, palm up.

El-Ward fi-l-Akmam looks frightened, but she must know there's only one way to get on in this world.

Irene takes from her belt some of the pink and green tokens that are the currency of Ka'abah and places them in the outstretched hand. The money tucked away somewhere in her robe, the woman's color comes back. She actually smiles. She cocks her head jauntily, looking up at Irene, a phenomenon that takes place at a height halfway between Irene's bottom rib and her collar-bone.

Irene says, "I want to find out about you, you know, as much as about the other people of Ka'abah."

El-Ward fi-l-Akmam looks baffled. "You are not from the Doctoress?"

Irene says, "Oh, no. We come from another country, to find out how people live here. The Wezeer knows about us. My partner is talking to the Wezeer and so I have come here to talk to the family. No, no, keep the money. I am not connected in any way with any Doctoress. And I would really rather know about yourself than about the Wezeereh, if you are willing to tell me."

El-Ward fi-l-Akmam says, "Not about the Wezeereh? But she's the important one. Look at all the things she's got!" She adds shyly, with a little laugh, "About me?"

Irene shrugs. "Why not? You live on Ka'abah. I want to find out how people live."

The maid hesitates and then says eagerly and hurriedly, with great energy, "If you want to know how people live here . . . ? Well, I can tell you. *I* know. *That one* has had an abortion—imagine!—and she's trying to get me to send for the Doctoress, to make her sterile. Imagine such wickedness! But these rich women are all alike; they'll do anything. They have no virtue. Let me tell you, if it was I who was married to a successful man" (here she grows more measured and more earnest) "you wouldn't find me being idle and wicked. I would be grateful to God and the good man!" (she draws herself up and almost spits this at Irene) "Nobody would have to medicate *me*."

"Medicate?" says Irene sharply.

But El-Ward fi-l-Akmam either does not notice or does not care. She goes on: "You can go back to your country and tell them that the poor of Ka'abah are trampled upon and that the rich gain every day. It's like everywhere else. If I were in her place I would spend money to beautify my daughters, and if from time to time

60

I bought something to amuse myself—I wouldn't waste money outright the way she does, oh no, do you know she once had me burn a pound token right in front of her eyes? and it wouldn't burn and I had to beat at it with a pan, to break it—well, if I bought some toy, I wouldn't break it and throw it down as soon as I was finished. Oh, no!"

"So you believe the Wezeereh—" Irene says, prompting.

"She's *sick*," says El-Ward fi-l-Akmam positively; "her personality is deranged. That's why the Wezeer hired me, because he knows I'm trustworthy. He's a very good man; he doesn't divorce her or send her back to her parents or knock her down. He has a conscience. All the man wants is respect and consideration in his own house, which is what any man deserves. *I* am respectful to him and he appreciates it. All he gets is trouble. From a woman who didn't grow up in the barracks; *she* wasn't crowded ten to a room with her cousins and female relatives yammering at her and slapping her when she misbehaved or made noise! These rich girls have all the space they want to run about in and *that one*" (she jabbed her thumb towards the courtyard) "even has a live animal toy she can talk to and waste food on. And they will take out her lower ribs, too, next year, so she'll be slender."

El-Ward fi-l-Akmam says all this with great energy, not as spite but as a lecture to a stranger on the advantages of the rich and the forbearance and virtue with which the poor face injustice. She glances towards her mistress, as if afraid, and then says shyly, in a low voice, "Do you want to hear about me?"

Irene nods.

"Well," says El-Ward fi-l-Akmam, playing with the tassel of her sash, "those who grow up in the barracks can still come to wear silk." She turns faintly pink. "I have my plans," she says. Irene, trying to find the reason for this

61

torrent of words, asks her if she often has someone to talk to, and El-Ward fi-l-Akmam only stares, laughs, says, "What, *here*?" and goes on with her "plans." The Wezeer, 'Alee son of Bekkar, will recognize and reward the devotion of his servant. Faithful service is always rewarded. El-Ward fi-l-Akmam, who was worn out taking care of her baby sisters and brothers when she herself should have been romping as a child, will save money given her by the appreciative son of Bekkar and will buy herself proper surgery; before she is much older she will marry and marry well and have many children. Children are the joy of a woman's life. She'll have servants to look after them, and she herself will see them once a day to oversee their education. She will have a splendid house ("like this," she says, coloring). She will have nothing to do but enjoy herself and form her personality. She will be able to watch the television without being interrupted every moment by the needs of a madwoman. She adds hastily that she means the Wezeereh, of course, though probably "mad" is too strong a word for the Wezeereh. But she will be as rich as the Wezeereh, she will have as many beautiful things as the Wezeereh, and she will be happy, as the Wezeereh has not the virtue to be. She will never go out; therefore rude men will not pluck her by the robe as she hurries down the dangerous streets. She will never work; therefore she will be able to enjoy herself continuously. She will elevate her relatives but not see them, lest their vulgarity corrupt her children; therefore she will have peace. Her husband will be inflamed by her beauty and will never hit her. She says:

"Oh! I have my plans."

Irene says (again), "You have few people to talk to," but at this moment there is a jingle of sound at the archway to the courtyard and in stumbles a fantastic little figure, unbelievably small and slender and straight as a reed. She wears a costume as elaborate as her mother's. It is Zubeydeh, with her eyes unfocused. She is smiling foolishly. She says, "I heard everything you said," and staggers to the middle of the room, where she falls down.

She says, "I took Mommy's old medicine."

And what a fuss there is! Zumurrud weeping and calling her a bad child, El-Ward fi-l-Akmam shaking her systematically, as if she's some kind of clock that has to be set right, Zumurrud throwing her embroidery on the floor, Zumurrud screaming, El-Ward fi-l-Akmam with hands raised in horror, calling on Heaven to witness the premature depravity of this wretched little girl, and Zubeydeh huddled on the floor, hiccoughing, as El-Ward fi-l-Akmam shakes her again.

The maid exclaims wrathfully, "How many times have I told you that you are not to be like your mother?" and Zumurrud cries, "No, don't be like me!" and begins to weep afresh.

Irene plucks the little girl from them—she weighs as much as an earthly seven-year-old—and sets her on the tile floor, where she sits gasping, opening and shutting her mouth like a fish.

Then, in the grip of the drug, she begins to chant something loud and rhythmical, crying, "Listen to me! Listen to me!" El-Ward fi-l-Akmam is furious and frightened and Zumurrud has turned ghastly pale; the mother puts her hands over her ears and says something to herself over and over; to Irene it sounds like "Oh, no, oh, no," and then something about a personage called Dunya.

Zubeydeh, smaller and less habituated than her mother, shrieks, *"I'm going to be a poet!"* at which statement El-Ward fi-l-Akmam comes out of her paralysis and springs toward the little girl, grabbing Zubeydeh with one arm and sticking the fingers of the other hand down Zubeydeh's throat; 'Alee's daughter gags and brings up a small, yellowish clot; then the maid bears her swiftly into the room behind, where similar noises recur. Little Zubeydeh is retching.

Zumurrud says, almost sober, "That is my daughter. She has some odd fancy to be a poet like her aunt Dunya. It's an idea little girls get. Last year Zubeydeh was going to disguise herself as a boy and fly offworld to become a miner. When my sister Dunya was young, she imagined the same fancies; we took her writing materials away and she bribed the maid to smuggle them in again; we took them away many times and my sister outgrew the idea. She's dead now. You can't always allow children to do what they want; it's not good for them."

El-Ward fi-l-Akmam returns with a limp Zubeydeh. The little girl looks even smaller, like a cat that's been washed. The maid is scolding: "What would brother Jaafar say!"

"My brother helps me," says Zubeydeh, barely audible. She is dumped in the middle of the floor and the maid, her eyes snapping, goes for materials to clean the tiles. El-Ward fil-l-Akmam is in a rage. She shouts at her mistress, as she goes, "Is it for me to do robot work? Am I shadow-life? Mistress, control your daughter!"

"Jaafar practices with me," says Zubeydeh. She is still quite intoxicated. Zumurrud looks odd; to Irene's practiced eye she looks as if she were afraid of her daughter. Zumurrud says in a low, hurried voice, as if fearful that someone will hear:

"Zubeydeh, all girl-children go through this stage; you know that. It is the turbulence of your new feminine identity establishing itself. Without a check from the presence of the male, that new femininity overblooms and becomes its own opposite; thus the little girl is tempted off her true path; she wishes to do fanciful and silly things like fight with a sword or compose verses. Her marriage adjusts and balances all this; once married, she becomes the woman she should be, in perfect balance with her husband, and her femininity finds its true expression in having children of her own, not in some phantom imitation of a life she can never have. You don't really want to be a boy, Zubeydeh, do you?"

"Yes," says a semi-extinguished Zubeydeh, from the floor.

"But don't you want a beautiful young husband?" says Zumurrud timidly. "Don't you want a handsome young man for your very own?"

"I want to marry Daddy," says Zubeydeh.

Zumurrud compresses her lips, smiles in fright at Irene, and takes up her embroidery.

Zubeydeh says plaintively, "Mommy?"

Zumurrud looks at her daughter, trembling.

"Mommy," says Zubeydeh, "when you finish that, what will you spend the money on? What *can* you spend the money on, Mommy?"

"When I finish this," says Zumurrud carefully, "I will sell it for a large sum of money and with that money I will buy something beautiful to amuse us."

"I know what you'll buy," says Zubeydeh, with baby cynicism. "You'll buy...another piece of embroidery!"

"If I only bought what I sold," says Zumurrud a little sharply, "that would be foolish. There would be no reason to do embroidery. I will buy you a beautification. I will buy you a pair of earrings."

"To beautify me," says Zubeydeh. "So I can get married. So I can afford to do fancy embroidery and get money for it. To make *my* daughter beautiful. So she can get married. So she can afford to do fancy embroidery. To make *her* daughter beautiful. To get married. To do embroidery. To get married...."

Zubeydeh begins to wail. Zumurrud, looking quite sober now, jumps off her couch, runs to her baby, and embraces the child of her heart. They cling to each other.

Zubeydeh says, "Mommy, I want to be a poet."

"No, no, no!" cries Zumurrud, turning Zubeydeh away from Irene's sight, trying to shield the little girl with her body. El-Ward fil-l-Akmam comes in, rag and bucket in hand; it is not right for machines to do personal tending and whenever possible this is delegated to people, but the stain Zubeydeh has left on the floor is of an intermediate character, so that it is just possible to have it cleaned by a shadow-servant. El-Ward fi-l-Akmam claps her hands loudly for the Household All, and says authoritatively to her mistress:

"Mistress, you are not well. Your medicine is wearing off. You must lie down at once and have another injection."

"I am well, I am well!" cries Zumurrud, drawing herself up.

"Your medicine is wearing off," says El-Ward fi-l-Akmam, clenching her fists.

"I know it," says the lady Zumurrud sharply, "and I also know that my husband, the Wezeer, will not reward an over-zealous service."

El-Ward fi-l-Akmam seems, for a moment, to be on the verge of effecting her will by force. The next moment she controls herself and retreats, exasperated, just as the Household All spins between them, dexterously avoiding in the room not only people but any object that might be damaged by its course. It cannot alter its search pattern, but in its spinning, hovers for a moment over the stain on the floor and then searches on, leaving the floor clean. Zumurrud claps her hands and the machine spins out. Zumurrud says haughtily and clearly, "I require no more service. You may turn the recording device on as you go.

You are a stupid, badly educated woman, El-Ward fi-l-Akmam, and I beg you to remember that although my medication affects my emotions, it affects neither my perceptions nor my memory. It is not the Wezeer's intent to make you mistress here."

The maid backs into the wall, swearing under her breath, and again does something unseen to something behind the curtains. She then goes into one of the back rooms. Zumurrud kneels down (to put her arms around Zubeydeh, who had simply sat down when released) and whispers, "Baby. Baby, look. Look at this strange woman!"

Zubeydeh does so, curiously.

"This is an ugly woman," says Zumurrud. "See how ugly? Her breasts are not large and beautiful, as your mother's are. She has no jewels and her clothes are ugly. She comes from a place where women have to work all the time and have no beauty or joy in their lives. They are not allowed lovely clothes and beauty spots the way we are. She has no mole, look. This woman spends her day ruining herself by doing hard, heavy work, like a man. She is sick all the time. No man is attracted to her. She is lonely and will never marry. The women there long for feminine development, but it is not allowed to them; they live in dull, drab rooms where they are kept all alone. Nobody loves them. If you keep trying to become a poet, you will be like this woman. You will miss all the good in life." Zumurrud, bending over her daughter, looks up at Irene in a desperate appeal for complicity. She says, "Isn't that true? Tell her. Isn't your life like that?"

"No," says Irene pitilessly.

"But it's true, it's true!" cries Zumurrud hysterically. "It's all true! No woman can become a poet in your world! You unveil your face only to wash floors! Your men hate you and find you ugly! They sleep only with each other!

Only the men are poets in your world and no woman is ever a poet!"

Zubeydeh says, soberer than before, with a child's rationality:

"Could I be a poet in your world?"

"Yes," says Irene.

Irene will always remember—not Zumurrud's face at that moment but the shock it gives—and then Zumurrud, who is afraid of her, pushing her out of the *hareem*, weeping incoherently, crying that it's all lies, and trying desperately to hold the little girl to her, her whole body shaking with sobs. In the entrance to the *hareem* is a veiled figure which turns out, when it speaks, to be El-Ward fi-l-Akmam, who unwinds her *izar* and her face-veil with a sigh.

The maid says sadly, "She's off again. Now I can't go out."

Irene is about to do something irritable when El-Ward fi-l-Akmam prevents any such phenomenon by sighing and shaking her head.

"Poor woman," she says, quite genuinely. She adds, "God sends trials to the rich as well as to the poor."

She says then, "Thank you, foreign lady, for lightening the Wezeereh's illness. I am only sorry you had to see this." It occurs to Irene that all this may be for the benefit of the bugging devices, but the maid's contrition seems genuine. El-Ward fi-l-Akmam continues: "Please, I ask you to go now."

On Ka'abah only the deformed, the incurably diseased, and the extremely poor do not marry. The maid seems none of these things; Irene therefore says, "I'll go, but tell me one thing. It's a rude thing and you needn't answer if you wish. If you don't wish, say so and I'll go. But why have you never married?"

The maid smiles. It's an incredulous smile. El-Ward fi-l-Akmam makes an odd movement with her hand; she attempts to duck her head. Her comely, healthy face turns red. Still smiling, she answers.

"Oh, Wezeereh," she says in a soft, hopeless voice, "can't you see?

"I am so ugly."

Public processions in Ka'abah are often merely windings through narrow, rocky ways. These are the streets. Heat and oxygen are provided as they would be to the interior of a hotel; the price of excavation is high and there is one Great Way for public events in which the side standard-bearers need not duck to avoid the ventilation ducts. Here crowds collect and people walk more than five abreast. To make war on Ka'abah one would not invade Within, but only attack the surface power stations that skim a fraction of the fierce solar radiation from Outside. Ka'abah is a burning rock that carries at its center a cave and a pool, and in the center of the cave, rising from the pool, is the woman, and in the center of the woman is Heaven. Hell is Outside. One of the powers dickering with Ka'abah for the privilege of keeping a fleet stationed Outside is Irene Waskiewicz's employer.

She spent the morning at GUM-Interpol, buying things. Their business is half remote orders and half cash-and-carry; not that there is one building, as on most worlds, but a collection of rooms and a certain number of hallways can be given a separate legal existence. There is the separation of merchandise as a convenience for servants like El-Ward fi-l-Akmam, a curtained gallery at each level where women may inspect merchandise from afar and have it brought to them if they wish; but Irene goes as a matter of course through the main body of the store. She is glanced at (she's a head taller than anyone there) and spoken to courteously several times (once in poetry) but this is no more than what she expects; Ka'abah is full of strangers nowadays.

There are veils, dresses, articles of furniture, jewelry, sexual objects, lighting fixtures, home machinery, toys, books, art, materials, trees, carpets, chemistry sets, pets, linens, television cassettes, university extension courses, parts for surface vehicles, panelling, enamels, drapes, drugs, a cafeteria, artificial flowers and plants, artificial birds, real plants, a prostitution bureau, a place to get tickets for television shows, and hologrammic panels of famous scenery.

Delivery on the last takes six to eight months and the stock is meager; Irene suspects that Ka'abites don't like to be reminded of Outside.

On the lowest floor, hidden away in a cubbyhole, is environmental equipment, including protective gear necessary for going Outside.

In the middle of the cafeteria is a fountain wired for light and constructed of three thousand separate pieces of imported crystal. No one has yet bought it because no one on Ka'abah can afford it.

Irene buys an artificial canary and two real plants, one broad-leafed and one trailing, all three items to be delivered.

She has sherbet in the cafeteria, avoiding the Ka'abites who are eating breakfast there.

In the book section she buys six cheap, self-destructing books on how to manage one's personal life (there are two to choose between for men, eighteen to choose among for women).

The Gang doesn't buy souvenirs.

Irene buys, in addition to her six how-to's, a copy of

the latest novel, another work (on the verge of being censored) which argues equally for economic Socialism and the use of representative images. She has these delivered also and leaves empty-handed. GUM-Interpol operates a luxury café as well as an ordinary eating place; she takes an elevator to the former and emerges in the central kiosk near Great Way. From a wall slot—this "shadow-life" is coded with a face carrying tiny features except for its vast mouth—Irene buys a bilingual newspaper and studies the political cartoons: predictable stuff, mostly self-applause. The letter column will be more revealing. There is a bad political cartoon of the Ka'abite Opposition holding an *oud* whose strings are broken. The *oud* is labeled "Economic Situation." Caption: "I only wanted to tune it." Great Way is some thirty yards across, filled with diffuse, artificial sunshine, as if it were a covered street in an uncovered city; this produces a strong, unconscious conviction that merely turning the corner will take one out into the open air and under a real sky. It is nine-hours-thirty and there are few early risers in the Interpol Café; thus she stops off there (it's around the corner in a side corridor), drinks coffee, and watches the short, slight figures pass her, some briskly on business, some peering into Great Way and discussing where to stand for the procession, two sitting in the corner of the café holding hands, one running with robes held up, rich ones in embroidered slippers, poorer (or soberer) ones in gray, persons with chests on their backs or Carries following them like pets, one figure whose *tarboosh* is askew, who's gotten drunk at this early hour (or last night) and suddenly sings as he rounds the corner. There's a clock, half buried in filigree, on the far wall; she compares the time it shows with her own watch. She orders raisin wine. It is a street, she thinks, which twelve-year-old Zubeydeh has never seen, which her

71

mother Zumurrud has perhaps seen once (on her wedding day) and which El-Ward fi-l-Akmam traverses perhaps once a month, uncomfortable and terrified, with a Household All doing ineffectual guard duty at her back.

The wine arrives, borne on gimbals to a recess in the center of the table. The center column sinks smoothly and the surface panel closes again. This central city of Ka'abah houses some ten thousand persons.

Then a small, veiled figure, brilliant in white and gold, edges in a terrified manner out of a doorway on the farther side of the street and walks with an odd, constricted gait to the edge of the café. She sways voluptuously. The surface of her *izar* is hung with jewelry and she tinkles as she walks, holding a fold of the expensive, gold-embroidered tissue of her *kinaa* in front of her face. Heads turn as Ka'abites notice her; a good-looking young man, who has sat down near Irene, pulls up his chair, the better to see this woman.

Following the woman is a great, hulking, hideous fellow in blue pajamas and gold *tarboosh*, intent on grasping her robe.

The street holds its breath. The young man next to Irene half gets up, his face flushed, his mouth open.

The woman turns, and seeing her pursuer, screams. Between the farthest tables of the Interpol Café she weaves as if intoxicated, screaming time after time, terrified but harmonious, like a willow-tree, gracefully falling from side to side. There is an odd motion inside the cocoon of veiling and she can be seen to throw a ring of gold at her pursuer.

Then she faints. The very young man who has been neighbor to Irene now gets to his feet in earnest, starting around Irene's table. Someone nearby whispers, "Is it a prostitute?" and then—suddenly laughing aloud—"No, no, it's the actor! It's Ala-ed-Deen!" as a whole camera crew of Ka'abites comes into the café from a door in the opposite wall. Hidden, they've been filming the scene.

The lady in white-and-gold gets up, plants herself in a chair, unveils, and shouts for coffee. His fellow-performer ("the famous Suleyman-es-Zeynee" whispers the young man next to Irene, awed) takes the gold *tarboosh* off his head and does likewise, though more quietly. The entire production crew—some twenty persons—has, it seems, been filming early so as to find the streets deserted; now they crowd into the café for food and drink, chatting loudly with one another. Ala-ed-Deen, brilliantly made up as a woman, vigorously swaps obscenities with the passersby.

The young man who had almost gone to the rescue of the lady now sits down next to Irene, flushed and delighted, and remarks aloud to no one in particular that actors always marry late and reluctantly and that when they do they require anatomical impossibilities of their wives.

The ebullient Ala-ed-Deen shouts back an invitation to try it some time, and the café roars.

The young man says to Irene, "Your pardon, sir. This youth is the son of the son of Bekkar. I am glad you have had an opportunity of witnessing this piece of art."

Irene bows and gives her name. The young man bows. He says, "This son is Jaafar." He adds, "I am awfully stupid, but I am only sixteen. I was ready to go to the lady's rescue! You must admit that such persuasion is really art of the highest order."

Irene nods. Jaafar, son of 'Alee, son of Bekkar, grandson of Bekkar (son of Willful Settlement in Cloud-Cuckooland, Irene thinks) turns around, awed again, to gaze at the actors, his mouth half-open. Irene knows the type; romantic, enthusiastic, innocently opinionated, easy to squash, and immensely loveable until suddenly at twenty-five he will turn unexpectedly into a carbon copy of his father. She supposes—seriously underestimating herself—that she was once as naive as that. Jaafar's head swivels back to the stranger, drawn by the demands of etiquette; he colors, looking at her, and Irene becomes aware that this puppy-dog finds her attractive.

Under false pretenses, of course.

She says dryly, "It is impolite to stare."

Jaafar closes his mouth and blushes worse. To be reprimanded for a breach of manners by a foreigner, an older man, someone one might find pleasing . . . he lowers his eyes.

Talk around them has turned to the coming procession; as far as she can judge from the bits and pieces she hears, the men will be dispersing soon to find places and the women will be watching on the television at home.

Jaafar says, behaving himself, "Oh, sir, women are lucky. They don't have to fight the crowds. My—um, a fellow's sister, say, if he had a sister, she'll have a much better view than either of us."

"Not better than mine," says Irene. "You forget; I'll be in it."

Jaafar sneaks a look at the actors again. Ala-ed-Deen has finished his coffee and the rest of the crew is mopping up the last bits of their food with bread (the Ka'abite sign that the meal is over). Some have paid and are getting up. Jaafar says, hesitantly, "Don't you . . . don't you think, sir, that there is a special emotion in the rescue of a distressed woman? I mean in art, that is, aesthetically. The poet says 'Beauty draws us by a thousand strings of helplessness.' I am attempting to write such a poem myself and this piece of aesthetic signification we have just witnessed will be of great help. I think I'll call it "Truth in the Café.' Do you think that's a good title, sir? Of course" (and here Jaafar suddenly retreats into his anxious phase) "I daresay you foreigners have very great art Outside. I know nothing about it and so shouldn't speak, should I?"

Irene resists the temptation to up-end him. It's impossible for her to be inconspicuous on Ka'abah, but there are degrees of memorableness and a sixteen-year-old held upside down by the ankles ranks pretty high. She says instead, wondering if even this isn't a little knowledgeable in a foreigner, "The poet says, 'One's eye sees, one's heart speaks.'"

Jaafar nods, fortified. It's not strange to him that a huge foreign man in uniform knows Ka'abah's poets; after all, doesn't everybody? He beams and opens his mouth self-importantly for a long siege of more poetry but Irene prevents him:

"Would you like to meet the actor?"

Jaafar deflates. He tries to speak, finally managing "Do you *know* him?" in a sort of squeak. Irene says no, but she may be able to do it anyway, and Jaafar, trailing her in agonized happiness to the edge of the café, waits while she speaks a few commonplaces and then makes the request in the name of interplanetary amity. Ala-ed-Deen has, with the magnetism of a star, the same rehearsed sincerity; close up his face looks handsome but overpainted, too bold and too brilliant. He is very short. As they talk, Jaafar painfully and the actor patiently and apparently rather tired, Irene retreats. The crew will, of course, remember her, but only as a foreigner. Jaafar will remember her as big and pale, but then all white off-worlders on Ka'abah are big and pale.

As she reaches the entrance to Great Way she sees that Ala-ed-Deen has veiled himself for the next take and is practicing a bit of mischief on the boy (possibly, she thinks, to head off another plague of quotations). Wrapped and bejewelled, the mysterious figure of the Distressed Woman thrusts its hips at the boy poet, and

Jaafar, beet-red, claps both hands over the front of his pants. The film crew roars. She wonders if this is something the actor has been threatening to do if his public bothered him too much; at any rate, the crew's memory of her will be somewhat muddled, somewhat shaken up by the events of the day.

And Jaafar, it is clear, will not remember her at all.

There are many one-person elevators on Ka'abah, usually used by women; there are also ventilation ducts. Elevators keep records of the stops they make but the ventilation system keeps no records at all. Taking a one-woman lift to a small corridor above Great Way, Irene punches tabs for another destination, instructing the elevator to stop at every possible place in between. Then she gets out, and while the elevator slides up its shaft, swings herself into the ventilation system overhead, lifting out the grille and snapping it back into place after her. She knows the map. There are handholds in the duct but they're for smaller people; she moves with difficulty until she gets to the broader vent where she can swing rapidly hand over hand. She repeats the process at the other end, jimmies the grille cover, and emerges into a narrow, featureless corridor. To the right there is a door. The lock here is magnetic and needs to be fooled open with an induction coil; inside there is another door, and inside that a sentry in a red *tarboosh* whom she puts to sleep with a spray. Ka'abah's too poor to have the proper experts. They're all off to see the wizard today, anyway. Beyond the sentry is another door, this one harder to open, and beyond that a computer bank, which doesn't need screamies because it keeps traces of all its own transactions. This one (she thinks but doesn't know for sure, doesn't have to know) is connected to the banking system; she sits in front of it, slips on gloves, and plays piano on the keyboard. It's unlikely that anyone at this end will be using it for the next few hours, so she instructs it to remember and perform incoming bits but not remember any of those that originate at the terminals.

Irene's real job is now over. She waits impatiently for a few moments until the board's ceased being busy—it clears—checks to see she's left no traces, wonders what information others in The Gang have sucked out of the files from the central terminals—then wipes out her previous instructions to the machine, locks the door (easy enough, they lock themselves, but she makes sure no record's being kept of openings and closings), sidesteps the sentry, re-locks the next door, and the next, and then goes back into the ventilation system. Ka'abah is easy; there's no dust underground. She retraces her way and comes out not where she entered but where she sent the elevator (few women will be abroad today, taking the Women's Lifts) and from there she walks visibly through major streets to Justice Hall.

The whole digression has taken seventeen minutes.

Ka'abites behind Justice Hall have been watching a parade form, with all the confusion attendant upon people wandering out of control and banners that won't stay up and groups that turn out to be too large and whose movements conflict, and in general the maximum confusion that can be created by a lot of people who won't stay put in a small space. Many get lost and come in late. Irene slips into place next to Ernst, who raises his eyebrows.

She says, "I got stuck in the elevator. I did something wrong; it stopped at every damned stop."

So now he knows.

She says, "It's so boring."

He says, "It's medieval. We walk for hours through these warrens with the little people throwing glitterdust at us; everybody shouts themselves hoarse and when it's all over the conferences begin and we have nothing to do. Public relations!"

Irene wonders where on Ka'abah the real specialists have been hidden until now, the ones who got the information The Gang wants—the information of which hers was only a part, and about which she knows nothing, for The Gang, in addition to its ostensible purposes (in which she doesn't believe) always gathers all the information it can. She wonders if she'll ever know The Gang's real purpose. She hopes her tampon will last the day, but it ought to; she's put in two of them. She thinks with amusement of leaving menstrual blood in a trail down Great Way.

She says absently, to Ernst, "Hell, you don't mean people. You don't mean 'everybody.' You mean men."

Jullanar, the daughter of the Wezeer, is to be married off to a handsome young nephew of the Cadee. His face is like the full moon, his gait is graceful as the letter Aleph, and above his brows he has a mole the color of ambergris. This poet first-class is called Noor-ed-Deen. When told of the marriage (in Act One) Jullanar weeps for joy; she attempts to compose original love verses but finds that her efforts pale beside Noor-ed-Deen's and the classics; she therefore contents herself with inscribing classical verses in her album and singing them at the grate of her window in the usual metre. (The Working Class Woman in Love is a subject for comedy, e.g., the play of the

Baker's Daughter, in which the protagonist is threatened with an unwitting marriage to two men at once, one of them old and one of them young. If the proletarian Young Woman in Love uses aristocratic metres, this is a sign that her real ancestry has been concealed and will be revealed in the last ten minutes of the play. Irene, who is watching TV alone with her feet up, wonders what Zubeydeh has made of stories in which women attempt to write poetry.) Outside among the jasmine the moon rises, and the effect of the moonlight mingling with the rose-shaded lamps indoors, the smell of jasmine, and the voice of Noor-ed-Deen (which Jullanar dreams that she hears, unearthly sweet, coming from the night outside) ends the first act.

Act Two opens with a servants' ballet, in which the news of Jullanar's approaching marriage vies with—and succumbs to—the terrible news that her betrothed is in love already, and with a man. (This is all pantomime.) Noor-ed-Deen's lover is a fellow poet and Noor-ed-Deen has declared that neither he nor his friend will ever marry. Jullanar is singing again at her window, apostrophizing the moon through the fretted grillework, when the news reaches her. She faints, thus causing a chorus of maidservants, sisters, brothers, and grandparents to lament for her in close counterpoint; she spends the rest of the act bewailing her miserable fate—to marry a Man-lover. (We intercut here with scenes of Noor-ed-Deen composing chaste but devoted poems to his male friend, and singing aloud his indifference to the beauty of women. We learn, in a timely flashback, that his character has been formed by having been orphaned as a child and never having had the presence of a mother to balance his youthful masculinity; his father, the Cadee's brother, is severely blamed for having allowed excessive devotion to the long-dead mother to have kept him from remarrying.)

In Act Three we find that Noor-ed-Deen has submitted

to the marriage out of filial duty, but has determined to flee immediately afterwards; the miserable Jullanar returns from the public procession of the wedding—at which, she says, she barely saw the streets and the cheering multitude through her veil, so distracted was she by Noor-ed-Deen's beauty—and after a famous classical aria, in which the bride (moving "her" voice rapidly from falsetto to tenor) pictures the rejection awaiting her, her miserable and lonely life as a spinster-wife, and her childless death in old age, Noor-ed-Deen is led reluctantly in and left alone with his bride. Here all the resources of the television studio are employed in a grand appeal to love (including, at one point, the ghost of Noor-ed-Deen's mother) in which the mother, the moon, the bride, a chorus of family outside the chamber, in short everyone but the groom, join. On her knees before him, Jullanar finally prevails upon her husband at least to take the one glimpse of her face that etiquette demands. He does so and immediately falls in love; Jullanar sings a song of thanksgiving to her mother, who bought her so many beautifications, and adds that she no longer wishes to compose poetry but only to spend her life "reading the poetry of love in his face." Noor-ed-Deen determines to find a wife for his friend without delay and fixes on Jullanar's cousin (whom we have seen briefly before) for the match, the lovers retire, and the play continues on the adult channels as in part a pornographic ballet, in part a song, and in part a montage of abstract effects. (Pornography is losing on Ka'abah and abstraction gaining.) Here Irene hears a blundering noise from the corner of the room, a kind of cockeyed stagger, and around the corner of the mercury bed comes a small figure clutching at the pom-poms and the curtains. It is Zubeydeh, making a funny noise, a sort of sobby hiccough. The overdecorated little girl leans on the television set, staring blankly at Irene; goodness knows how she found the room when everything outside the *hareem* is out of bounds to women. Has Zubeydeh taken her mother's pills again? Irene pushes the television armrest control, the picture dwindles and dies, and Zubeydeh—who by now has made it to Irene's knees—grabs the edge of Irene's tunic and stammers something unintelligible. Her face is grey. Irene takes the child up into her lap; tears roll silently down Zubeydeh's face and the funny noise continues as Irene rocks her; then she slips to the floor and pulls spasmodically at Irene.

"Follow?" says Irene; "Okay, show me," thinking that something must have happened to Zumurrud—she hopes it's not an overdose—and hand in hand with Zubeydeh—what cold little fingers she has!—Irene follows the child out of the room. Zubeydeh's face-veil has come off and hangs askew from one ear. It surprises Irene that the little girl can find her way so easily out of the *hareem*, but then they probably come out when nobody's there, like mice from the wainscoting or like the furniture that children think dances at night when nobody's there to see it. At the entrance to the *hareem* Zubeydeh hesitates for a moment—Irene wonders why she doesn't consult the photopanel set near the guardbot—and then hits the wall again and again with the heel of her hand.

A gap opens in the corridor wall. A sliding panel. Zubeydeh, her color flooding back, screams, "There! There!" and pulls Irene through, stooping, for the ceiling is low even for a Ka'abite; Zubeydeh hauls her along, crying "It's Aunt Dunya!" and bangs on another part of the wall. There is a small, shuttered window set in the end of the corridor as if in place of a door; this slides open to Zubeydeh's pounding and Irene bends to look in. The little girl is crying, "Daddy did it! Daddy did it!"

At first Irene can see nothing. The walls beyond are

bare rock; there is an undecorated, naked bulb in the ceiling and someone has left a few crumpled pieces of paper on the floor and what look like smears of food. There is an odd smudge along the wall, some sixteen inches off the floor, as if furniture had been moved there repeatedly over the years and had scraped or in some fashion partially smoothed the rock. At the back of the room is what Irene recognizes as a crude sanitary facility: a tiled pit with a faucet, a ventilation fan, and a shower-head set into the wall. There's a mattress in one corner. There's nothing else except a heap of old clothes, and Irene wonders if she's stumbled on to one of the early rooms of Ka'abah, the temporary quarters used before borrowed money carved halls and living quarters from the bare rock.

Then the heap of clothes begins to stir. It fits itself into the smudge on the wall—so that's how, Irene thinks—and moves slowly along the floor. From time to time the woman whom one can't even see inside the rags becomes still, not stopping in any human attitude but ceasing the way a snail might do upon encountering an obstacle. Then the heap shivers a bit and for a few moments rocks back and forth, a movement in which Irene sees a faint echo of Zubeydeh's extravagant grief. And again the slow creeping along the wall.

Little Zubeydeh has wrapped her veil around her face and is rocking back and forth, too. She gasps, "*She* told me!" and Irene turns at the sound of footsteps to see the Wezeereh—El-Ward fi-l-Akmam is away, apparently—pacing up the tunnel with the blank steadiness of someone beyond even the euphoric effects of her medication. Zubeydeh runs to her and starts pounding at her with her fists: "You did it! You did it!"

Zumurrud says, "I heard everything." Irene finds, to her own surprise, that she has palmed a weapon, a glass-

and-ceramic-filament affair that dissolves walls, and is holding it on the Wezeereh as if the Wezeereh were about to become a dangerous person.

Zumurrud says, without expression, "This child wants to be a poet. She's crazy. She's as crazy as my sister Dunya. When Dunya was thirty she ran out into the streets and started to take her clothes off. She said God had given her a mysterious secret and she must show it to all of Ka'abah. My sister was on medication. We gave her electric shock, too. We had everything done, but nothing helped. My husband, the Wezeer, has spared no expense for Dunya but we had to lock her away; she soils herself and will tear to pieces anything you give her. I come to observe Dunya every day, and if she has a disease we put anesthesia through the ventilation duct and have her treated. It smells very bad in there. I took my daughter to see her because I want her to know what happens to women who go mad in our family."

Zubeydeh shrieks, "You did it! You were jealous of her! You had her put away!"

"Don't be foolish," says the Wezeereh, swaying a little on her feet. "Your father did it."

Zubeydeh attacks her mother, beating at her with her small fists. "Liar!"

"Your father did it," says Zumurrud.

Irene glances in the window again; the bundle of old clothes crawls slowly around the room. "Why didn't you stop him!" screams the daughter, "Why didn't you, why didn't you!" and launches herself at her mother again. Irene reaches a long arm between them. Zubeydeh starts to weep more naturally and Zumurrud, her face flushing, puts her arms around the child. Their ornaments jingle, their veils billow, their necklaces become tangled together. The Wezeereh says heavily:

"Your Aunt Dunya wanted to be a poet."

83

She adds, "We kept taking her papers away from her. They weren't good for her. And then we knew we had done the right thing because she went mad."

With a high, shrill eeeee-ing sound Zubeydeh tears herself loose and barrels down the corridor, yelling between her teeth. Irene, careful not to bang her own head, goes after. Behind her the Wezeereh (she glances back) remains stolidly expressionless. In the central room of the *hareem* Zubeydeh is deliberately tearing off her clothes, pulling jewelry off her robes and stamping on it, crying wildly, jerking ornaments off tables and throwing them to the floor, pulling savagely at her own hair. There is a jingle of bells in the next room. Irene says quietly:

"You are frightening Yasemeen."

Zubeydeh screams long and loud, in angry despair.

Irene says, "You're frightening me, too," and sits back on her knees so as to be nearer the child's level.

Zubeydeh stops. Her sobbing subsides. She says:

"I hate my clothes! I hate my jewelry! I hate Yasemeen!"

Irene says, "I hate them, too. But I like you."

Zubeydeh says, "I will be a poet! I won't give in!"

Irene wipes the tears off the child's cheeks with her forefinger. She says gravely, "Will you show me your poems? And explain them to me? I know the poetry of my own country but not yours."

Zubeydeh says anxiously, "I don't want to be a poet for my own sake. It is for the greater glory of our country."

Irene nods. Zubeydeh begins slowly to pick up her broken ornaments, to smooth her dress and put herself back into order. She says, still crying a little, "Daddy doesn't want me to be a poet, but that's only because he's afraid I'll fail. He doesn't understand, but I'll convince him. I know it's not good for women to be poets, but I'm different."

She adds puzzled, "Your face looks funny."

"Does it?" says Irene. "Well, I expect it does. I was thinking about a great woman poet in my country who talked with Death and with God. She rode away into Eternity with Death at her side and never came back. I can try to remember some of her poems for you, but I can't remember them now. Her name was Laura Dickinson."

She says then, "Zubeydeh, promise me one thing. When you speak to your father about Aunt Dunya, make sure I'm in the room with you. Promise? And in return I promise that I will speak to him about your poetry. As soon as I can."

Zubeydeh looks confused but nods. She says in a low voice, "I bet he doesn't know about it. Not really. I bet he thinks Aunt Dunya wasn't a real poet. She probably wasn't. But I promise." She goes running into the courtyard, shouting, "I'm going to get my poems!" and then, peering around the archway, "I'll make Daddy understand!" and then, incredulously radiant:

"Do you *really* want to see my poems?"

Irene says to Ernst, "First-rate poets don't get put in cages. Second-rate ones do. She doesn't question the system, only insists she's outside it. Daddy doesn't 'understand.' I've read the poems."

Ernst says, "Are they any good?"

She stares.

"Irenee," he says, "Irenee, please, do you think I am going to put her in a cage! I am curious only. May I see them?"

She hands them over, saying finally, "As far as I can tell, they're your ordinary juvenilia, the kind of thing you'd get from any bright and articulate twelve-year-old. You know the type."

He says absently, leafing through them, "Nightingales. Roses. Heroines. Patriotism."

She says, "I'm sorry. I know you won't put her in a cage. But you understand—"

She stops, stops all over, and adds carefully as he continues to study Zubeydeh's life-work, "I know I'm over my quota. But I would like.... I feel very strongly. And that woman, that dilapidated schizophrenic—"

"It's your decision," he says dryly. He adds with sudden, humorous energy, "Well! *Very* good for a twelve-year-old. But how does she suck the top of her pen through her veil?"

Irene finds herself saying, "God damn it, Ernst, the *kinaa* doesn't *grow* on them!" and after a short silence, "Well, I'm taking her back with us if I have to smuggle her out in a crate. And the aunt. If I have to pistol-whip the revolting little son of a Bekkar into it, which I wouldn't mind, by the way."

"Yes, of course," he says, tapping the sheaf of papers to even them up. Zubeydeh's handwriting—or rather her calligraphy, which is an important part of writing poetry on Ka'abah—is still childishly round. Irene has known Ernst's attitude toward the poor, the mad, and the tortured for years; it leaves nothing to be desired. She feels unjust. She may sleep on the floor tonight; Irene can sleep anywhere at any time, now. There are times she can't bear Ernst, times that seem to come out of nothing, to point to nothing. It's temperamental. She'll show him the madwoman tomorrow. The mercury bed may be leaking, and what other bizarre luxuries can be found in the corners of Ka'abah's stony rooms, their immense weight supported by solid rock? Unless 'Alee's house is on the lowest level.

Ernst says, "It is shocking and appalling. There's so much one wishes to do. Well. Take the poems. Tell her I'm impressed. I am, you know."

She thinks: *Not to give in. To forgive.* She says, "Yes."

She says with an effort, "Yes, dear, I will."

In her best clothes, choice poems up her sleeve, Zubeydeh trots along the corridor with her hand in Zumurrud's. Zumurrud has scrubbed Zubeydeh's face until it hurt and then covered it with the veil. Zumurrud has dismissed El-Ward fi-l-Akmam. She has stuck gold butterflies (on springs, so they seem to be flying) in Zubeydeh's hair until Zubeydeh shrieked with pain and is now telling her how to behave in front of the foreign lady: to subside gracefully on to the cushions, to hold the skirt of her robe with one hand, and never, never to look directly at the foreign man.

Zubeydeh says, "I know all that," sulkily tugging at her mother's hand, trying to make Zumurrud slow up. She thinks that sometimes it really is easier to get along with mother when mother's medicated. She wishes she could live with only her father. At the curtains to the visiting room Zumurrud stops and elevates her right arm, shaking it delicately, thus ringing the chimes on her Visiting Bracelet; inside Daddy will hear them and say, "Come in, thou." The Visiting Room is beautiful; Zubeydeh has been in it only twice before, but she knows it's the most beautiful room in the house. Zumurrud, of course, has been in it many times before, to supervise its cleaning. Yanked through the curtains by her mother, Zubeydeh tries to catch a glimpse of the carved molding that portrays an undersea scene with the abstract curves of red and blue imitating the curl of the waves, but she has no time to find it. She does manage to catch a glimpse of the benches and pillows, the little tables, the tabourets, the tesselated floor, and best of all, she gets a real look at the foreign man through her face-veil as she gracefully bows and then finishes the bow by lowering herself on to a cushion on the floor. Her mother says curiosity is the worst female sin. Zubeydeh thinks she's done pretty well by getting her rear to settle right in the middle of the cushion without any wobbling on the way down or last-minute shifting. She hopes Zumurrud won't find it necessary to slap her in public; mother can be beastly. Actually the foreign man is disappointing, since he looks so very much like the foreign lady; it shocks Zubeydeh's sense of what is proper that the two of them are so alike and she is genuinely scornful to find that the foreign man has no beard. A man without a beard looks like a eunuch or a youth (Jaafar, for instance), and one would expect him to be married to a youth and not a lady. She knows perfectly well that the foreign man and the foreign lady are married, even though Zumurrud insists they're not. She feels surreptitiously for the papers in her sleeve. The strange man and woman are sitting with Daddy on the far side of the room and everybody is making social noises; then the side curtains are pushed open and Jaafar comes in. Everybody says, "Welcome, thou" all over again. The foreign lady seems pleased to see Jaafar, as if she's going to laugh, and Zubeydeh wonders why; but then Jaafar's coming in must give everyone pleasure because Jaafar is such a dear. If it weren't such a formal visit, he'd pick her up and whirl her around as he usually does; he'd call her "Little Sister," "Baby Bit," or even—as he does sometimes—"Jingly Scribble." Here she gets her poems closer to hand, because that's going to be important, and reminds herself to show Jaafar the one poem she's never showed him, a bad one in free metre about a silly subject. It goes:

> Sleep is a dear blessing.
> When I sleep the night-light becomes the Moon
> And then I imagine I am
> Outside.

Some day (she thinks) she'll change it to the beginning of a poem spoken by Budr-el-Badr dreaming of her husband far away in Baghdad. It occurs to Zubeydeh that if she is ever going to be a television playwright (one of her ambitions) she ought to practice by taking down in her mind what people are saying; she imagines her play being performed in a television studio, announced as the work of Jaafar, son of Bekkar, grandson of Bekkar, great-grandson of Bekkar. Secretly everyone will know it is hers, of course. Dutifully Zubeydeh opens her ears and sets herself to listening to the grown-ups' conversation— she assumes that everybody has a switch in their heads with which they can turn off their surroundings—and also watching Jaafar and trying to find words for the expressions, alternately attentive and eager, with which her brother is listening to Daddy.

Daddy is saying, "...when our guests leave tomorrow."

Zubeydeh's poems fall down into the bottom of her sleeve.

Zumurrud pokes her sharply: "Sssssh!"

"But—" squeaks Zubeydeh, nonplussed, and is rewarded with another (and sharper) poke. Jaafar is mooning at the foreign man. Tomorrow! She wonders what is the best thing to say. She knows that at bottom it's a matter of the right words, as in the Play of El-Barmekee where the milkmaid calms the raging crowd by speaking persuasively. Her heart feels as if it will knock through her ribs with fear and excitement. She remembers the promise the foreign lady got from her, and so, waiting for an apt place in the conversation (Jaafar will discuss poetry with the foreign man; Jaafar is smart) she fidgets on her cushion, her poems ready to hand. Everybody in the family knows about them but nobody is supposed to know that anybody else knows; she's aware of that. Suddenly Zubeydeh finds herself crying out anxiously in the middle of a classical quotation from Jaafar:

"I want to say something!"

Immediately Zumurrud is shaking her. Zubeydeh can't see much past her mother, especially through the veil, and especially since she's being shaken like a milk churn, but she does see a large, pale hand come to restrain Zumurrud, one without jewels or paint on the nails, the foreign woman's hand. It ought to be Daddy's hand. Zubeydeh understands for the first time that a "woman" is not always a "lady" and that the foreigner may really do something horrible, like scrubbing floors, in her own home. Zubeydeh thinks (with a certain literary thrill) that this person could be a *jinneeyeh* or even a *ghooleh*. The foreign voice, harsh, low, and queer, says:

"Please, Wezeereh, please. It is useless. We all know your daughter's secret."

"What? What? What?" says 'Alee, the way he does when he's flustered by something (Zubeydeh often thinks her Daddy is comical; she's seen him do the same thing after unsuccessful attempts to catch Yasemeen).

"But this is no secret," says Zumurrud hastily. "Oh, no! This is silly. This is nothing. She wishes merely to show you her squirrel. She's a naughty girl."

There are times when Zubeydeh cannot stand her mother. She has told Zumurrud carefully and explicitly about the foreign woman's promise. But instead of being reassured like any sensible person, Zumurrud appeared to be more frightened than before; Zubeydeh thinks to herself bitterly that her mother is rotted by fear, like an ill person. She knows there is no real reason for that. So Zubeydeh, with an unconsciously supplicating gesture, grabs the foreigner's dress and shouts:

"I'm going to be a poet! *She* said I could!"

—and when Daddy (who has been sitting on a bench, out of consideration for the guests) rises to his feet, hand on heart as if he were going to begin an oration, she throws herself vehemently to the floor by the foreign woman's feet, thinking that might do some good.

There is a moment's silence, in which she can hear Daddy's hard breathing, but he doesn't say anything. Then she hears Jaafar say in the voice she so hates, the oily, excusing voice, "It's my fault, sir, I encouraged her. Punish me. Oh, sir, she doesn't mean it; it's only a game—"

There is a slap somewhere above her head and the sound of someone blubbering. Then there is father's voice, saying a little shrilly, "I will be master in my own house!" and Jaafar saying in a crushed voice, "Yes, sir," and father shouting, "You will never speak to your sister again!" and Jaafar answering, "Yes, sir," and father declaring, "Everyone is in conspiracy against me," and Jaafar snivelling, "Forgive me, sir, forgive me," and Zubeydeh gets up to see that Jaafar, his face averted, is blubbering sincerely. Zubeydeh takes no account of her mother or father. Furiously she shouts:

"What about Aunt Dunya!"

'Alee turns pale.

"You murdered Aunt Dunya!" she screams, hoping he will deny it.

'Alee snatches at the air, as if he could hold and contain this furiously dancing little daughter. He cries, "Zubeydeh! Stop it! You are shaming me."

He adds, in a soothing voice, glancing at the guests, "I will speak to your upset. I understand that it is a frightening sight; I have seen it once myself. But you must understand that nobody drove your Aunt Dunya crazy; there is bad blood in your mother's family, and that is why I am so afraid for you. Your Aunt Dunya went mad through scribbling and we had to shut her up. Do you want that to happen to you? Do you want to break my heart? Do you want to break your mother's heart? Do you want her to beg and plead for you as she once had to do for her sister? Do you want me to shut you up anyway with my own hands as I had to do to your aunt? Do you want your poor brothers to be shamed—"

Zubeydeh has taken her poems out of her sleeve and is waving them at her father: "Daddy, they are real poems! *Real* poems!" She holds them out to him and sees his face change; he glances round again at the foreign people (who all this time have been watching with the detached, alert glances of jinneeyeh who have seen everything wonderful and horrible in human life) and 'Alee says, controlling his voice:

"Very well, I will read your poems," and takes the pile of papers from her. She waits in triumph and dread. She wonders if any little girl, any poet, any human person, has ever had such a glorious vindication. As in the Play of Meymooneh, in which the young man, chained to the floor of a dungeon, scrawls great poetry in the dust with his forefinger and the Governor of the Palace reads it and sets him free.

'Alee raises his eyes. He says, "Daughter, do you believe I have read your poems?"

She nods.

"Do you believe," he says, "when I tell you that I have read them carefully? Do you think I am a good judge?

Remember that I earned the Eighth Level award in poetry when I entered public life."

"Of course you're a good judge," she says, puzzled; "that's why I gave them to you." 'Alee is shaking with some grave but fiery emotion; she wonders which of the poems it was that did this to him.

"Will you trust my judgment?" he says again.

Zubeydeh says nothing, uneasy. Finally she nods. He looks through the papers again, carefully scrutinizing them, and then—with a decisive gesture—tears the sheaf of papers in two.

He says solemnly, "Alas, my daughter, you have no talent. Your poems are worthless. They are no good at all."

"Liar!" shouts Zubeydeh. She does not even consider hitting her father's chest with her small fists. She draws herself back, and very efficiently, using her head as a battering ram, runs into her father's stomach. It is surprising how easily he falls down. The next thing she knows, her mother has snatched her up and is hurrying her out of the Visiting Room, although Zubeydeh explains as patiently as she can that the foreign lady wants them to stay and that her poems are back there, torn up, and she wants them. She can mend them with strips of gauze and some paste. She manages to stamp on Zumurrud's foot, thus gaining a moment in which she glimpses the foreign *jinneeyeh* standing at the entrance to the Visiting Room, arms folded and back turned to them. She seems to be preventing 'Alee from getting out. Zubeydeh shouts, "Liar! Liar!" again at her father, knowing that he is one, a bad one, and Zumurrud hits her in the face with a volley of slaps. She starts to cry. Everyone is against her. No one, neither mother nor father, is willing to admit the truth. She starts to cry more hysterically then for it seems to her that she will wake tomorrow in the cell with Dunya, fouled by the madwoman's excrement, daubed with her food, with a mad, whispering voice in her ears saying horrible poetry until Zubeydeh's own brain begins to turn, until she gets dizzy, until she too goes mad, and then there will be no poetry, no marriage, no friends, no happiness, no sanity, but only madness forever and ever.

In the *hareem* as El-Ward fi-l-Akmam holds her down and Zumurrud goes for the whip, Zubeydeh finds herself weeping hysterically and clutching at El-Ward fi-l-Akmam's hands. "Beat me!" she cries. "Thrash me! Thrash it out of me, it'll do me good! I'm mad, I'm mad, I'm mad...."

Irene stands with her back to the curtains, arms folded. She's not threatening anybody. If 'Alee chooses to take it that way, that's his business. She says over her shoulder to Jaafar, "Go away, child. *Nicht für kinder.*"

Jaafar says quickly, "First, I'm not a child. Second, I'm not responsible. Third, I didn't know she was going to do this. Fourth, she's crazy. Fifth—"

The father raises his hand. Jaafar winces. His face reluctantly averted, he mutters something that resolves itself to Irene's hearing as, "When I marry, *I'll* be master."

She says, "Beauty draws us by a thousand threads of helplessness.'"

Delighted into courage, the boy says, "Do you know that? Are you a—" but a look from his father sends him scuttling out.

'Alee, in front of Irene, says, "Permit me."

She doesn't move. Ernst, bored, is sitting across the room on a bench, guarding the other door.

She says colorlessly, "Son of Bekkar, I cannot let you leave the room. First we must take away your daughter."

'Alee stares.

"She is being mistreated," says Irene, "and I want her."

'Alee laughs in disbelief. In Irene's hand appears a black object which he does not need to recognize; with a flip she reverses it. He says, "Nonsense! you cannot shoot me." Across the room the other *jinn* meditates, elbows on knees, his huge barbarian head supported by his hands.

"Ernst," she says, "he will not give me the visa."

'Alee, now genuinely alarmed, steps backwards, away from this woman. He says again, "Nonsense!"

"Which arm shall I break?" says the female *jinn*.

"If you break my arm, I will not be able to write the visa!" shouts 'Alee.

The female *jinn* says, "I will not break your writing arm."

Involuntarily he puts his hands behind him, aware of the brittleness of his bones; he stutters, "You wish to sell her!"

"Ernst, your gun," and the female monster advances on him with a black object in either hand: heavy pieces of metal which will descend upon his flesh with excruciating force. 'Alee is ashamed, but nothing in his life has prepared him to deal with this.

He cries, "I am a man of peace!"

She smiles; she says, "I am a woman of war," and raising both fists threateningly above her head, throws from her the two objects, as if they impeded her strength. As 'Alee tries to back off, her great foreigner's hands descend on his shoulders and her ropy arms go around him; she begins to squeeze him in jocular fashion, smiling a broad smile like that of the black-faced demon in *The Thousand and One Nights*. His ribs cracking, he can hear her talking to him, telling him in friendly fashion that he's a reasonable man, that he'll give away his daughter, that of course he'll give her what she wants; half-smothered, he can smell her bodily smell and feel her breasts against his face. Disgust horrifies him. He imagines, without being able to help it, his delicate child Zubeydeh and this rapacious woman linked in some excruciatingly sexual fashion that he can't understand, and remembers with terrible shame his former curiosity on the subject of the bodies of foreign women. He had even, some days ago, been mildly aroused by this one. He knows now that she wants to rape his daughter and in spite of himself his imagination presents him with several ways in which this act could be performed. When she lets him go, breathless and bruised, he stands at first not moving. He thinks *Now I am gaining time*. He feels a smile on his face, like something alien. Then he says, blinking and in a timid voice, "But you must not take my daughter away against her will. It would provoke a diplomatic incident."

He adds hoarsely, unable to suppress that dreadful smile, "I am broad-minded. I would not forbid Zubeydeh anything. But you must not kidnap her."

The woman says, "No one will take her against her will, son of Bekkar. Write that she has gone mad and that we are taking her away to a hospital to be cured. Say it's an honor. Your neighbors will believe that."

'Alee essays a little laugh, but his voice fails. He says only, "She will never go."

"Write!"

He goes to a table at the side of the room and gets behind it. It is his desk. Hastily he fumbles with quill and paper and writes. He finishes the paper and holds it out with a forced laugh, saying, "My sister-in-law you may keep!"

"Write!" she says. "The visas for both."

He writes. He seems to be out of breath somehow and

he scrawls painfully. He considers marring his own signature but cannot; he knows Zubeydeh won't go. Perhaps he can appeal to the male, who may himself be a father, the father of a baby *jinn*. Men should not do this to men. He imagines the male *jinn* commanding the female to leave his daughter; he imagines rescuing Zubeydeh himself, turning on this demon foreigneress and wresting her weapons from her.

Trembling, he hands Irene the visas. She holds them out for her partner in crime to take and read. The great, coarse arm approaches again and he winces, but this time she doesn't touch him; she only says, "Now you'll sleep a little, son of Bekkar, and when you wake, your ingenuity will enable you to make up a story that won't disgrace you in your neighbors' eyes."

'Alee says, bowing, "Yes, we must all sleep on it, mustn't we? Decisions must never be made lightly. Yes, that is true. When will you be coming for her?"

The *jinneeyeh*, who somehow during this has gotten hold of the black objects again, now points one of them at him. Through a sudden weakness he sees her come at him like an express train, with arms out like scoop-shovels. Then she wavers and recedes. The world tilts and turns over. They're going to take his daughter right now. They're going to do unspeakable things to her. She will become a public person, a soldier, a paramour, she will lose all her virtue. From the center of Ka'abah the soft woman, who gives meaning to it all, has been stolen. Something soft in his body has been stolen. The woman's face, above him, is as big as the moon. He sees Zubeydeh helplessly dangling from the foreign demoness's teeth, in the process of being eaten, only to feel that the flesh is in his own mouth, between his own teeth, that he is killing his own daughter. Zubeydeh cries out, "Daddy! Daddy!" but he can't save her. He can't stop. Only a father. Only a father can. He's no longer because they've taken it away. No father. He can do nothing, only submit.

He does.

Curiously turning with his foot the relaxed figure of the son of Bekkar, curled in artificial sleep on the tesselated floor, Ernst Neumann says, "Would you have beaten him, Irene?"

She says, "That little man excites me," but there is nothing sensual in her face or bearing; she looks as though her coldness could plan ten times worse than the hottest hate.

She says, "You bet I would."

She says then, "We'd better go."

In the semi-darkness of the single, tinselly lamp, Zumurrud has opened slit eyes under the veil. Her dream of a cat stays on her face, molding the features. She sees the foreign monster pick up Zubeydeh in the sleeping room at the back of the *hareem*; the little girl sneezes and puts her arms around the foreign woman's neck. "Mommy?" she says. She rests her head on Irene's shoulder, digging her chin in. The foreign woman turns and meets Zumurrud's gaze; then the strange person shakes her passenger gently and Zubeydeh wakes up.

Zubeydeh looks down at her mommy.

She says, slurred, "You beat me."

Zumurrud says, "I'm dreaming." She adds, "I don't know you."

"Wezeereh, we are taking your daughter with us." This is the strange woman, who now shifts Zubeydeh in her arms, crackly veil and all. Zubeydeh's charm bracelets catch on the veil.

Zubeydeh wriggles; "Really?" and she pulls her head back to look at Irene's face. "Good!" she says.

"We need your permission, Wezeereh." The foreign woman is carrying her baby as if the little girl were so much straw. Zumurrud remembers with resentment how heavy the child was to lug about, even as a two-year-old; she says finally, "I don't want to be interrupted while I'm dreaming. My dreams are good for me."

Irene says patiently, "If your daughter wishes to go with us, will you let her go, Wezeereh?"

"No," says Zumurrud spitefully.

Zubeydeh breaks in: "Mommy, they'll let me be a poet!"

"Oh, don't ask *me*," says Zumurrud, with heavy irony, "don't ask *me*," and she turns away on the bed, drawing a corner of the embroidered sheet over her face in mock humility, as she would the veil. She says, into the mercury mattress, "I have no authority."

"Mommy!" shouts little Zubeydeh angrily.

Sitting up so rapidly that the decorative sheet falls to the floor, Zumurrud whispers, "Yes, take her from me! Let her abandon me! Let her never make a marriage, let her disobey the Wezeer and bring sorrow to her mother's heart! Leave me with nothing!" And she beats herself just under the collarbone in illustration.

"We wish you to come with us also," says the foreigner.

Zumurrud is silent. Her mind returns to her dream: a cat in a cat garden with cat servants, a free cat rummaging in garbage with cat allies, a heartless cat who had walked along a fence made of real wood in the Outside in some kind of loving mist and had sung in earsplitting shrieks.

99

"No," she says at length.

Zubeydeh has begun to cry. "Put me down," she says, and wriggles on to her mother's couch, one knee on, one knee off. The beds are without legs, right on the floor; there's no trouble with draughts underground. Zubeydeh pulls at her mother, but haughty Zumurrud, with the ferocity of a cat, turns her important face away.

She says finally, "I can't leave; my boys need me."

"Stupid!" says Zubeydeh under her breath.

"Go then!" cries Zumurrud, turning on her daughter frantically. "Suffer then! Become unsexed! Write your poetry! Become a soldier or a sailor if you like, but don't expect me to abandon my lifelong project of forming a feminine personality. I will not abandon my family!"

"*I'm* your family!" shrieks Zubeydeh.

A big foreign hand descends on them both. "Quietly!" says the stranger woman. "My colleague is outside the door, since we do not wish to violate your customs, but if the boys wake, he may have to come in."

"Who cares!" whispers Zubeydeh distinctly, but Zumurrud, in dignified fashion, picks her *kinaa* up from beside the bed and wraps it around her face.

"She's medicated," says Zubeydeh in a hopeless voice, slumping back on to the floor. "You won't get any sense out of her."

"I am not medicated," says Zumurrud earnestly, "and my sense is this, little daughter: do not go. The Wezeer will beat me. Your father is a good man, but whom else has he to beat? Jaafar will be lonely. You will never marry. You know what is here but you don't know what is there. You cannot even speak their language. They will take your fine clothes away from you and set you to washing dishes like a servant-girl; never again will it matter that you are well-bred and come of an important family. You will never have children. And in return for this, they will

100

let you write poems in a language nobody there can read and nobody there cares about; what good are poems when they win no prizes? When they have no readers? You will hate the new language and not be able to write in it. As for me, I will die of loneliness without you; El-Ward fi-l-Akmam will take my clothes and my beautifications and reign here as mistress without anyone to check her; I will have no daughter's grandchildren; I will have no one to talk to but my sister Dunya, and soon you will see me in the cell with her, a madwoman deprived of her daughter, a poor, sick woman with no one to care for her. And I can tell my mad sister Dunya that once I was happy, because once I was loved; once I had a daughter."

In a creaky whisper, with head bowed, Zubeydeh says, "I'll stay, Mommy."

Zumurrud stares. The cat speaks out of her: "Oh, take her away before she believes it!" and she turns her back on them. She adds, "Fool!" and then, "Get out."

"And you?" says that inconvenient foreigner.

"No, I must stay," says Zumurrud in a different voice; "I must stay," and looking about the gold-flecked walls of the *hareem* sleeping chamber, walls that sparkle dimly even in this dim light, she almost adds aloud: *My dreams are here*. She wonders what Dunya sees on Dunya's walls. She says, "My medication helps my life. I will probably be well soon. And as you know, my family could not get along without me."

"Mommy, *come*," says Zubeydeh in agony.

"No, you must get along without me," says the mother, lying down on her bed; "you must do for yourself now." She adds, "It is like getting married. You must leave your family home," and she draws the embroidered sheet over her shoulders.

"Wezeereh, we have two visas," says the woman, "one for your daughter and one for your sister Dunya. We can use the second for your sister but we can even more easily use it for you. We can get you out of these rooms into a different world where you will not have to stay shut up and where you will not have to be medicated. It is, believe me, for all its faults, a better world." She speaks earnestly and for a moment Zumurrud is almost swayed. But she knows better. They will put her to work. She will lose everything. She says with sublime altruism, "No, take my poor sister Dunya; take her," and with a pleasant feeling because of her own compassion for her sister, lies waiting for sleep to come. She hears the foreign woman's hesitation, hears the big body finally get up (*What an ugly creature!* she thinks, with a tinge of enjoyment), and hears Zubeydeh sob and whimper as the two sets of footsteps recede.

The Wezeer, of course, would not have her put in the same cell as anyone, let alone her own sister. She thinks about that. But she knows that when the Wezeer wakes from his bed to find his daughter really gone (the visas are, of course, forged), he will be in sad trouble; she imagines herself comforting him, ordering about the servant, getting food for him, making things easy for him, until he says, "What a good wife you are, Wezeereh!" A good wife is appreciated. It may be possible to get rid of that scheming servant-girl and have another woman brought in, an older, more motherly woman who will sympathize with the Wezeereh and who knows what a woman's life is like. Together they can persuade the Wezeer to resume relations with his wife's family, and perhaps they can get something she has always longed for: a simulated, hologrammic view of a mountain or desert Outside; that would make the room perfect. The Wezeereh is full of plans. She is momentarily grieved to have no daughter. But Zubeydeh will write letters; she will become a famous woman out there, in that other world, and in a few years she will come back and visit her mother: older, richer, her figure heavy and full like a woman's, with a beautiful and important husband, with many fine clothes. Zumurrud slips back into her cat dream, in which cat friends tell her admiringly that she's a stubborn cat, all right, in which the walls of the sleeping room melt into the illimitable vistas of Outside, and—for she is a dangerous cat—she goes off to have cat adventures, to bear famous kittens and seduce handsome toms, but all somehow in a key that doesn't matter, in a way that doesn't really count, for she's also alone, and what really matters are the trees and the plains, the endless forests, the rivers she follows for miles, all this mixed up with a lot of explanation and self-justification, mixed up, in fact, with endless talking, and with the sensation of walking, walking forever, never stopping, pulling a little harness with bells on it like Yasemeen's, like a cat she saw once in a picture in her childhood, a cat in a shop who pulled a little rotisserie, or like Dunya.

Zumurrud turns in her sleep and sighs, sunk forever in her beautiful, troublesome, unsatisfying dreams.

Halfway to the front door, Zubeydeh remembers Yasemeen. "My squirrel!" she cries. She stands stockstill, corrugating her brow, her hands clasped in front of her. Then she says in a little voice, "My brothers," and pulling the foreign woman by the hand, "Please, my brothers," knowing bitterly that they can't get the bells off Yasemeen (it was hard enough getting them on) but she can look at her brothers silently while they sleep. She's frightened of waking her father. She explains that the eldest, Noor-ed-Deen, is away, that he is going to be married soon, that he is rather severe, though kind, which is only proper for the eldest, and that he is very handsome and remarkably conscientious, with a Fifth in poetry.

She pulls the foreign woman through the corridors by the hand, exclaiming, "Here, here," to the room where Jaafar sleeps with his brother Yahya; Yahya is thirteen and Jaafar sixteen, and she only wants to look at them while they sleep. They will miss her; they don't have as many nice things in their lives as she does in hers. For example, their sleeping room is not nearly as beautiful or decorated as the *hareem*. Zubeydeh says, "Boys have a much harder life than girls; they have to obey and work," and she plucks at the foreign woman's clothes. "There, right there."

Jaafar is asleep. His brother, across the room, is curled in a ball under the covers, one plump foot and one dimpled fist thrust out into the air of the room. There is a lamp set in the wall.

Zubeydeh begins to cry quietly. She tries to memorize the look of them. Yahya is still chubby: a slow, stubborn, thick-necked little boy whom she loves now, despite his habit of bellowing out everything he thinks important, Yahya shutting his eyes (in rage) and shouting for candy in his deep, child's voice, fat Yahya pounding around the courtyard, as clumsy as a girl.

The tutor resting by the head of Jaafar's bed swings round, lights up, and issues one deep, musical, warning chime.

Jaafar's eyes open.

She whispers, "Brother, turn it off! Turn it off!"

Jaafar, uncomprehending, says sweetly, "Hello, sister," and she dives at the tutor, fumbling at its casing, without the slightest idea of what to do with it. Jaafar reaches up and pushes a button in its back; the machine shuts off, swinging round to the wall again, and presenting to the room the grave, intellectual face of its particular shadow-life, in which the vision screen figures as a long beard.

"What's the matter, Scriblet?" says Jaafar. Then he sees the foreigner, behind his sister. "Ssssh!" says Zubeydeh sharply.

She adds, speaking low, "I'm going away with them. I'm going to be a poet."

Jaafar sits up, alarmed. "Does Daddy—"

"No," says Zubeydeh. "At least I don't think so. But I'm going anyway."

"Oh," says Jaafar, comically holding his head, "when he finds out . . . but aren't you *lucky*, Little Scribble!"

She says, "This lady is taking me."

He says, "Will you come back and see us?"

She nods, starting to cry. She sits down on the bed. Jaafar, his face going all weepy too, puts his arms around her. She hears him say in a broken voice into her veil, "You're the best sister a fellow ever had."

He lets her go and says then, rubbing his nose, "Scribble, you do understand why I couldn't stand up for you in front of Daddy. Don't you?"

Hot thoughts rise in Zubeydeh, but she nods reluctantly. It shows, though; she can see that in Jaafar's face. She pulls away and averts her gaze from him.

He says impatiently, "Now don't go all girly on me, Little Bit. You're better than that. You're above it. You know that when I got married I was going to send for you as our housekeeper and friend, and my bride would probably be glad not to be alone and to have you for company. And you could teach her to write, if she was intelligent."

Zubeydeh says, "I don't think you—" and he shakes her.

"Of course I was going to!" he says. "But I can't do anything until then, can I? If I went against Daddy, what good would it do? But I would've certainly sent for you, you know I would, no matter what he said."

Zubeydeh says, "If he let me."

"Well, it doesn't matter now, does it?" says Jaafar reasonably. "You're going away!" He says again, with sudden energy, "You *lucky* thing!"

Zubeydeh weeps. She manages to say, "You are the best of brothers." Energetically she flings herself into his arms and they hug each other again, Jaafar rocking his baby sister from side to side as he used to do when she was a toddler. He stops and Zubeydeh says:

"Oh, Jaafar, you'll be all alone," thinking of Yahya, whom nobody likes except Mother, and even she is nervous and annoyed around him, and then there's Father's severity and Mother's illness, and Noor-ed-Deen's grown-up condescension. She pats Jaafar's face.

He says awkwardly, "Oh well, Little Bit, I can go out a lot, you know. And I'll tell you something that's wonderful: I've fallen in love."

"Who is he?" says Zubeydeh, delighted, clapping her hands together but lightly, lest Yahya wake up. "Oh, tell me!"

Jaafar smiles. He pats her head and for a moment is silent. Then he says, "I'll write you a poem about him, Little Bit. He is a true, good friend. I don't know how we shall get together because he's to be married and is very upset about it, and I'm too young to live alone, you know, but we'll manage. I don't want to meet him in cafés; I want to live with him always like the two brothers in the play of El-Barmekee. He's my real, true love."

Zubeydeh feels an impulse of great compassion. "Poor Jaafar," she says softly.

He says thoughtfully, "Do you know, dear, I always think it a shame that you girls can't have part of the country to yourselves, to live together and have love

106

affairs, as we do. And we could pay you a good lot of money to raise the children until they were five, and then we could take the boys, maybe, I don't know. And have big parties a few times a year in which we all got together and danced and recited. Or maybe all of us could just live as we pleased, with no fathers or mothers any more."

"Love affairs?" says Zubeydeh, puzzled.

"Yes, of course, sister," says this silly brother earnestly; "With each other. And you could keep a business, the way men do, and ride about in your own car, and keep your own accounts. And have a beautiful woman lover and the two of you work together and perhaps recite your poetry in public together."

"That's absurd," says Zubeydeh, annoyed. "Women don't have women lovers and they don't keep businesses."

"Well, then, a man lover," says Jaafar argumentatively. "You don't have to marry him, Little Bit; after all—"

"That's stupid!" says Zubeydeh sharply.

Jaafar starts to get out of bed. "Look here, Scriblet, just who do you think—"

"Oh, sure, now you'll say you're *older*!"

"I *am* older—"

"No more now," says the voice of the foreign woman; "Not now; say good-bye," and Zubeydeh feels that big hand close on her own. Zubeydeh pulls the corner of her veil over her face, to hide her tears. She whispers, "Say good-bye to Yahya for me," and when Jaafar looks dubious about this particular project, "Oh, Jaafar, Jaafar, Mommy can't come and I'll miss her!"

Jaafar says uncomfortably, "Well, now—come on, Little Bit—" and she says, "I know, I'm going to be a poet," and her brother, "That's right, dear," and they embrace once more, and then Zubeydeh is somehow outside the room, crying hard, and being trotted back to the *hareem*.

There in the corridor is the fascinating foreign man, as tall as a mountain, casually carrying a long box under one arm.

"What's that?" says Zubeydeh, through her tears. "Is that for me?"

"No, it's for your Aunt Dunya," says the foreign man.

The foreign woman lets go Zubeydeh's hand, plants herself in front of the man, and says something, seriously and sharply. Zubeydeh can't understand the words; this must be their native language. The foreign man answers mildly and the foreign lady becomes more emphatic; she skins her lips back over her teeth, her head juts forward, and she chops at the air with one hand. She says something something something Zumurrud something. Zubeydeh thinks that the lady will lose the argument, although the man looks like a nice, pliable man, but if he gets really roused the lady will, of course, have to give in. She suspects that they have been married a long time. She wonders if they have any children. She wonders how they will get Aunt Dunya into the box, and whether or not Aunt Dunya will smother in the box; the idea comes to her that the foreign man will have to wash Aunt Dunya first so she won't smell, and the process of anesthetizing Aunt Dunya and then taking off her rags and washing her under the shower head strikes Zubeydeh as so horribly disgusting that she tries not to think about it. She knows that the foreign man is getting angry—she can see it in his face—and although the foreign lady is muscular, she isn't as muscular as he is, so Zubeydeh wonders idly how the lady ever gets anything from the man without beautifications and lovely clothes.

Suddenly Zubeydeh is flattened against the wall of the corridor by a huge, invisible hand: a great siren-sound that rises and falls, the alarm bell of the *hareem*. She shouts, "It's the box! The box!"

The foreign lady is bending down to listen to her.

She shouts, "No, it's *him*!" and then, "The Police will come!" for she knows that the alarm is registering a mile away through the rock, in the local police station, a precaution that had reassured her very much when she had been told about it as a small child.

The foreign man smiles and says something jocular.

The foreign lady does not drag her by the hand this time, but merely elevates her, with astonishing ease, into her arms. She is carried through rooms at great speed. At the front door (which she recognizes by its decorated curtain) Zubeydeh finds she cannot face the outside world and buries her terrified face in the lady's neck, crying, "My squirrel! My squirrel! I want her!" Nobody listens to her. The foreign lady and gentleman go much faster then, because the roof is higher (she supposes) or the halls are longer. Shutting her eyes tight, Zubeydeh grabs at the lady's clothing for dear life. The siren sound is fading in back of her. Suddenly she feels something hit her on the back and hears a jingle of bells; there are the familiar bunches of tickly grab along her back and a bounce on her chest. Something jingly is holding desperately onto her, as she herself, with her jingling bracelets and necklaces, is desperately holding onto the foreign lady. She opens her eyes and finds herself looking into a runty, gray face crowned with a red, velvet cap, into bulgy, brown eyes and twitching, pointy ears. It is Yasemeen, who has come along for the ride. Zubeydeh won't be entirely alone. She dares not let go long enough to catch hold of the jouncing squirrel, but Yasemeen seems to have made up her mind to hold on; Zubeydeh thinks that she and Mother can feed Yasemeen peanuts in the new world. Wherever they are taking her. And remembers.

And begins to cry again.

Joanna Russ

• • •

The Port of Entry of Ka'abah is just under the surface, inside the rock, another series of rooms. A labyrinth. The sensation of never having left 'Alee's living room. From a filigreed gate to a series of cubicles, each bigger and barer than the last, through search booths and X-ray rooms, finally up a many-person elevator and into a vast space as big as a small warehouse or a large gymnasium, with a clerestory that admits artificial sunlight around the top, with potted orange trees sitting in dusty beams of light around the perimeter, doors spaced along the walls, telephone booths, a café with gilt tables. The central floor space is divided by a system of benches and flimsy barriers; seated in one of these arrangements, Irene Waskiewicz is setting up a family, said family consisting of her colleague, her tag-along passenger, and her passenger's passenger. One look at the place and Zubeydeh has made her *izar* thicker and rounder, performing a mysterious vanishment of Yasemeen somewhere into the cocoon. Irene is keeping track of the little girl by the feel of a small hand grabbing at her clothes.

She says quietly in her own language, "Conscience, you have exceeded your authority."

He replies in the same tone, "I gave you advice, Irenee, nothing more."

She says, "Without your advice, there would have been no delay and hence time to take the mother." She adds, "God, I resent that!"

There is a moment's silence. Then he says slowly:

"She didn't wish to come, Irene."

"Wish!" says Irene Waskiewicz, jerking her hand away from Zubeydeh's. "What can that woman decide or that

110

woman wish? You don't know, Ernst; you may think you know, but believe me, you don't."

He says mildly, "I do run across it from time to time."

"I run into it," says Irene. He nods, agreeing with her. She says, "No, it runs into me. Right into me."

There's another silence.

He says, "After all, Irenee, I didn't know we were going to be interrupted so soon," and Irene turns on him, half rising with her fists up, the same way she used to do in high school when she was enraged. Ernst looks as quiet as before but she sees that he's shifted his weight to his feet; he appears to be sitting but he isn't sitting.

Controlling herself and sinking back on the bench, she says, "Well!" and then, "You should have agreed; you should have agreed instantly. What that woman decided wasn't a decision; you know that!"

He says dryly, "There is a difference of opinion."

She says nothing. Her neck and shoulders are stiff with the desire to strike. From a speaking-box near them comes a rapid, insistent series of buzzes; then the speaking-box, another piece of shadow-life, this one with a long chin, vertical mouth, and slit eyes, all on top of a stalk, calls their names and adds a number. It repeats the information several times.

Startled, little Zubeydeh says, "What? What?"

"It's telling us where to go," says Irene, trying to soften her voice; "Girl-child Zubeydeh, non-son of 'Alee, son of Bekkar, son of Bekkar, that's you, long name and all. We go over there," and she takes the little girl's hand. In the far wall is a series of numbered doors; Irene grasps Zubeydeh's hand more firmly and the non-family with its non-marriage and non-son (but without its non-coffin) progresses towards the proper door, somewhat hampered by Zubeydeh's short legs.

At the door there's another barrier, with two customs

officials behind it, one in a red *tarboosh* and one in a blue. Irene pushes Zubeydeh in front of her, at the same time displaying the little girl's papers.

Yasemeen pops out of hiding and streaks to the top of Zubeydeh's head where she sits, quirking her tail. The customs official in the blue hat (to Irene's eyes they both look like 'Alee) leans forward, inspecting the squirrel disapprovingly.

He says, with satisfaction, "You cannot go aboard with that."

"Look at your papers," says Irene impatiently. "You'll find the squirrel listed on them. We've been inspected five times."

The official in the blue hat smiles broadly and shakes his head. "Oh no," he says; "It is not this person's rule, but no, no, not with the squirrel," and he crosses his arms on his chest. Irene's fingers itch; she sees the official in the red *tarboosh*, who is seated, peer at his colleague and grin to himself.

"Now look here," says Irene, losing her temper, "we've been inspected five times and X-rayed twice. We have been passed. The animal has been inspected. You'll find it described in detail on the papers, the whole, bloody process. We have also, I might add, posted a bond in the usual manner and I must now request most politely that you let us through."

The official in the blue takes the papers from Irene and inspects them carefully, holding them close to his nose, apparently favoring one eye. A myope. He looks suspiciously at her and reads the papers again. Finally he puts the papers down on the barrier and smiles. "No," he says, "no squirrel." Irene lets go Zubeydeh's hand. She lifts her right arm and deliberately brings the edge of her right hand down on the barrier, breaking it cleanly. Red hat starts and blue hat steps back. "Stamp this paper," she says, and with a sidelong glance, blue hat does. Blue hat looks scared. Red hat's mouth is open. With Ernst behind her, Irene frog-marches Zubeydeh into the featureless hall beyond; Ernst says quietly, walking behind her, "You're rather going it, Irene."

Irene thinks: *I will be murdered by my own rage.* She shouts at him, calling him a pig, a *nosferatu*, a self-indulgent, ignorant male *golem*. She says she's coming back for the mother and the aunt if it takes the rest of her life.

At the end of the hall they step into the long, flexible tubing that leads to the ship, a tough spiral covered with plastic skin. Here the artificial gravity of Ka'abah abruptly ceases; in one moment the floor drops beneath them and the push of inward-pressing air from the vents completes the disorientation. Zubeydeh shrieks violently. Yasemeen is leaving spots of dung on her veil. Irene catches the child up in one arm, pulling herself from handhold to handhold along the wall; what a thing to forget! She thinks, *I'm sorry, baby. Sorry, sorry.* She thinks of Zubeydeh and Zumurrud clinging together in the free fall, terrified but holding on to each other. Zubeydeh continues to shriek. At ship's port Irene flashes her I.D. at the wall and hurtles down the proper corridor, braking at the end with her feet. She hopes heartily that Zubeydeh will not throw up. Into the squirrel cage and on with the power, Yasemeen floating helplessly in the air and squeaking shrilly, her paws flattened. The mistress has fainted.

The walls of the booth blur; better put it on full power. She can't see Zubeydeh now, except as a streak. Irene punches out the medical number: tranquilizers, anti-nausea, anti-vertigo pour as mists into the air of the cage.

Zubeydeh doesn't know; no one has ever told her about gravitation. Or about temperature, or about the

113

simplest physics. Irene thinks, *Don't worry, baby*.

She anchors herself with one finger to the hook in the wall and wonders how she'll make it up with Ernst; life lately has somehow become a long process of making it up with Ernst. She winces, remembering her own words: pig, *nosferatu, golem,* ignorant, self-indulgent. Bad words. Angry words. Her anger frightens her. She thinks, *My expensive weapons, my expensive training, I'm exceptional, I should know better*.

She thinks idly of her own mother.

She remembers shouting at Ernst and then suddenly is not so sure; floating next to spinning Zubeydeh it occurs to her that none of it happened, that her anger fooled her, that at the last minute she held it all back.

She never said any of that aloud. And that's shocking.

She thinks, *My expensive position, my statistically rare training, my self-confidence, my unusual strength*.

And I'm still afraid.

Of what?

To shower in low weight, even in a strong current of air, is an eerie experience; the water piles up lazily around your feet and the waves sometimes reach your shoulders. Ernst enjoys it. He comes out of the cubicle with the mild erection that the teasing fear of it always gives him and takes off his breathing mask; Irene, who has been before him, is sitting cross-legged and naked on the stateroom rug. She smiles sleepily at him and they embrace, Irene also moist from the shower, tender and vulnerable, arching her back in the low gravity. She's oddly helpless and shy. He feels the kind of desire whose severity used to scare him in his 'teens; he was so sure then that he'd never find anything to do with it. Uncharacteristically he pulls her on to him—he usually has no chance to do this with Irene—and the central star of his sex begins to eclipse the taste of her saliva, the feeling of her breasts poking at him, the pleasure of the sinews under her fluid belly. She makes a sound that isn't like her upon being entered, a sort of low complaint, and shuts her eyes. She says, "I'm not sure...."

She says, "No, wait...."

For once he can't. The room blurs. Stars and spangles. Coming out of the fog, he manages to say, "Lord! Sorry. I'm so sorry," and enters it again. He's had no chance to save anything for a second full time. He says, "Oh, dear. Oh, my dear. Damn! In an hour?" He hears her voice— "No, it's all right"—and she's swum away from him, across the tiny room, wiping herself, getting into her clothes, taking up the positions of an acrobat. She says, "It's archetypal, Ernst; we just met something archetypal, that's all," and her tone is unreadable, so he's forced back on the words, which make no sense. Unless she means her passivity, his hurry.

He decides that she'll tell him, in time.

He thinks of Irene hauling down the flag (although you need a new metaphor there), the classically comic situation—what do I do with my genitals now?—and wonders if he should help, when the door of the stateroom clangs open and Zubeydeh, hovering in the doorway, shrieks and covers her eyes. Irene laughs—"Family life" she tells him—and throws him his shorts, which he puts on; pretty Zubeydeh, in blue pants and white tee-shirt, peeks.

She says flatly, "If you're busy, you should lock the door."

Then she says, dropping her hands, "That's better, look at me," and starts to walk on her hands, feet in the air.

Ernst says, toweling his hair, "So that's what you've been up to!"

Zubeydeh says importantly, upside down: "The servants here are insubordinate and much too free. My father would know how to deal with them. They won't let me see my squirrel. She's in the baggage room. I yelled at a steward today and he actually picked me up and shoved me out the door, imagine. What insolence. Tomorrow I shall go into the weightless section to see how far I can jump."

"The stewards here are all poets," says Irene sharply, "remember that. Treat them with respect."

With an angry look at Irene, Zubeydeh interrupts: "Will I be this light on the new worlds, Uncle?"

Indulgently he shakes his head.

She says, "I don't mind going about without my veil— *she* made me take it off" (another venomous look at Irene) "but tomorrow I will get back into my old clothes. Nobody pays any attention to me here." She adds shrilly, coming right-side-up, "Uncle? Uncle! You're not listening!"

He says, "Zubeydeh, if you stamp your foot, you will go right through the ceiling. I have to shave, so sit cross-legged on the floor, lock your toes together, and bounce quietly until I come back."

Pacified, she giggles. "Shaving!" She makes a face. She sidles against him seductively, laughing, making eyes at him as if she were still wearing the veil. She whispers, "Dearest Uncle!" He places her on the floor with both hands, which makes her wriggle extravagantly, and listens to the ensuing conversation (from inside the sanitary cubicle) while putting depilatory on his beard.

First Irene's voice: "Zubeydeh, that's a falsehood. I didn't make you do anything with your veil."

There's the sound of a brief scuffle, as if Zubeydeh were throwing things or hitting Irene, and then Zubeydeh's voice, very high-pitched: "You want me to be ugly!"

Irene says something low and reasonable that he can't make out.

There's a silence.

Then, "I'll never learn the nasty language!" Zubeydeh cries shrilly. "I hate it! It's ugly, like you! I don't want to grow up like you!"

She adds, more deliberately, "*You're* not married. Nobody would marry *you*. You have to work hard and do these awful things because you're not married. You left my mother behind on purpose because you wanted to take her place but I won't let you, and you told me my father hated me but it isn't true; he loved my poetry. He was just afraid for me, that's all. He was going to give in. And you made me come away, you lied to me, you insisted, you forced me, you took me away!"

There is the sound of another scuffle, perhaps Irene losing her temper.

"I hate you!" shouts Zubeydeh energetically, and as Ernst comes in from shaving, half his beard vacuum-plucked and half bristly (the depilatory persuades the follicles to let go) Zubeydeh hurtles at his knees.

"I want to go back!" she yells. Her face is ugly and angry. He suspects that nothing will change her mind except agreeing with her. She tries to rattle his knees. "Take me back!" He starts to pry her fingers loose but the little girl is tenacious; with a half-look at Irene (who's not enjoying this) Zubeydeh cries, "You let her decide everything! You're not a man! You're *henpecked*!"

This estimate of his character exquisitely tickles Ernst's sense of humor but it doesn't seem to have the same effect on Irene, so he says shortly, "Zubeydeh, stop it," and the little girl bursts into heartbroken tears. She collapses, floating above the floor, and clutches his feet, sobbing breathlessly, "Oh, Uncle! Uncle!" and then, "I'm sorry, Uncle, I'm sorry." He leans down and sets her on her feet.

He says over her head to Irene, "Can't she have a holiday from the language lessons?" and Irene shakes her head. "Better not," she says. He gently shakes Zubeydeh, who is showing an alarming tendency to crumple. "There, dear, did you hear? She's right. You've got to learn. You're going to need it soon."

"If she wants to flirt with the stewards, she needs it right now," says Irene.

He puts his forefinger under the pretty, miniature, dirt-and-tears-streaked chin. Zubeydeh looks up at him, her eyes swimming. She's a heart-tweaker, even at twelve. He says, "Irene is right. Go with her and do what she tells you."

Zubeydeh gives him a deep, tearful, eloquent glance. She says, "If *you* say so, Uncle." She walks proudly past Irene, obviously making the latter's fingers itch. Irene involuntarily makes a fist, then just as involuntarily hides it behind her. An extraordinary performance! Zubeydeh, head high, unknowing, walks out.

He says, raising his voice, "Zubeydeh, you think Irene is unpleasant because unpleasantness always happens when she's around. That's because she's the one who's protecting you from unpleasantness. I only play with you. And until you understand this, I want you to obey her in everything, whether you like it or not."

Irene is looking at him, fist hidden behind her. She says slowly, "Conscience, I want to thank you for giving me so much authority. I hope to prove worthy of it."

One of the recurring sticky patches in his relation with

her. She withdraws; she gets sarcastic. He knows that it's something left over from the old days, something unself-confident and self-wasting; he can only respect what he doesn't know and wait, tolerate and wait; this has happened before. She'll tell him, in time.

He says, feeling his way, "Sklodowska, don't beat me!" but the nickname doesn't please her. She says only, "Ernst, I don't know what I'd do without you."

"You?" he says laughing, overcome in spite of himself with the silliness of it, Irene pining away for lack of anyone, "you? Why, you'd die of loneliness. You'd lose your profession, like Othello. You'd go right back home. You'd skulk around for the rest of your life, thinking about what you had lost."

She says, "Yes, I think I would," and goes out and closes the door.

Sailing vessels, submarines, airplanes, spaceships: all these means for the exploration of space are like Ka'abah inside; space in them is expensive. Ernst Neumann and Irene Waskiewicz, private passengers paid for discreetly by somebody, sit together in the tiny lounge, served by pale-eyed, hulking, hairy people, another interesting strain of the humanity that's spread so far sideways, so far forward in time, so far back. Seats are curtained, for privacy, stacked about the inside of a sphere in a staggered pattern that allows anyone to see to the center of the room; there are mirrors everywhere, hologrammic scenery, and an attempt at forced perspective, like that in a Japanese garden. The ship is Cetian, not that anyone lives there, but a watch-station has been put into decent orbit around the star and the ten people who run the instruments have title to a lot of property that isn't theirs, a service arrangement for which they are paid a large fee. As Ernst knows, Irene has dismissed the whole business long ago, impatient and cynical, but he intends to make a stab at understanding it one of these years. Both sit with drinks in bulbs which neither touches; Irene has spent the last twenty minutes in sketching out Zubeydeh's future, a little jumpily, as if preoccupied; Ernst drifts in and out of the conversation, occasionally laughing or otherwise appreciating it. Zubeydeh will marry a millionaire. She'll make his life wretched. She'll keep a salon and write. And wear her native costume. And be famous. And be called "Zooby," which she'll hate. She'll do everything she feels like except fuck anyone else and he won't be able to get rid of her.

Irene says, "You see? I've settled it. Totally Victorian." Ernst stretches, relaxing. Irene remarks:

"You know, Ernst, it's very odd; I don't know any women."

Ernst says idly, "What?"

"At Center," says Irene. "At R & R. There's the one linguist out of twenty. And the anthropologist we all studied with, years ago. And all those staff women, of course, you know, the ones who tattoo you, take your retinal prints, give you your guide-rod, the ones you always see in the background doing all the little jobs, but no women."

"That's plenty of people," says Ernst, yawning, "isn't it?"

"Not anyone in The Gang," she says. "Not anyone like me."

"You're unique."

He takes her hand in his and then drops it. He's too tired to court her.

She says, "I'm sorry, Ernst. I'm in a bad mood."

"Are you yearning for civilian life?"

She says sharply, "Sometimes you're very stupid."

She adds quickly, "I'm sorry. That's not what I meant."
Both fall silent. He thinks ruefully that she's right, he's
getting stupid and old or he'd make an effort to handle
these things better, but Ka'abah has exhausted him, it was
no vacation, and he'd rather not handle anything thorny
for a few days. Particularly not coming from a partner.
He thinks *Age is selfish.*

She says, "Damn it, Ernst, we don't know a soul
outside The Gang. We don't really know who pays us, we
don't know the effects of our work, hell, half the time we
don't even know what the work is."

He says, roused, "No, Irene, that's too—"

Turning around sharply in her seat: "No, it's not. We
know names, right? Like you know the name of your
bank. Do you know its investments? We know a history;
did it really happen? Where do you find out? In the
museums? How can we tell when an artifact's faked? We
know the theory of possible worlds—yes, in popularized
form, that's to say, no form, because we certainly can't
operate the machinery or plot a course and we don't
understand either the machinery or the course."

He says, "Kopernik, the world fades out to mystery in
every direction. Do you want to change that?"

She says, "You sound like—" and then, clasping her
hands together in her lap and staring downwards, "You
sound conservative today. Is that deliberate?"

He says gently, "Yes, it is. I am beginning to wonder
about the wisdom of remaking cultures or even people's
lives. That little girl's, for example."

He sees her looking up at him, eyes unfathomable,
head tilted to one side. Doggedly he goes on: "Now, I do
not mean leave her there, of course. Don't beat me for
nothing. Let me hang myself first. You know I would

rescue everyone if I could. But you must face it that she's out of her language, out of her culture. What sort of adjustment is she going to make after spending her whole life in one room? And there's the Freudian business. I mean I really do not like what she's doing with the cultural pressures suddenly lifted; this little girl may turn into a deep-sea fish and explode all over us before we can get her back into some kind of tank. And I like least what surprises me most: that she genuinely hates you. That child hates you; you know she does."

Irene's head bends; her gaze is directed down into her lap, into her folded hands. She says softly, "Yes, I know."

He waits to see if she'll speak, but she doesn't continue. So he adds thoughtfully, "You know, Irenee, I've been too many places, I think. Too many that were like one another but not quite. Too many contexts overlapping but not quite. New rules, new languages, things always changing. I've had an overdose. So when I say there's a value to staying put, you've got to understand what I mean. We have the child now and we can't undo it, but don't be too optimistic; things can't be broken and reset that much, people uprooted so thoroughly, not people's expectations, not their hearts, you know."

She says whimsically, "Do you intend to be respectable, Ernst? To get settled and keep bees?"

He says, disliking the implication that she's rallying him, "I'm tired."

He finds his hands held. Irenee says, "So suddenly? I don't believe it. Ernst, you've got indigestion."

She smiles and holds his hands. He thinks: *Well, once in a while I've a right to be a stubborn bastard*. Her hands loosen their hold. She says, no longer smiling, "I suppose we're not ourselves."

"The influence of Ka'abah," he says. And feeling that he really ought to respond, he frees one of his hands and folds it reassuringly over hers. On her face is a faint, unhappy echo of Zubeydeh's expression when she said, "Uncle! Oh, Uncle!" It surprises him. He doesn't think explicitly: *This is not the woman to be my successor* but things flash in his mind, *Are women*—and *Women don't*—, thoughts he knows are treasonous to Irene. And then there is the strain and sympathetic misery of finding her unhappy. He pats her hand.

She says, "Ernst, I'm sorry," and he—heartfelt— "Irenee, you don't have to apologize to me."

The terror of The Gang says, through dignified tears, "Yes, I know, I'm sorry. I'm sorry, I'm sorry. I know. I'm sorry."

Fast shuttles have water tanks, houses have beds, staterooms on liners have rugs or ruglets and tethers to keep sleepers from wandering over the spidery furniture; in low weight you can sleep anywhere. Irene has had a call button installed next door for Zubeydeh to push if she gets scared; usually they leave the connecting door open, but it tends to swing shut by itself and when this happens, Zubeydeh screams. Irene expects a peaceful night, as Zubeydeh has with her the little friend she's found, a six-year-old named Michael, unless of course Michael pushes the button. Michael is traveling alone between sets of parents, a big-eyed, apparently self-possessed little boy, the temporary victim of some domestic emergency he cannot explain; when Irene asks him he only stares. Sometimes he tells her his name and address. Sometimes he goes into a long, hesitant narrative about Che, and Mishkatel, who's a rabbit, and other people, assuming that Irene knows them all. Once he said, "I have a dog," and stared until Zubeydeh pulled him away. Between Michael and Zubeydeh communication is still primitive; she uses gestures, she pushes him, she yells.

She bullies him.

123

Irene wakes, not knowing what's waked her; as soul knits back to body she sees a strange child's face, like a baby moon, taking up her field of view. Ernst is awake on the other side; she can feel him moving. Michael is scared of Ernst, possibly because Ernst is so big, and Irene usually deals with the little boy alone. Michael is pulling strongly at the jacket of her pajamas, his odd little face expressionless, his owl-eyed glasses askew; he says in his queer, hoarse voice, which is so deep for a six-year-old's: "It's Zooby."

Irene decides that the child's face is odd becuse it has no expression. "What?" she says.

"Zooby," Michael repeats and then something or somebody outside her field of vision snatches him back. There's a muffled grunt and a squeak. She gives herself a moment to wake up. Ernst appears to be asleep, but she knows that the slightest trouble wakes him faster than it does her; she says, "It's the children. Don't bother," and unsnaps the tie around her waist. From next door comes a steady, furtive, bumping sound mixed with the murmur of someone talking in a low voice. The connecting door has been shut. Irene wonders if Zubeydeh is trying to kill herself by dashing her brains out against a bulkhead. She puts her hand to the door and finds that it is latched as well as shut; quietly she frees the latch so as not to alarm either child. The second stateroom is tinier than the first and the lights have been turned low; Irene first checks the room (as usual) for exits and entrances, concealments, anything grossly wrong. Then she sees the children.

Then she sees what the children are doing.

Zubeydeh, dressed in her Ka'abite best, is exquisitely glittering and filmy, an Eastern fairy in the cave-like darkness of the room, all slow-floating gauze and sparks of jewels. She has backed little Michael against a bulkhead and is telling him in a cooing and disagreeable voice that he has been a bad boy and must be punished. Michael's pants have been pushed down around his knees, hobbling him, and Zubeydeh is pulling at the little boy's limp penis; from time to time, his shoulders hunched, Michael tries to protect his genitals with his hands, and when he does so, Zubeydeh strikes the hands sharply away and pushes him. His hands and his head knock against the wall. Her bracelets jingle.

Before Zubeydeh hears or sees Irene, Michael does. He tries to duck sideways along the wall and the little girl yanks him back. The muscles of her arms and back go rigid for a moment; then clever Zubeydeh turns about swiftly, with a clashing of ornaments, and stares at Irene. Her expression is ugly. She starts to yell, her voice rising: "Get out! Get out! Get *out!*" With one arm Irene puts the little boy behind her; with the other she slaps Zubeydeh, who spins about in the low gravity, her Ka'abite dress twisting. Zubeydeh grabs the knob of the door and begins to scream hideously, her body jerking in a temper tantrum, sometimes wallowing on the rug, sometimes off it, sometimes thrashing in the empty air. She tries to get at Irene but can't stabilize her position in the low weight, so she claws at nothing. She screams repeatedly.

Irene gathers up the trembling little boy, who says into her ear, in a hoarse, tickly caw, "I feel funny."

She says to him, under Zubeydeh's din, "Do you know how to use the cubicle?"

"Yes," he says, so she lets him down, and as he scurries past, she takes on an armful of infuriated twelve-year-old, who claws her face and bites her on the arm with sharp teeth, drawing blood. Zubeydeh screams, going rigid in Irene's arms. She jerks from head to foot. Irene wraps arms about her in a bear hug and shakes her hard; Zubeydeh's teeth rattle and she yells the tail end of some word in Ka'abite over and over as if it were being shaken

125

out of her. Then she goes limp. She begins to cry
normally. Irene lets her down on a ruglet, meant for a
pillow but just Zubeydeh's size; several of the little girl's
glass bracelets have been smashed and are drifting down
to the floor in pieces, her white-and-gold robes are badly
torn, and one ear is bleeding where the earring caught on
something and was half ripped out. "I'm bad, I'm bad,
I'm bad!" she cries, and begins to beat herself weakly with
her fists.

Michael comes out of the cubicle with his pants done
up and Zubeydeh turns her face away, tears leaking out
from under her eyelids; Irene takes the little boy's hand
and leads him to the door, saying in a low voice, "Ernst,
Zubeydeh has been tormenting him." Neumann will hear
and take care.

She goes back to the little girl, who has curled up on the
ruglet with her face hidden; from inside her own arms
Zubeydeh says quickly:

"I know! I was bad!"

Irene says, "You were bad because you scared him and
hurt him. If another child wants to touch you or be
touched by you, that's fine, so long as it's friendly and not
angry."

Zubeydeh mutters something unintelligible. She
straightens herself so that she can see Irene and her chin
trembles. She says, "Well?"

"Well, what?"

"*You* know."

"No I don't," says Irene.

"When will you...will you...." and the little girl
bursts into tears, crying, "Don't send me back! Don't!
Don't! I'll die!" She twists herself about and knocks her
forehead against the ruglet.

"But we can't send you back!" says Irene. Zubeydeh
stops in mid-knock: "What?"

Irene repeats, "We can't send you back," and adds, "We are not legally entitled to send you back. I don't want to but I couldn't even if I wanted. Your visa has written on it that we must deliver you to the Trans-Temporal Authority at a place called Center and if we didn't, we would be doing something highly illegal. You won't be living with us any more when we get to Center but we'll see you from time to time. And once you're there, you can claim refuge, which means nobody can interfere with you until you're a grown-up woman. And then, of course, nobody can send you anywhere against your will."

Zubeydeh lifts herself on one elbow, her mouth open. *"Really?"*

"Yes," says Irene a little shortly. "And don't ask me why we didn't tell you before. We *did* tell you, and you didn't listen."

Zubeydeh drifts back on to her sleeping mat, half lying down, half propped against the wall. She is looking not at Irene but at something invisible hanging a few feet in front of her. Then her gaze focuses on Irene and she says:

"Will *he* visit me too?"

"Of course."

"I don't want him to," says Zubeydeh soberly.

"I thought you liked him."

"I do," says Zubeydeh softly and she turns her face away. "But I'm through with all that."

Irene suppresses a smile.

Zubeydeh says earnestly, "Love is no good," playing with a rent in her dress, poking her finger through it. She looks down into her lap. She clasps her hands in her lap and says, "No, I'm through. It's like The Play of the Baker where the lady says she needs love so much that love has become her law. I don't want to be like that."

She's silent for a moment. Then she says painfully, "I've decided not to marry Uncle Ernst. I feel too much for him. I feel that he's a god. So when he doesn't like something I'm doing, I have to stop; I know he disapproves of it and I can't go on doing it, I just can't. Because I need him so badly, you see, and if I lost him, there would be nobody else."

"There's always someone else," says Irene dryly. "Stop being romantic."

"No, I'm not," says Zubeydeh simply. "It's just common sense. Why should he like me? Nobody else does. But lots of women must like him."

Irene brushes the little girl's hair back from her face. "Try standing up to him and getting your own way."

Zubeydeh shakes her head. "They can do without us," she says. "Uncle knows that. When he wants to show me he disapproves, he just gets very quiet; that's to show that he can withdraw his love. He doesn't have to fight about it." She adds mournfully, "That's why I dragged Michael around, because he's so little and alone that he needed me. I thought he couldn't do without me." Her face twists. "And now he'll never have anything to do with me again!"

"Indeed he won't," says Irene, "and don't you go pushing yourself on him or getting mad because he won't play with you. If you ever get so angry again, come tell me about it and you can hit me all you like; I can protect myself. But if you do anything bad to anybody else, maybe I can't send you back, but I *can* wallop you within an inch of your life and I will. Now take your dress off and get into your pajamas."

Zubeydeh unwinds herself, neatly folding the fancy textiles with a care and deftness that surprise Irene. She supposes that the little girl has been trained to do it and that she might even do a better job of mending and washing (which the dress badly needs) than any grown-up off Ka'abah. Zubeydeh stows her dress carefully in the floor chest, smoothing the wrinkles, and then climbs into her sleeping shorts and jacket; she bestows herself gloomily on the ruglet, cries a little, and says:

"I can't sleep. I'm not covered up."

"Don't fuss," says Irene, "I'm going to stay here tonight," and she goes to shut the door. In the bright light of the room beyond, Conscience Neumann sits cross-legged like a bear in a cave, drowsing, with a stuporous Michael, fast asleep and breathing noisily, cradled in his big hands. Michael's glasses are off and he's been wrapped in a blanket. She thinks that her Conscience makes a fine Madonna, and with what she recognizes as envy, closes the door. *I'm too old for a Daddy.*

Zubeydeh is half asleep. Irene thinks vaguely, *Poor little fellow.* She glides to the cubicle to find out how the little boy's terrified body betrayed him: did he pee? throw up? leave a turd on the floor? but whatever he did, it's gone; there's nothing in the cubicle to clean up. Irene goes back to the room to snap herself in next to Zubeydeh, but Zubeydeh's eyes are open.

She says, "Irenee, I want to kiss you good night," and Irene bends obediently down to receive a living necklace of arms and a smack on the cheek. She puts her arms around the warm, fragrant little girl.

Zubeydeh says, "Will you be my Mommy?" and as Irene jerks back in surprise, "You don't have to answer right away, you know."

She adds, "You think about it," and burrows into her ruglet. She says, "I want a sheet." Irene fetches one from the wall storage space and fastens it over her; Zubeydeh says luxuriously, "Oh, that's *better*!" and yawns. "Irenee?" she says.

"Yes?" Irene is snapping the tether round her own waist.

Zubeydeh says softly, "Irenee, why did you tell me to stand up to him?"

"Because you should," says Irene, reaching above her to re-set the wake-up call. "Everyone should stand up to everyone."

"But *you* don't," says Zubeydeh, wriggling under the sheet, which action makes her rise and fall as under a drumhead; "You don't really. You always give in."

Irene starts to answer, but the little girl is fast asleep.

A bed is an island. A patch of rug big enough for two people is an island. Irene drifts out of the uneasy sleep of low weight to fool around with her colleague; she says something unintelligible and tries to reach him, but succeeds only in unsettling her weight and bumping against him, which wakes her.

"What is it?" he says.

She says sleepily, "Ernst, let's . . . let's . . . Ernst, let's blow up the world."

The next day in the lounge she says to him, in a tone she herself feels to be brittle:

"Zooby tells me I always give in, so I'm not going to give in this time."

He looks properly attentive. He's holding his drink cradled absently in his big hand as if the glass were baby Michael. Then his gaze begins to wander about the fake rocks and spot-lit cataracts of the lounge; somehow he's no longer looking at her.

She says, "I have always found these places aggressively dull. Ernst, you're not listening to me. You can't find this place that amusing."

She thinks, *How many times have I said "You're not listening"?*

He begs her pardon.

She says sharply, "Perhaps my voice isn't loud enough to attract your attention."

How many times have I said "I'm sorry"?

"I'm sorry," she says finally. His gaze comes back to her. Then Ernst puts one hand over hers and states:

"Irene, you needn't apologize to me."

She says promptly, "I don't want to apologize to you. I want you to listen to me. It's not a favor."

He puts his drink in the receptacle arm of the chair; he spreads both hands helplessly and says, "Behold, I'm listening!"

She says carefully, "I told you. Zubeydeh accused me of always giving in. But I won't, not this time."

He says, "Very well. What do you want me to listen to?"

She says, exasperated, "That I'm not giving in."

He nods. He waits expectantly. The silence lengthens. It occurs to her that she doesn't know what on earth she was going to say. Possibly what she wants him to listen to has gotten lost in the fight over listening, so she goes back to that doggedly.

"I shouldn't have to ask to be listened to," she says. "It's absurd."

He agrees courteously. "You shouldn't. And of course you don't have to, because I'm listening."

Rage. Defeat. Fear. Something is getting to her. She wonders if it's a replay situation, something from her earlier life. It can't have anything to do with him. She knows that she's perceiving him through some kind of distortion, that it's not fair to him, and that nothing she can trot out now will justify all this fuss. She tries to remember what she started with, and can't, and then notices that Ernst has picked up his drink and is looking round the room again. Out of patience, she gets up and snaps open the curtain.

He says mildly, "Where are you going?"

She says only, "You act like a Ka'abite."

He smiles. "Why, Sklodowska, I have no plans to chain you to the bed and put a veil on you."

She doesn't answer. She longs to knock the drink out of his hand, but in low weight that's not only messy; it's unsatisfying, like playing golf with balloons. She says sharply, "I'm going, that's all," and flips the curtain back into place, hoping (absurdly) to break the mechanism. She thinks, *My God, I'm an idiot, he didn't do anything wrong*, and wonders if she should find someone on board to have a love affair with, for revenge, but she can't imagine touching anyone who doesn't look like Ernst. The bare idea of it gives her the horrors. She swings through the corridors in long, absent-minded glides, pushing off from one hand-hold to another, wondering where to go. Is Zubeydeh in the gym again? Bothering the stewards? Visiting Yasemeen? Parading up and down the dining room in full drag to get stared at by the other passengers?

She thinks: *How did I fail?*

Then she thinks: *And at what?*

Zubeydeh remarks, hanging by her knees from a horizontal bar in the gym, her tee shirt rucked up under her narrow arms:

"Yes, Daddy yelled a lot. You could tell when he was angry. But Noor-ed-Deen didn't. He just looked away until I stopped. He wouldn't even speak to me until I stopped. I mean stopped whatever it was. That's the way an older brother should discipline you. He didn't beat me, you know."

She says severely, coming upright like a snake in the low weight, "Husbands don't beat their wives, Irene. That's silly and barbaric. That's what outsiders think about Ka'abah."

She adds, "We're not really so different from other places, you know."

She knows that Ernst often reflects back to her her own vagueness or lack of self-confidence—as partners do—so she decides to be slangy and sharp. She has a plan this time. She says, "Ernst, I've decided. I want to get into Trans Temp's files. The Gang's files."

He laughs, delighted, "Kopernik!"

"I'm serious," she says. "I've picked enough locks and tampered with enough machinery that I should be able to do it by now. And I want your help."

He's silent.

"What I really want," she says pedantically, counting on her fingers, "is first to find some way of smashing Ka'abah. And don't tell me they won't last past the third generation; the banks won't let them fail. Second, I want to find out the real purpose of The Gang. Third, on Earth—"

He interrupts: "You're joking!"

She says quickly, breaking her own resolution, "Don't make fun of me!"

He says, "I'm not, Irenee."

She says steadily, recovering herself, "And don't tell me I'm unrealistic or immature. Where I come from those are fighting words. I don't like Ka'abah and I don't like my home and I want to do something about both of them."

He says slowly, "But surely you know that all places are bad, Irene."

She says, "Then we will have to do something about all places."

"That's a very, very big job."

"We are supposed to be very, very able people."

He shrugs. They're in the lounge again, in that early part of the artificial day called morning. Zubeydeh has gone to breakfast. When people sit in a tent with barely room for their elbows, they are forced into confrontations.

She says suddenly, breaking her resolution again, "Ernst, don't float away."

He raises his eyebrows politely.

She says, her voice breaking in spite of herself, "Ernst, you matter to me, you really do."

He smiles, a little absently.

"No, tell me," she says, "do tell me, why are we in this? Why be in it at all? It doesn't change anything."

He says, "Lady Lovelace, are you going to cry?"

She stares at him. *What?* The digression throws her; it throws her badly. *What is he trying to do?* She remains silent while Ernst goes on, remarking that Trans Temp has produced their jobs, that she mustn't forget that, that nobody can know the entire purpose of an organization so big.

Silence. Irene is astonished.

He says in a lighter tone, "Well, as for me, I like my job. It lets me dream that soon I will retire and raise bees. And take special care of the queen bee. And your job lets you rescue little girls who want to be poets."

"But not the mother," says Irene.

"Well, my dearest dear," he continues in the same deliberately lightened tone, "we can't save them all, can we? Think! All the rebels, all the refugees? No planet would hold them all. The universe itself wouldn't hold them."

She says promptly, "Then to hell with the universe!"

More silence. A prolonged embarrassment. She's not sure whether it's hers or his, but she likes what she said anyway. Then she feels a hand on her shoulder; it occurs to her that Ernst is trying to be kind. He's patting her gently. He says, "Am I allowed to speak?"

She doesn't answer.

He says, "You make it hard for me when I am not allowed to call anything unrealistic, Irene. But I must say: Ka'abah has changed you. I know this, as a friend. And remember your family—"

She shouts, "Family! What the hell has it got to do with my family? Do you think everything is Rose and Casimir?"

She sees that her outburst has annoyed him and thinks, *I won't say it. I'm sorry, I'm sorry, I'm sorry, so many times I'm sorry.*

"You're shouting," he says.

She says, "That's the lie I got all my life!"

She adds, "So I'm allowed to rescue poetic little girls. What about the unpoetic ones? What about their cousins and their sisters and their aunts?"

Ernst has wrapped one hand around the other; he's serious and worried. She thinks that he must also be going deaf. She wonders whether his next remark will prove it and, sure enough, he says quietly: "People have their own ways of getting along, Irene."

Dunya. Zumurrud. Yes.

He says quickly, leading her to believe that he hasn't completely lost his sensitivity to other people's feelings, "I don't mean the madwoman, of course. But other people, sane people."

Like my mother. Like Chloe. Like me.

He says, "You know I have been against.... Well, it's done and she's here now, but where are we going to send this little Zubeydeh? Where can she possibly fit in?"

Irene says, amazed, "Hell, where can *I* fit in?"

He puts one hand over hers. "Sklodowska, don't talk about leaving!"

She stares at him again.

He says, "It's my fault. I'm the Watcher, the Conscience. I ought to have known something was happening when you got so absurdly angry at that little man. When we get back it has to be more than R & R, you know. It must be a check-up."

He adds energetically, pained and compassionate, "Talking about getting into the files! Talking about leaving!"

Silence. A long silence.

She thinks, fascinated, *Now he's going to flatter me.*

He says, "I keep forgetting that you're not a super-woman."

She says, "No. Only just me."

"What an extraordinary woman!" And then, "You know, highly gifted children are never born into an easy world, despite the sex. Like you and the little girl. It is not the sex."

Shakespeare's sister.

He says, holding her hand, "Are you sorry you joined us?"

She thinks, *He's old, that's all it is*, but hears Zubeydeh saying: Daddy loves my poems.

He says, "Please know, dear, that I will never let you get into such bad trouble as fooling with The Gang's records. That's dangerous."

She says, "Would you turn me over to the authorities?"

She adds, "Then I would be dismissed and I would be a nobody. I would be one of those ladies we never speak to."

136

The moment is over; he doesn't take her seriously. He hides his face comically in his hands. His hair, through which she has always loved to run her fingers, stands up like an expensive, rough-cut, grey brush. She stands up, wondering how she could run away with Goliath only to end up with David again, how she managed to get married after all, and who she'll be when she's not in The Gang.

She says, "I'm going."

Then she says, "Oh, Ernst, you make me feel sixteen again."

Zubeydeh, who is hiding in the stateroom in full Ka'abite sail (pursued by the steward at whom she threw her breakfast pie), says:

"Women always go crazy. My mother was crazy. I go crazy, too; I become my Bad Self and put on my dress and do something awful. When Mommy ever said anything wrong, Daddy would explain to me that it was her craziness speaking. Jaafar told me all about it; it's harder for a woman to form her feminine personality than it is for a man to form his masculine one because women's bodies are made of lighter molecules than men's and it's harder for women to incorporate their masculine element into their characters than it is for men to incorporate their feminine element into theirs. Besides, we have our monthlies and that drives us crazy, you know. I don't have them yet, though. I'm not really crazy; I just *look* crazy because I'm a poet and that's different, but mother's craziness was horrible. The men know. They can spot it. We're just not as stable as they are. Jaafar would say, 'That's just like a woman,' whenever I pigged out on some candy. And I would get *mad*. Of course he'd say that

137

about Yahya, too. But Yahya was still trying to subordinate his feminine element to his masculine element and that was very hard for Yahya because he was so fat. Women need discipline because of all those light molecules and if we don't get it we really will go mad and end up like Aunt Dunya. I dream about Aunt Dunya. I dream I'm back in her cell, although I don't dream it very much any more. Daddy used to warn me about going mad and tell me that was why I had to give up poetry and get married; women are always wanting to do something crazy and we never know why. That's why we're so interesting."

Zubeydeh peers through the keyhole, keeping her eyes skinned for the steward. She says:

"I hit him right in the face with my pie because he called me a baby. I don't like pie anyway. I know I look five and sometimes I act eight, but still I'm not a baby. That's an insult. I can run a lot faster than he can. In fact, I tripped him. Discipline is one thing but this is another. Actually I don't mind going crazy now and then and becoming my Bad Self; I think it's good for me. Poets need something like that. Anyway, the gentlemen are always calling the ladies crazy and that's wrong."

She adds, "Irene, do you ever *enjoy* being crazy?"

There's a hydroponic garden aboard, with trays of plants-in-water arranged like the stacks of books in a library: one on top of another. Passengers aren't allowed in, but Trans Temp can get you in anywhere under any name; as she shows her I.D.'s to the machine and human guards, she thinks: *Without these, I'd be nobody.* Beyond the bulkhead are the plants, whose senses don't reach far enough to tell them they're in the wrong place. White roots are visible through the glass containers. There's just enough room to walk between the shelves. Lights are above the human observer, set at an angle between the rows; there's the hum of the air recyclers. Irene walks between beans and clover, studying the plants, running her fingers through green traceries, wondering where she's seen them last. On Earth. Some Earth or other. So much for Anne Bonny, the pirate's bride, and Chloe, who is red clover here, stringy and scattered. As if Irene has been dodging for years but has finally run out of luck. Rose will be sixty-two or sixty-three if she's still alive.

Irene weeps a little. *If Rose is alive.* She wonders how Rose will take to the little oracle in the funny gown if Irene goes home, if Zubeydeh wants to come along, if Rose is alive, when she and the baby poet again become nobodies. There's nothing to lean on in the garden except the shelves, which are strung on wires, and which her very breathing disturbs. A big, floppy, dark-green vine which she doesn't recognize, probably something tropical. There are standing circular waves on the surface of the liquid in which the white roots bunch: the hull is vibrating.

I'm far too old for a Daddy. She recalls visiting a greenhouse with Casimir, who liked and was interested in the flowers but complained about ruining his shoes in the dampness. There was the same strong, odorous greenness. Zubeydeh has said, "The gentlemen always think the ladies are going crazy." The thought of that baby oracle, with a figure like a string bean, talking about ladies and babies and gentlemen, sets Irene laughing; if she didn't fear for the wires, she'd lean on the shelves and smack the pots. That little girl is a genius. She tries to recall Rose, tries to recall Casimir, wonders if she's recalling anything properly. It's not possible, no, not even for Trans Temp, to walk back into nineteen-fifty-three and introduce forty-five-year-old Mrs. Rose Waskiewicz to an astoundingly talky little genius with a monobrow and a veil. Sidewise, yes. Crabwise in time. Rose (she's figured it out) will be sixty-two and a half exactly. Only in a dream can one make the telephone ring over wires long since dismantled, on an instrument junked years ago, in a house long since torn down to make room for a parking lot, so that even the wallpaper is a ghost and the old Kelvinator next to the phone is a ghost, too; only in imagination can one make the dead phone ring and hear the long-gone voice say, "Honey, it's for you."

Young Mrs. Waskiewicz stands in the kitchen in nineteen-fifty-three, looking out into the living room past the clunky old television set in its plastic case (new then), past the china shepherdess perched on a doily on the dinette table, and says to an ugly seventeen-year-old who's sprawled in the overstuffed armchair with her muscular legs out in front of her, wishing she weren't too old for comic books and could still read *Sheena, Queen of the Jungle* and *Rio Rita, Girl Espionage Agent:*

"Irene, it's for you."

She thinks, *I'd better get home before my mother dies*.

To come so far. Like Elf Hill. And all for nothing. To spend your adolescence dreaming of the days when you'd be strong and famous. To make such a big loop—even into the stars—and all for nothing.

She thinks: *What a treadmill*.

Irene has taken to studying in the ship's library: a cubicle with a viewer. She's trying to get away from Ernst, who keeps following her around, looking worried. She looks up from her bibliography of women poets and painters to see that he's hanging around the doorway and has stuck his head into the room in a friendly way; now he takes her glance as an invitation and crowds into the room with her, so she says coldly:

"When we go back to Center I want to change partners. I want a female partner next time."

She sees his face (at the height of an Alp) becomes shocked, but he tries to hide it, saying as a joke, "Why, Irene, there aren't any women as extraordinary as you."

"Let them recruit some," she says. She adds, "If I wanted a black partner, they'd find one. If I wanted someone who spoke Zuni, they'd find one. What's so strange about this request?"

He says, "But it's not functional," and then, joking, "What on earth would you talk to her about? Would you talk about beisbol?"

She dives into the viewer hood.

He says in a more serious voice, "Irene, is it that you think a woman would be more sympathetic in places like Ka'abah? Do you think she would feel more as you do? It's true that I don't feel quite as you do—I don't take the same things to heart—but then, Irene, nobody does feel exactly as anyone else, and I have never stood in your way. Have I?"

She says, "I've never inconvenienced you."

A hand on her shoulder, tentatively; "Indeed you haven't," he says.

It makes her unhappy to analyze him. To see his age and stubborness, the way he insists on her weakness. She starts to talk about how *Women know* or *Women are* or *Women understand* and then stops. That's bad manners. She learned that was bad manners in high school. It's polite to pretend there's no difference, at least in your speech. If you don't, you may find yourself forced to

141

admit that women are good for nothing, even now, even here, even she herself. She says, coming out of the hood:

"You've stood in my way whenever it inconvenienced you. Yes, you have. That means small things, but small things mean all the time. Ernst, you don't *listen*. And you like me being aggressive as long as I don't cross you. Then you don't mind. Hell, Rose always told me I'd have to find a man who didn't *mind*."

He says, "Why are you dwelling so on the personal?"

"Zubeydeh's mother—"

"Irene, if you keep coming back to—"

"It's feminine!" says Irene. "Right? Dwelling on the personal! That's why I feel so abjectly tied to you even though we're both free, right? That's why I'm always the one who feels like a fool and who always gives in. Give me the Clewiston Test when we get back to Center; see if I'm mad. I'm not; it's just my feminine nature!"

He says, "Irene, if you have always felt this way—"

She says, "Oh, use your head, Ernst! Who else can I sleep with? Where else can I go? Can I join the U.S. Marines? You've got a dozen possible jobs and a hundred possible women and you can live anywhere!"

He says carefully and with dignity, "You exaggerate my freedom, Irene, believe me. I may have a few choices not open to you, only a few. But I love you and want to stay with you and work with you. Obviously this is not reasonable if we fight. When we get back to Center you may put in for any change you want, obviously, but they'll wonder, you know. I wonder myself. I can't help it. I wish you would tell me rationally and systematically what is wrong; I'll do my best to understand. They won't be as indulgent there, you know."

She thinks in amazement, *Threats. He's threatening me.* She says, "Are conditions the same for both of us?"

Seriously he nods.

142

She says, "Then I'm a constitutionally inadequate person," and goes back to her viewing. She's only pretending to look; Ernst's presence against the curving wall is exquisitely irritating—the room's impossibly crowded in any case—and he excites her without pleasing her. She wishes he would go. She says finally, emerging from the hood, "Look, dear, if conditions aren't the same, that's it. That's the sexes, that's the races, that's class. Right?"

He's trying. He's certainly not dismissing it. Physically he's a beautiful man; she likes to look at him. She wonders if Ernst will come out with a platitude, finally, and what it will mask, whether he's saying in the privacy of his heart, "I'm selfish, Irene. I'm too old to change." Or, "Don't you love me any more?"

He says thoughtfully, "Yes, there's some truth in that." And then, "I do not believe in the innate differences between races, of course."

He ponders. Finally he says to her, shaking his head:

"Irene, you dress as I do, you work as I do, you're paid as I am! If you were in your mother's situation. . . . But we go back to Center, we lead the same life, we have the same training, we exchange memories like the others, we're isolated people."

He adds, "If there's a difference—"

He says then, simply, with a grave smile, "I'm glad of the difference."

She gets up, keeping her temper. She swings the viewer hood back into the wall. She says to him, "Ernst, I do love you," and he, with an exasperated, helpless shrug, "I suppose there's something—" and then, "We must talk about this, Irene," and she: "That's what I've been *trying*—" and having stood up in the library cubicle, she has, of necessity, walked right into him. Ernst is pleased. The contact gives him pleasure.

Then she must wait until he steps out of the way, which he does politely. She pushes past him: alas, never a good operative because she loses her temper. One woman painter (Irene has read) spent her life painting Judith cutting off Holofernes' head, but Irene won't cut off Ernst's head; he uses it little enough as it is. By an impulse fast becoming habit, she decides to go looking for Zubeydeh, who will say: *Of course he's right* and elaborate her light-molecule explanation of women's nature. But no, Zubeydeh has never accused Irene of being mad and Irene suspects she never will; Zubeydeh makes room for both of them in her theories. Perhaps life would be supportable with Zubeydeh on an uninhabited island: Zubeydeh and Rose and Chloe and one of the nameless women from R & R. They can call it Paradise Island. And Ernst is one of the few men she's ever met who likes women. Most men don't. Most women don't, most boys don't, most little girls don't.

She feels a tug on her sleeve. She's passed the gym and is somewhere near the dining room, another sphere like the lounge but with its own spin added; people stay there for an hour or two after eating. It's the little girl in tee shirt and shorts, her long hair floating tangled behind her. Irene is beginning to dread the chore of combing it out; Zooby shrieks so.

"Hello, I'm back," says Zubeydeh.

Irene has been trying to find some dreams. She's gone through her mother's dreams, Chloe's dreams, some of Zubeydeh's dreams, and finally what she recognizes as Ernst's dreams, which fact makes her so angry that she wakes up.

There are no dreams. The stateroom night-light is on. Ernst is dreaming his own dreams next door. Will Irene kidnap Ernst when she leaves The Gang, and make him come with her? Sedate him, gag him, tie him up while he sleeps? Will she kill him? Will he have to kill her? Will she apologize? Will he break down? Will he have her committed? Zubeydeh would enjoy tying up Uncle Ernst, while maintaining all the time she did it that ladies never did this to gentlemen, although gentlemen did occasionally do it to ladies.

Irene wakes again. Zubeydeh's asleep on the other rug. Careful not to stir the little girl's tangled, black hair, Irene untethers herself and drifts across the cabin; the night-light is a dim, sourceless radiance and the machine hum of the air recyclers comes right through the walls. Irene floats out via the handholds, scarcely touching the floor; the corridor is empty, as the whole passenger section will be this time of night. She thinks she will take a walk between the curving walls, so like a giant hotel on Earth; the gymnasium, the lounge, the hydroponics garden, all three will be empty. Halfway to the garden a computer terminal shows up ahead, glowing dimly at waist height, and she slips her cover I.D. into it, intending to ask for a library print-out of the ship's map for Zubeydeh. Irene herself knows her way around. There is a moment's silence and Irene impatiently presses the request button again; above the card-slot, a rectangular tab lights up red:

Rejected.

Momentarily annoyed, she fishes in her clothing for another I.D.; either the terminal has gone wonky or the computer's entire passenger section has. The former is more likely. She tries a second I.D., waits a moment, and sees the same red tab light up:

Rejected.

The terminal is out of order. Three hundred yards

down the hall is another; she tries it. It accepts her cover
I.D., waits a moment, and then lights up red:

Rejected.

She tries her other I.D.'s:

Rejected
Rejected
Rejected
Rejected
Rejected
Rejected
Rejected
Rejected
Rejected
Rejected

The print-out dish has been gathering identical
flimsies. She reads them:

*Your access to the central computer has been formally
cancelled. If you wish to have this ruling reviewed, please
contact the ship's officer from your cabin. Your cabin
terminal will accept this request or any other emergency
request. Your ordinary voyaging and meal-time privileges
are still in effect.*

Someone's been prying at the computer terminal in his
cabin, some child's been hogging the access channels, and
they think it's her.

But not all eleven of her.

She thinks, *But I have no such power.* She has never
had the numbers of Ernst's I.D.'s, not even when she was
his Conscience. Yet he must have a record of hers and
must have gotten it from Trans Temp at Center, months
ago at the very least. Keeping them all the time. Holding
her identities in the palm of his hand. Trans Temp guards
against the different one, the unstable one, the female one,
the Wife-stealer! She remembers 'Alee peering in horror
through his beard: *Where are your children?* Center must

have been asking the same question, asking it for years, expecting that any moment she would revert and turn back into Rose. It occurs to her that they may even be right, that nothing in her life accounts for the intensity of her anger, that Center is not Ka'abah, that Ernst is a man who loves and respects women. He has good judgment; once he judged her worthy and now he judges her mad. *The gentlemen always think the ladies have gone mad.* It occurs to her that in some sense she doesn't really exist, now that Ernst is no longer her ally, that the little beauty she had from him is gone and that no woman she has ever known would back her up. Her mother was, after all, quite mad, certifiably mad, and Chloe was mad, Chloe fell down when you talked to her; nobody can blame Ernst for losing patience with a madwoman.

Irene presses her fists into the pit of her stomach and bends over, sliding down to the foot of the wall. *They never*—she thinks. *They didn't really—*

The gentlemen always think the ladies have gone mad.

She says to herself stubbornly, *But I want those I.D.'s back.* A wave of heat washes over her. They may be right about her, but all the same they're fools and Ernst is a fool; does he think her skills disappear when she's off duty? Or that she's crazy and stupid both? Apparently they do. Ernst must believe that she daren't do anything without him, that she loves him too much to call a bluff or ignore a threat, that the fear of abandonment will bring her back. They think she can act only under orders. Irene wants very badly to throw up, but instead she rolls the print-out flimsies into cobwebby balls and swallows them one by one; there's really very little substance to them. She is now supposed to go to Ernst, who is older and wiser than she, and say, "I'm sorry. I won't defy you any more. I'm not cut out for this work."

Irene cries. She lets herself go. They all swear they love

you, they all swear they don't want to control you. She thinks, *How Chloe loved opera!* and what a ghastly fake mess it all was, the soprano dying in glory and the mezzo stuck with an unsympathetic brother or a job as housemaid, while all the coloratura had was the joy of singing *Addio! Addio!* and stabbing herself, dying of T.B., starving, eating poison, throwing herself off a cliff, what the devil could Chloe have been thinking of?

The tears stop. She slaps the wall open-handed time after time: a way to get rid of your feelings without breaking your bones. She sits and grabs her own ankles, pulling arms against legs until the muscles crack.

She stops. The job's still to do. The hall curves like the cave of *'Alee Baba. Open, simsim!* and if she does it right there'll be no trace at all. She gets up and wipes her face with her hands, then starts patting her pockets for pencil and paper, but the library will have that. And she can lock the cubicle door. It's going to have to be a beautiful job, a love of a job, a classic for the textbooks like a perfect game of Go or Chess, like walking backwards in a labyrinth in your own footsteps. A line she read in a book years ago comes back to her, though it was a book she didn't like and paid no attention to at the time, Chloe's gift, something all about men and male creatures, as all the books were:

Killing the spider all by himself in the dark made a great difference to Mr. Baggins....

Well, somebody ought to live it from the spider's point of view, that's all. Like Dunya in her foul cell, like Zumurrud spinning daydreams from wall to wall. Someone ought to let the sane ones know. Someone ought to make them find out.

She thinks, *I'll make them find out.*

• • •

In the library cubicle, with the door locked from the inside, Irene queries the computer, without I.D. card or number, about a minor emergency. She says one of the lights has gone out. She has already made fourteen similar requests from various terminals in different parts of the ship. They are requests the computer is bound to accept with or without I.D. and Irene has coded them incompletely, thus leaving all fourteen lines open. None can be cleared or snapped shut before the routine delivery to consumer affairs in the morning. Irene carries her tools in her clothes, always; thus she has with her now a device that measures the amount of time the computer terminal has taken for an answer or response that looks instantaneous; this will give her some idea of the topography of the current program and what areas overlap. She attaches the device.

Using the terminal for yet another single line, Irene demands political access to consumer complaints but without specifying I.D. card or number; when the computer queries *Who?* and gets no answer, it thriftily leaves the line open. There are now fifteen lines filed as one. With Zubeydeh's number, but not using the card itself (which she does not have) Irene now demands to be incorporated into the short-term memory as spokesperson for passenger unrest; the demand is denied on the grounds that Zubeydeh is not inserting her I.D. card into the card slot.

Irene now reminds the computer that Zubeydeh's card has been reported missing some time ago; in fact, a request for a duplicate card for Zubeydeh was among her original fourteen requests.

The green *Verified* tab comes on and Irene repeats her demand; for a moment she's afraid that Zubeydeh may have been spotted as a child (the machine has this particular difference built into its short-term response memory) but the little girl has an adult visa and so Irene won't have to do the whole thing over again with Ernst's cover number. She now has fourteen from the library terminal; although the origin of requests is automatically noted on the short-term memory, the computer does not—as yet—discriminate between real and imaginary persons on that basis or "understand" that all fourteen lines are open on the one terminal. Irene thinks *Very sloppy programming*. But of course if you make the number of complaints too high, or attempt to use the file of fourteen to go beyond access priority one, there are automatic guards.

Irene is now spokesperson, under Zubeydeh's number, for fourteen nonexistent passengers. She has access priority one to a second-level line, which gives her a way into the permanent memory. The programming "expects"—or rather its creators expect—that at this point any genuinely disaffected passenger will use that priority either to search the permanent memory for legal precedents or demand an immediate connection to someone in authority. Irene transfers the entire line to another part of the permanent memory and gets out her tools; now is the time to search out the other access codes and get some idea of the thing's internal structure. She starts in on the standard questions. It is also possible to approximate certain codes—those which are used often don't vary that much from place to place—and the operations the machine rejects give her the best clues of all.

It takes several hundred operations to break through the legal library and into other main tracks in the permanent memory; from there Irene—who already knows some of the access codes—kites her way into the twenty-four-hour memory in some thirty separate operations. Then she erases the automatic record that she has done so, erases all her operations up to that time, plants a call for a connecting ferry soonest, marked verified by a minor official whose business it is to know such things (she doesn't know him, only the access code), and about to reverse the cancellation of her I.D. numbers, hesitates.

Taking an ink pen from her own pocket she adds a handwritten *1* to the last digit of each of her cards; adding the new numbers to the passenger list is easy. Anyone who queries the computer by her old number will get the information that her cards have been cancelled. Anyone trying to use the old numbers or duplicates of the old cards will likewise find that they've been cancelled. A simple request to see the passenger list will reveal that something's been cooked up, but Ernst will probably not think to do that, at least not for a while. She adds an "e" to "Irene" on her cover I.D. and inserts the name into the passenger list along with its new number. She inserts it out of alphabetical order; the ship now has an Irene and an Irenee, only one of whom the computer rejects. The other cards get random letters at the end of the name; she inserts those names likewise. She thinks, *Simple, machine-recognizable shapes. And I know we don't go discriminating inks.* Passengers have (usually) access to very little; hence the simplicity.

Irene does not totally trust her memory, or the notes she's been making on the library scratch paper, and so checks routinely that the last traces of her meddling are gone; she runs the standard test questions and some specific queries of her own, then erases the record that such questions were asked. She will have to do the final erasure on faith; otherwise one can go on forever checking the erasings and erasing the checkings—it's like trying to erase your footsteps in flour by making more of them. She goes through the final operation and ignites her notes at the cubicle's memory hole in the wall. They burn to ash on the ceramic-topped table and she rubs the ash between her fingers, scooping it down the waste channel at the side of the table. It's done.

She's stiff all over. Her eyesight's blurred. She shudders all over, her usual sequel to hours of effort. Her checking has, of course, included trying the cards themselves, but a sudden doubt makes her do it again; she slips one Supercard into the wall slot and asks for....

She asks for the weather. Some giggle hidden in the room, Irenee wanting to know the weather in space. The amber tab lights up and for a moment she thinks she's failed—she's never been as good as Ernst, she can't be as good as Ernst!—and then she sees in the print-out dish that the machine is simply remarking (quite reasonably) *Request incomplete.*

Of course. The weather where? That's the whole point. Irenee laughs. She terminates the request and slips the used pencil down the waste channel; anyone might have used it but she doesn't, somehow, want to leave it there. She has, according to her watch, about an hour before "morning" when passengers will begin to stir; if Ernst has not noticed her go out, he will certainly notice her come in; best not to hide it. She'll say "I slept somewhere else." Let him think what he pleases. She can look embarrassed enough. There will be a record of extra power expended in the library, perhaps enough to light one incandescent bulb for the time the job has taken. She should've had a library tape running for the six hours, but easy enough simply to say she spent time in the lounge; you don't need an I.D. to get in there. She decides to sleep a few hours in the lounge until the first breakfast shift wakes her; that will do for an excuse. She can do without sleep. Still, it's

better to remove the traces and she can look sulky enough
for this fool to be fooled. She can say "I'm sorry" enough.

For the time being, anyway.

Sleeping with your colleagues has its disadvantages.
For one thing, they notice it when you stop. Irene has
kicked Ernst out of bed for three nights running on the
pretext that Zubeydeh is having nightmares. Irene herself
is prone to tears at odd times and would like to wear dark
glasses, but this would only bring on more questions from
Zubeydeh. The little girl is pleased by the change in
arrangements and has taken to confidences and curiosi-
ties at bedtime; tonight she asks about Center. Irene finds
that she knows the place almost too well to talk about it;
she says it's like a park, like a fancy hotel, with bungalows
dotted about between the trees and the administration
building in its center. Like a summer camp. Nobody
knows how to get in there and nobody knows how to get
out, although somebody must. It's a fairy tale.

Zubeydeh isn't satisfied.

Irene says, "Okay, I'll tell you; there are clerks who set
the settings to send you out or get you in. From one
probability to another. It's not in this universe, Scribble;
it's on one of those strange parallel strands that lie
somewhere clear on the edge of probability, and that's
why nobody can get there. You remember Earth, the
world I came from? Well, it's part of Earth, a dry place,
what I would've called California. But it's one on which
people never developed, so there's nobody there but
Center. It's like a garden in a desert: there's grass so thick
you can feel the texture in your teeth by just looking at it,
but it doesn't rain much. They water it. And the hills, too,

they're all planted. Little hills with rocks to sit on, and small trees, everything to a smaller scale than most places; you would like it. They have a school there, for Trans Temp, but nothing much else and they don't bring much in—I suppose it costs too much—because we don't keep up with the new movies or the new books from our separate worlds or what's happened in those worlds since we left. I suppose there are too many different worlds for it to be practical; they'd have to keep somebody in each one. And everyone's from somewhere else. So we don't really know what's happened to our homes. We end up knowing everybody's past, though; we sit around and swap stories."

She thinks but does not add: *And drink, like other exiles.*

Zubeydeh, sitting on the rug in her peejays, is scornful.

Irene says, "Well, yes, I suppose we're all very stupid for not finding out more. But it's probably not an important place; I think the real center is elsewhere; this is just a lovely place to be, for resting. And the clerks don't know much."

Zubeydeh makes a face.

Irene says, "But you'll like it! Honest. It's a nice place. There are lectures and old films. And everybody speaks a different language, almost, so you can learn anything you like, although most people do end up sticking with those from near their homes; it's nice when you have things in common. That's why I always end up staying with Uncle Ernst, I suppose."

Zubeydeh, who has for the last few days been talking a lot about prostitution, sometimes titillated, sometimes angry, (Irene does not know where she learned about the subject) looks sly. She looks away. She says, "Are the women pretty?"

"Yes," says Irene, "but they're not paid companions.

People who work there enjoy our company, that's all."

"Uncle Ernst's company, you mean," says Zubeydeh, not looking at Irene and then she adds under her breath, muttering, "Two for the price of one."

Irene says nothing. It won't do to give Zubeydeh an opportunity to start; everything has led to salacious giggling in the last few days. And after all (Irene supposes) Zubeydeh's right. She's always right. If no one has ever gone out into the surrounding hills—where one could probably live well enough with a few simple tools—it's undoubtdly because Center has such superior attractions: booze, dope, women, security, and then the reassignments that open up the whole universe. Even for her there is so much; she thinks of the peacefulness of Center, the steep hills in the twilight, the few yellow lights coming on in the little town in the valley where you can go to buy groceries or old magazines, where the people talk tactfully about your being "from the University" though if her memory for faces holds, it's the same people as in the administration. Certainly it's the same euphemism. When Irene is lucky she gets to go to Center in the summer, not in the winter rain (although the small trees are green through February and flowers bloom the year round). She remembers the long twilights in summer, the purple hills turning black against the Western afterglow, fold upon plummy fold. Trans Temp knows what their sophisticated super-people really want: safety, peace, joy, a living picture-postcard.

Irene feels small fingers on her face. Zooby-dooby has sat up and is saying in a shocked tone, "Why, Irene, you're *crying.*" Zubeydeh flings herself into Irene's lap, a little too actively compassionate for comfort. The kisses are nice, but the knees and elbows dig in.

Cautiously lowering her voice, Irene says, "Zubeydeh, if Uncle Ernst and I . . . if we separated, would you come with me? Wherever I went?"

Suddenly the affection is over. Zubeydeh is making a show of delicacy. The child carefully withdraws herself from Irene's lap, going from the age of eight to precocious adulthood in the one movement. She puts dignity into the set of her shoulders, the turn of her head, the Ka'abite beauty with her passionate glance, haughtily refusing the go-between.

She says, "Irene, I do *not* want to marry you."

Irene is speechless.

Zubeydeh says quickly, "Now don't tell me I'm imagining it! I know there are ladies like that; I heard about it in the library. I'm very quick with languages. When a lady is disappointed in a gentleman she sometimes turns to another lady, but it doesn't last. I never believed it could happen, but it does. I can't read printed words, but there was a play on tape in the library and I understood the talking. And Michael helped me. We're friends again. I let him look at Yasemeen when I go to see her. I don't think you and I should get into an arrangement like that because we're friends and I would hate to do anything that would put our friendship in jeopardy. That's first. And second, you're a good bit older than I am, so what will I do when you die? And frankly, I prefer you as my mother."

Irene collects herself. She must not laugh. She says, "Zubeydeh, dear, I prefer you as my daughter. Truly I do. I'm not one of those ladies, at least I think I'm not, but if you meet one later and want to go away with her, it'll be fine with me. When you're older, I mean."

Zubeydeh is evidently relieved. She clutches her knees and lets out a Whoof! of breath. "Oh, well!" she says, and then "Oh, *yes!*" She adds slyly, "You really ought to tell me why you and Uncle Ernst quarrelled, you know."

Irene shakes her head.

"Shit!" says Zubeydeh, using one of her newly acquired words. She adds, "Anyway, I know why."

Irene lifts both hands helplessly.

"Prostitutes!" says Zubeydeh.

That night Irene dreams about Center. There are jolly-girls but no jolly-boys. Zubeydeh is always right. Irene herself is wearing false padding on her shoulders and crotch and wandering around the outside of what is obviously a summer camp; Center has become the interior of an asteroid, the clouds, fake clouds, the hills, a designer's masterpiece, the sun and moon, artificial projections, the blue sky, an engineer's triumph. The gravity is as light as Ka'abah's. Irene decides that there must be a way out, at least for freight, and careful observation should uncover it, especially if nobody's ever bothered before. She doesn't fancy herself as a detective, but thinks she's competent. Center is time-retardant; thus she has no trouble moving faster than anyone else, but upon finding the door in the basement that will lead to Outside, she sees through it the same big, barn-like dance floor she's just left, with the same people frozen as before. She strips off the cumbersome padding, which she resents, only to be given the false shoulders again by somebody: *Wear these long enough and you'll get epaulets*. Again going to the basement she finds the same door, finds herself again in the same summer camp, in the same Outside, with the same beautiful women and the same successful men, only nobody's moving. And so on. And so on. Until it occurs to her that she does know somebody who can get her out, somebody very important, who's got the secret. She thinks it must be Ernst. And

157

wakes up finally, hearing herself cry out in her sleep for this person: *Zubeydeh!*

Confess it; this is all very much nicer as comedy. Jaafar stuck-up but kind, Zubeydeh running her head into her Daddy's stummick. You don't want to know how Irene hates looking at that good man and neither do I; it tears her in two. She's hanging around the corridors to the Communications Room, waiting for news of her ferry. How she checks repeatedly with the computer to find if Ernst has made queries about her: none so far. She thinks, *I'm getting paranoid.* How she's tempted to make friends with the Communications people, but is afraid Ernst will find it out if she does; she's not yet sure what she's going to do when the ferry comes: explain everything to him, sneak aboard with Zubeydeh and Yasemeen, tell him he can come too, reason with him, tell him she's having a love affair with another man, whatever. I've contemplated giving Ernst stomach 'flu and letting the other two run while he's retching, but I don't think so. Not really. I don't think it happens like that. I think they meet in the hall leading to the Communications Room after Ernst's private query to the computer has let him know about the ferry; it's in just such abstract, softly lit, gently curving spaces that the worst things happen. Where there's no place to run to and nothing natural to ameliorate the human conflict: human walls and ceiling, human lights, human handicrafts, human ideas. Here are these two larger-than-life figures of the woman and the man, both in black this time and looking just a little like the living cards in *Alice in Wonderland:* belted tabards over long underwear. They're not—at the moment—wearing their guns. Both are tall, the elder (fiftyish) with grizzled black hair and high-bridged nose, long-limbed, with the deep-set dark eyes and high cheekbones of a desert prophet, the other a stockier sort, almost twenty years younger, with that Slavic dish-face in which the nose is a mere dab, the eyes a washed-out blue, and her hair that fine, no-color, spun sort that Russians go in for when they forget to be blond. She's trying to reach the Communications Room and he's barring her way.

They're no longer on Ka'abah.

She says, "Get out of my way."

He's unbearably disappointed. Hoping for weeks that her words would supply the enormous deficit of information in her behavior but no luck; Irene's entirely lost her ability to project.

She says again, at a higher pitch, "Look here, will you get out of my way!"

He prepares to listen because you must always listen, but it'll be the same plausible nonsense: publicly true perhaps, some of it with a germ of truth, but privately impossible. He has a horrible feeling in his gut; one way or another he'll lose her. And Center will use the incident as an excuse never to recruit women again; he knows that. He blames himself, knowing that he should have seen all this coming earlier, that she needed more understanding than he could give, that he's been lax, lazy, even withdrawn, that he hasn't really challenged anything she's said or done.

On Ka'abah they would call it unmanly.

In his mind's eye she's surrounded by madwomen: Zubeydeh's mother, Zubeydeh's aunt, Irene's friend, Irene's mother, maybe Zubeydeh herself. They're sealed-off, self-possessed, unhappy women, sinking back into that sinister matrix Irene herself has always abhorred, something unformed and primitive, a paranoia so complete that it closes over its victim like a swamp; he thinks that there's no he-and-she of it left. No familiarity.

Irene shouts, "Ernst, get out of the fucking way!"

In the low gravity of this too-wide corridor, motion away from the walls will be a slow caroming, like two shuttlecocks trying to close with one another; he recognizes the defensive stance she's taking as one he taught her. Everything about her is heartbreakingly familiar: the turning-in of her knees, so graceful in slow motion, so awkward in running, the intent look on her face, her amplitude of hip and buttock, and the hidden face under her clothes: two blind eyes, a dimple, a hairy mouth. He's remembering Irene in bed. The absurd littleness of her hands and feet.

Surprising him, she kicks backwards, down the corridor away from him, and he sees her slip something into a computer terminal in the wall and speak rapidly into the grille; she crouches over it to muffle the sound of her voice. She grins and her whole body relaxes. The surprise of it, the chagrin of it, an almost instinctive response to her unguardedness takes him down the corridor after her, but Irene is already in the air, having chosen a technique of horizontal, twisting attack in which her lower center of gravity gives her the advantage. She was always faster than he. He evades and finds himself on his back, not a bad place to be but not much advantage in this weight. He knows better than to get up. It's borne in on him that Irene is really serious; she's trying to hurt him. She doesn't need the friction of heavy weight for a good kick and he's seen her pivot in the most graceless, unorthodox, and effective ways. She has said in the past, *I fight well because I'm bad at it and I practice. You play at it.*

Hurt Irene? He'll have to. He rolls and grabs for her and she evades him; there is another tangle and he pins her down with his body, giving her no leverage for motion as in a practice session in which, years ago, this parody of lovemaking reduced her to tears. But he's forgotten the gravity; she has enough leverage to heave them both into the air, where they sail statelily about in a circle and he is markedly at a disadvantage, with nothing to push.

Irene gets a knee in his back and one arm around his throat. She starts to strangle him.

He bucks her off.

It occurs to Ernst that her strength, although not as great as his own, is becoming a serious nuisance; Irene doesn't seem to care what she's doing. She's mad. Irene is the student and he the teacher; it's the teacher who remains romantic about the student's inexperience and the student who (although learning nothing) can mimic the teacher's mannerisms with deadly accuracy.

They go again lazily head over heels in the air.

Ernst is distracted by memories: Irene making love, Irene asleep and dreaming, Irene flirting. It's unfair having to fight someone your very thoughts disarm you against.

To you—

to an observer—

to you, if you were there—

—they would look like dancers, half the time on their heads, arms and legs flying. Both of them seem to have forgotten why they're there or why they're fighting or what they're trying to do. Ernst is no longer wondering whether they can fix her at Center (if he can get her there) and Irene has given up her attempts to get her foot into his groin, Ernst automatically protecting himself and never giving her room enough.

Neither follows the straight-line trajectory of innocence, the one Zubeydeh would take if she came careening into the corridor like a bullet, skree-ing madly, her veils flying, her jewelry knocking against the walls, to smash her head into this mad couple, into Ernst's stummick.

Zooby could do this; she's been practicing running in the corridors. She's been knocking people down and getting herself into trouble. She could easily bash into the lovers and knock them into a wall, from which they'd rebound in nauseating over-and-over fashion, and there next to them would be a screaming twelve-year-old sailing off at an angle, a whirling little mass of jewelry and gauze like a condensing galaxy, a cloudlet filled with the gold sparks of her pins and earrings, a starlet.

But Irene and Ernst are alone; therefore they fight. In such a contest of strength and skill it's always significant who wins and who loses. It's crucial that the man is stronger than the woman or the woman stronger than the man. Ernst's age weakens him; there's not much to choose between a woman of thirty and a man of fifty. Her endurance is greater than his, but nonetheless he's stronger and his muscle hurts her. She's coming out of a thirty years' trance, a lifetime's hypnosis. She used to think it mattered who won and who lost, who was shamed and who was not. She forgot what she had up her sleeve.

Sick of the contest of strength and skill, she shoots him.

In the ship's corridors, the messages left in odd places by the dust and the stains on the wall, by scraps of paper the passengers have dropped, are all obsessed with death. Or to be blunt, with murder, of which the above is a very unpleasant example. The gratuitousness of it. The tediousness of it. The inevitability of it. The tiredness of it. There is a labyrinth and the labyrinth is swimming with it

162

(tears in the eyes). Thoughts about erasing him from the ship's records, moving her and Zubeydeh's possessions from the stateroom, changing the number of their room. Yasemeen now lives in the purser's office (because of good behavior), inhabiting a cloth-lined box, with a traveling hamper for occasional journeys up and down the ship: a cage within a cage within a cage.

I wish I could talk to her. I wish I could nudge her. I wish I could walk down the corridor with her and whisper, *Hey, baby, you wanna fuck? Hey, Miss, you...uh...dropped your panties*. Though I wouldn't say that. I *couldn't* say that. What I want to tell her is what it's really like, what happens to you, the ises and isn'ts of guilt. The way the victim hangs around afterwards, which is preferable to your own dead self hanging around afterwards. I would tell her that it's not unbearable. I would tell her that depression is how you treat someone you hate, not feeding her, not entertaining her, not valuing her, not making life good for her. I would nudge Irene from the side. I would tell her that her deed has not closed her in. That she is not pursued by Fate. That Zubeydeh is very important, that she must listen to Zubeydeh, that she must get Zubeydeh out of here.

There's no Zooby in the stateroom. And her Ka'abite clothes are gone; Zooby's being bad again. Irene packs the little girl's underwear, nightie, and manual toothbrush in the miniature duffle bag Zubeydeh bought days ago at the ship's chandlery; the duffle is almost too small to hold even that.

Ernst would have enjoyed—

He would've—

—would have—

Well, no, not really.

It occurs to me that she only stunned him, that soon he'll get up, facing nothing worse than a temporary embarrassment (because they can't find him in the computer), that he'll come looking for her, penitent, contrite, having learned his lesson.

Well, no, not really.

Irene walks down the corridor, swinging the duffle from one hand. Zooby will be in the dining room or the gymnasium. There's the work with the computer to do, which Irene does, and then she thinks how they threaten you, all those parent and doctor and artist and teacher and movie and boy friend and girl friend shamans, telling you about guilt, telling you how the taboos will revenge themselves. The ladies go mad with guilt if they leave the gentlemen or stop caring about the gentlemen or say nasty things about the gentlemen; the gentlemen run the ladies over with cars or shoot them or rape them or break their necks or strangle them or push them off high buildings (the taped stories in the library). There are crises of terror and screaming. Zubeydeh gets nightmares. Gentlemen put cigarettes out in other gentlemen's eyes. In the domestic stories the ladies throw themselves in front of trains or get put in madhouses by concerned families or get sent to doctors to be cured or they leave business because they are too fragile and break down or because they are evil and hurt men *and Zubeydeh reads these*. She loves them. She perches the viewer on her exotic nose and eats them up.

Irene is shaking with a rage so absolute that she almost breaks her hand against the wall. This is not a comedy; Zubeydeh will never come across it in the library. A comedy is where Ernst would marry Irene in the end. Irene slings the duffle around her neck and hastens down the corridor until she's striding in air; she's wasted enough time. Zooby will be in the dining room or the lounge, showing off her squirrel to the most people she can find at once; look for a small figure in floating white like a fairy or a ghost. Ernst (thinks Irene) was kind and gentle, he was a truly good man; nonetheless he was going to return her to Center (for her own good), stick her in a desk job (if they had one), or maybe just send her home. It strikes her as reasonable that after twenty years Ernst could decide to send her home and Center would of course do it; she mistrusts Center and always has. As the ladies of Ka'abah would say, there are the gentlemen who, weeping, send you back to your parents because you are not stable enough; there are the gentlemen who refrain; there are the gentlemen who push you down a flight of concrete stairs; there are the gentlemen who (for your own good) lock you up, either on Ka'abah or not on Ka'abah.

She shakes her head vigorously, to clear it. Something is coming down the hall. In the hall outside the dining room is a procession like the illustration to a children's book: a Victorian fairy carrying a red-coated elf in a cage (who stands up, clinging to the bars), and tagging along with them a weak, mortal, little boy in shorts and glasses.

Irene says, "Zubeydeh, give Yasemeen to me. Take the duffle. We have to catch a ferry in the Transportation Room."

Zubeydeh says, "Michael wants to come."

Irene says, "But he's not ours."

"I wasn't yours," says Zubeydeh sensibly.

Michael pushes up his glasses, which have slid down on his nose. He watches the big people, his eyes moving from one to the other as they talk about him. Irene does not find him an appealing little boy; his shorts are too big, his glasses enormous, and from time to time he snurfs audibly. Michael is a runt.

Irene says, "Zooby, what have you been telling him?"

"Nothing you didn't tell me," says Zubeydeh sharply.

Michael begins to groan. He utters strange, creaking sounds, as if his breathing mechanism had gone wrong.

Something inside Michael isn't working; he holds on to Zubeydeh's veils with both hands and tears slide out of his weak, distressed, owly eyes, tears absurdly magnified by his glasses. He works his lower jaw stertorously from side to side. Why Michael can't wear contact lenses like everybody else is a mystery to Irene; perhaps they cost too much or his eyes can't tolerate them. Or his family doesn't care. Zubeydeh says, "I know he wants to come; I asked him. Don't you?" and the little boy nods. She says, "You're sure, aren't you?" and he nods again.

Zubeydeh pats him and then directs a warning look at Irene, a look that says "Now it's done." Irene is not to quarrel. Michael is coming. Zubeydeh looks as if she knows that determined people can perfectly well walk off with other people's children, that other people's children can certainly walk off with other people, that five-year-olds can sensibly decide on their own to leave one set of grown-ups and go with another. Such an arrangement is good for everybody. She says "Can he come?" in a formal tone of voice, looking benignly at Michael, and when Irene shakes her head, Zubeydeh frowns. "No," says Irene patiently.

"Look," she adds, "this child has a family. People don't like having their children disappear on them; they're not used to it. That's why the ship's officers keep tabs on everybody. They won't release a child this age to us; they have records of who he belongs to and if we try to just walk off with him, they won't let us. They'll check on him. They'll ask the computer who he is. And we can't crate him and pretend he's a plant or a bookcase, you know. Besides, he's a boy; nobody's going to stop him from being a poet or keep him in one room, the way they did to you."

Zubeydeh looks dubiously at Michael. Then, pushing him behind her, she reaches up and pulls Irene's head down to the level of her own. She whispers:

"He's afraid of grown-up men. He says they're mean to him, and he wants to come with us."

She adds excitedly, "Irenee, what if they teach him to beat his wife and go with prostitutes!"

Irene says helplessly, "Zubeydeh, I don't—" and the little girl promptly backs off, arms akimbo, narrowing her eyes. She says:

"Why do you hate him?"

"I don't hate him," says Irene. "I just won't take him."

"You hate him," says Zooby.

Irene says helplessly, "All right, I don't *like* him—"

"*I* like him," says Zubeydeh aggressively. Michael is clinging hard to her gown, which bunches up in his sweaty hands. Zubeydeh pushes him away, then smacks him to make him let go of her; she shoves Yasemeen-in-the-cage at Michael—he drops the cage, making the squirrel chatter—and pushes the little boy behind her. She says, pale and intent:

"Either he goes or I don't."

She adds with composure, "I know he smells, Irenee, but that's because there's nobody here to give him a bath and he's too young to do it himself. He doesn't know how. I tried, but the Hot button was too hot and we both almost got scalded. He would've drowned anyway. He needs someone to look after him, like the little orphan boy in the Play of the Street-sweeper. Where the Sultan's wife first beats him with a stick but then relents and adopts him. But I don't want him along because of that; I want him because he's my friend and I'd be lonely without him. And why you can't take him when you took me, I don't see! Anyway, if you don't, I won't go either." And she puts her hands on her hips, one foot forward in the militant posture that Irene suspects comes out of a Ka'abite play. The Maiden Defying. She can't imagine what, on

167

Ka'abah, the maiden could have defied, except perhaps a bad mother who is unkind to a male child. Michael, peeking around Zubeydeh, can be distracted by Yasemeen even in the midst of crisis. Squatting, he extends a fascinated forefinger toward the squirrel.

"How will you earn a living?" says Irene to her daughter.

Zubeydeh says, "I'll give poetry readings."

This is Irene's life-work: to collect women and little girls from the far corners of the Universe. But not little boys. Her decision must show; Zubeydeh cries fiercely, "He's a good little boy! I love him!" and grabs Michael's hand, ready to dash away down the corridor. Her narrow chest heaves. Zubeydeh knows he's a good boy. Zubeydeh is willing to give poetry readings for him, to scrub floors for him, to work for him and sacrifice for him. Irene could pick Zubeydeh up with one arm, immobilize her with two, carry her off screaming. Irene could check with the computer's passenger information and invent a fake lading for Michael, match fake information with real and then lift out the real. She could do her work badly and make some small error, enough to keep him: when they query the computer about Michael they'll find he must stay on board ship. Zubeydeh will be heartbroken. Zubeydeh has no aunt, no mother, and no brothers; if she loses Michael she'll have no little friend, either. The little boy has wound himself (caged squirrel and all) so much into the folds of Zubeydeh's gown that to tear him away would be to ruin the folds of her Ka'abite dress, the only thing she has left from her home to remind her of her mother. The rest is inside Zubeydeh's narrow skull. Her face is furious and pleading, her brow is corrugated, she's holding hard on to Michael, her arms flung about him in a dramatic attitude: the *Poet Protective*.

They'll find Ernst any minute now.

If he's alive, he'll be getting up off the floor any minute now.

"All right," says Irene, her mouth stiff, "go to the Transportation Room. I'll bollix the computer. Wait for me," and she gives the Ka'abite family group a sweep of the arm that sends it down the corridor, Yasemeen chattering frantically. Irene hears, over her shoulder, from Zubeydeh:

"See? I told you. She likes you!"

And thinks, wrenching open the cover on a computer terminal:

All I have to do is make one mistake—

The Transportation Room is featureless except for the customs barrier and the uniformed customs official. These are not the same as on Ka'abah. The barrier is a metal ledge set into the wall and it glitters with buttons and switches; the official is a pale man Irene's own height, his brow ridges heavy, his pale eyes small, the hair on his face shading into blond fuzz on neck and temples. He could be one of Irene's neighbors at home, so strong, so sexless, so male, so precise, so powerfully antiseptic is he. He reminds her of her father. He goes into the routine questions:

"Are you a family unit?"

No, but it follows me around.

She nods.

"Your names, please?"

She gives them.

"Your numbers, please?"

She gives them.

"Do you have a permit for the animal?"

169

She nods.

"Your identification, please."

She hands it over.

"The others, please."

She lays them face down on the customs barrier.

Zubeydeh's visa is eaten by the computer and spat out. Irene hands over her own card. Michael's identity card is on a string around his neck; it has become grimy in the weeks he's been on board. The official displays, at this time, the only human reaction Irene has yet seen in him; distaste at having to handle Michael's card.

The computer eats it indifferently and spits it out.

It spits out Irene's card.

Zubeydeh tries to thread Michael's card on the string around the little boy's neck, a problem, as the card has no hole; Irene takes it away from her and snaps it to the string mounting. She takes Michael's hand and Zubeydeh's hand; the customs official has put on a pair of glasses and is playing a complicated arpeggio on the keyboard set into the customs ledge.

Lights on the keyboard go on.

Other lights go off.

He hits two more keys, stops, looks something up in a manual chained to the edge of the customs barrier, plays on the keyboard again, looks at the family group over his glasses (Michael fingers his own glasses in vague imitation) and touches three more keys. He looks doubtful.

"Where's Uncle Ernst?" says Zubeydeh.

Irene says, "Must we go everywhere with Uncle Ernst?" Michael is letting his weight down onto her hand, squatting, swinging from her hand, then pushing himself up, then letting his weight hang down again. He's a heavy little boy. Irene adds, to Zubeydeh, "I'll explain later," the time-honored excuse with children and Zubeydeh knows it, for her monobrow wrinkles spectacularly. She's going to get angry. She's going to speak. She's going to say something smashing. Irene says, "Aren't you worried about your little brother?" to shut Zubeydeh up, but here the customs official takes off his glasses and slips them into a receiver in the keyboard. He smiles—suddenly becoming considerably more human—and says in a cordial voice:

"We are compatriots."

He continues to smile benevolently. "Ladislas Janowski," he says, extending one hand. She takes it briefly: dry, hairy, well-manicured. He says, lecturing her:

"You have made a mistake, Mrs. Waskiewicz. I will tell you what you have done. First you have suggested worry to children. Second, you have allowed the wrong information from your son's visa to be entered into the computer when you came on board. Here"—and he points to the computer print-out—"is the wrong code for indicating his relationship to you. You have said 'neutral' instead of 'offspring.' And his age is incorrect by several years. But I will not detain a fellow countrywoman."

"Thank you," Irene manages to say. Zubeydeh stares frankly. Irene hits the baby poet a good clip on the leg with her own foot and Zubeydeh jumps; Mister Janowski is handing out to the children pieces of silvery metal shaped like stars with a pin on the back of each to use in pinning it to clothing; it's the ship's symbol.

He says, "Have a good journey, Mrs. Waskiewicz."

"Thank you," says Irene again and starts blindly out. His hand on her shoulder stops her.

"That way," he says, pointing. "Through there. *Lekkiej drogi*. Have a pleasant trip. The children will not experience any loss of gravity. We have put a few units under the boarding corridor, to avoid sickness. Your little boy has dropped his Captain's pin."

171

"Michael, pick it up!" says Zubeydeh, and then in a whisper to Irene, "Irene, is Uncle Ernst coming at all?"

"He's not," says Irene in a low voice, "and don't you make a fuss!" From somewhere in her memory she dredges up: *"Kziekuje bardzo"*.

Zubeydeh says equably, "I won't make a fuss." She looks thoughtful. They step through a hole-in-the-wall and are in a featureless silver corridor at the end of which is another iris; "down" has become faint but if you try, you can find it. There's a slight, positive air pressure at their backs. Zubeydeh says, "Did you have a fight with Ernst, Irenee?" They step through the second iris: another corridor, more sharply curved this time, another ship. A married woman with a daughter and a son, a family group. Zubeydeh says in disappointment, "Oh, it's just the same," and then, with more interest, *"Did* you, Irenee?"

She adds, "How did you get away? What did you do? Did you have to *kill* him?"

Zubeydeh says in the middle of the night, in her pajamas, in a stateroom just like the other one, "He's not dead. I don't believe it. He'll come after us."

Irene hears herself saying, half-asleep, *"I* wouldn't."

Near them Michael grunts; he's always making odd sounds at night: moans, creakings, the fluthery sound of a small boy getting tangled in the bedclothes, his loud and enormous snufflings. For a while I thought Irene, Zubeydeh, and Michael would take a different kind of ferry: a battered old tub full of flowers and animals driven by a pipe-smoking Eskimo called Anarré, but I couldn't invent her language (does she speak English or Eskimo?)

so I gave it up. The rugs are the same, the night light's the same; only the ship's smaller and it goes faster. It's differently shaped, too. Zubeydeh says:

"Did you *really*, Irene?"

"Yes, I did really," says Irene. "Now let me sleep." Zubeydeh grabs at Irene's arm and Irene hears sobbing in the dark; her adopted daughter is crying. Zubeydeh crawls into Irene's arms, her small body shaking like a cat's delicate bones, a bird's bones, her voice shaking too as she says, "I m-miss him!" Irene listens for the echo in herself but there's none. She cradles the little girl.

"Why!" demands Zubeydeh.

"Things are complicated," says Irene. "You can't judge people by only some of their actions; it's a difficult business. You've already seen some of it and I'll tell you about the rest of it in the morning."

Zubeydeh says plaintively, almost hiccoughing: "Did you have to?"

"Yes," says Irene.

Zubeydeh blows her nose loudly, Irene does not want to think what on. Then the little girl says in a low voice, "Do you miss him?"

"No, not really." That's probably the wrong answer, certainly not a Ka'abite answer. She feels around for the tissues. She finds herself saying, "No, not at all."

"Irenee, do you"—and Zooby sounds hesitant and scared—"do you think you'll ever—with anyone—again, you know?"

Not a baritone. She says, "I don't know, dear."

"Do you think," says Zubeydeh even more awkwardly, with thumping and creaking sounds, as if she were turning over in the dark, "do you *think*—well, like the lady in the play?"

"The lady in the play?"

"The lady who fell in love with the other lady,"

Zubeydeh at last brings out.

"Why, I don't know," says Irene. She thinks. *The real Ernst is somewhere else, the real Ernst has yet to be found. Ernst is the real enigma.* She says, "If I feel it coming on, I'll tell you. Now go to sleep."

Zubeydeh says, blowing her nose again, "I suppose you're right to be so cool. Even if it does look inhuman. What must be done must be done. Sultan er-Rasheed closed Baghdad to the plague, you know. And the poet Shems-er-Nehar passed his own father in the street without speaking to him. I suppose." She adds in a different tone, the pitch of her voice rising, "Irenee, are all men beasts? Ernst and my father and all of them? And the men who run Ka'abah? And Jaafar's selfish."

"Are you using a Kleenex?"

"Yes, of course," says Zubeydeh. "Do you think I'm a savage?" She adds insistently, "Are there any good ones, Irene?"

There's the old joke: *Is everyone corrupt? Well, I don't know everyone*, but Zubeydeh answers her own question with every appearance of relief at the answer, freeing Irene for sleep and dreams (always about her childhood home in which Ernst has so far failed to put in an appearance). Zubeydeh says:

"Michael's all right."

A trip is a time to bathe Michael, to buy him a rubber duck with his name on it, which he pursues nearsightedly around the bathtub, occasionally dipping his breathing-mask into the water. He falls asleep on Irene's lap as he fell asleep in Ernst's, ready to believe that in the end some adult will take care of him but not really confident, always quiet, always sober. Irene waits for his first naughty deed as a sign of his liberation; meanwhile she takes to kissing him absently on the top of the head (a much pleasanter task now that he's had a bath), which Michael accepts stolidly, perhaps with an interior spasm of relief, but nobody sees it. He's a staring, solemn, heavy, perhaps even stupid little boy. Irene doesn't want him. She thinks of the Sultan's wife, who displays her goodness and maternity by adopting the male orphan.

It's blackmail.

She didn't take him. She didn't do it.

I made that part up.

The ferry lets you down at night, secretly. You've screwed a little of the local currency out of Center and one inferior, yellow diamond for your "vacation"; before leaving you drop your I.D. cards and all the documents in the hatchway; you take no change of clothes, knowing you'll have to get rid of what you have on as soon as possible anyway: sell everything, throw everything away, convert everything to cash. The margin of time before Ernst's murder is traced to you gets slimmer and slimmer. You know you're going to have to buy a forged I.D., that in so doing you'll have to cope with customs years ahead of your own, in a city you've never visited, speaking slang you no longer know. You wonder if there's a law against owning unset diamonds, as there used to be against gold. They drop you off twenty miles out in the desert, at night. Zubeydeh is shivering audibly in the pea coat you bought her on the ferry. Under the little girl's coat, made into a flat parcel, is her Ka'abite dress; that too must be sold or thrown away. Perhaps you'll bury it in the sand. You're in a dress and coat, although you've drawn the line at high heels; you're wearing penny loafers with your nylons. At the edge of the highway you sit down—inconvenient in a dress—and let the little girl sit down by you, gathering her sleepy body to you for warmth. You rehearse your excuses: "I've been in the hospital, I've been in Europe, I've been sick." Back to Square One. Always back to Square One. It occurs to you that you're not in the right world, not the right one at all, and with a sudden, exquisite pang of fear the possibility becomes a dead cert; it's the wrong stars, the wrong town, the wrong continent. You won't be able to speak the language; nothing you know will be of any use. You start to shiver against Zubeydeh, bitterly ashamed of your own nervousness because there's Gemini setting in the West, there's the jewelry of Cygnus on the opposite horizon, against the Sierras. Albuquerque is twenty miles away; at this altitude, in this dry air, you can easily see the plume of the Milky Way, all frost and diamonds.

Why the nerves? You've done this kind of thing a dozen times before.

(But only with Center behind you, only with a partner, only with arms, only with immense resources to draw on should anything go wrong. It's different now that you're a thirty-year-old divorcée with a child to support.)

Rose always warned you never to run away from your husband.

Then there's the sound of a truck coming down the dark road and you nudge off Zubeydeh and get to your feet. It must be near dawn. You know without pleasure that this is your own world. You place yourself carefully in the path of the oncoming headlights, ready to step back at the last moment, but the truck slows down and stops. The driver becomes visible as he opens the cab door on your side: a big man, checked shirt, thick neck, red face.

176

In the spill of light from the cab you read what's painted on the side of the truck: *Coors Beer.* "Need a ride?" Another baritone.

"Yes," you say, in a voice that sounds rusty even to you, wincing as you would not have eighteen years ago, worrying about rape as you would not have then, either, because rape then was a punishment so bad it only happened to other women. You put out your hand and Zubeydeh takes it; you step with her into the light from the cab so that he can see you both. "Going to Albuquerque?" You expect the city to have another name, be another place; he'll say he's never heard of it and what highway do you think you're on anyway—you half hope you'll be able to plead *nolo contendere,* the wrong planet, the wrong language, turn around and go back—but instead he nods.

"Lonely on Forty this time of night. Where you from?"

Instead you say what you've rehearsed for the past weeks—no, years—and it's as true now as it was when you were seventeen:

"I've been away."

Irene Rose Waskiewicz lies wakeful (with her daughter sleeping) in a cheap hotel room in Albuquerque. The neon light coming through the curtains from a sign across the street has fascinated Zubeydeh; she hung out the window for hours after supper, dividing her attention between the sign ("We Move Our Tail for You") and the old television programs on the hotel set, of which her favorite was *Mary Tyler Moore.* Zubeydeh has decided that she wants to be Mary Tyler Moore. The one armchair in the room, a big overstuffed one upholstered in green vinyl, holds boxes of new clothes, mostly for Zubeydeh, magazines, local newspapers, the telephone book. There's been no time to do anything yet, no time to read the newspapers, get a job, find a women's bookstore. The passage from waking to dream has developed a knot, a hitch, that Irene has been trying to smooth out for some time now: at times it's Zubeydeh's even breathing beside her and the sense of responsibility it imposes, at times the suspicion that Ernst was not really killed, the speculation that Center may think they've merely run off together (but why should they?), the feeling of helplessness away from a big organization. If Ernst is not dead, if Center doesn't know he's dead, if no one's looking for her, if this new mode of written address for women means anything, if the world is really different. She thinks she must've been a fool to quit Center so fast, not to lie to Ernst, make love to him, string him along until she could get her hands on the information about the whole business. If there is such information, if there is such a whole business. Now it'll take longer than one woman's lifetime; now she'll never get to it except the hard way: a civilian attacking from the outside. A nobody. An unimportant and powerless person. She has no idea yet that she can find other unimportant and powerless people. She wants it back, even with Ernst attached to it, even with the lying and being snubbed and being thought mad; there really is nothing else. To console herself Irene daydreams that on another ship in another universe Ernst is keeping Zubeydeh company while she practices her English on children's books he's gotten from the ship's library, that the ship's goat has eaten the last pages out of every book save the one Zubeydeh's already finished *(Ding Ling, Woman of History)* and so ruined all the plots, and that Zubeydeh doesn't know this. They sit on the grass under the birch trees of Reclamation Level and Ernst smokes mutated dandelion floss, peacefully contemplating the daisies. It's not a good day, however. Yasemeen has escaped from the baggage compartment to join the other squirrels (who live in the chartroom) and will soon narrowly miss falling into a pot of soup in the galley. Someone will put too much salt in the dinner brown rice. Ernst is sad; he holds a note from the Captain, who is not Irene, declining their evening lovemaking on the grounds that she really ought to spend more time with her children. It's a sloppy ship. The navigator pads about naked save for a beard and old red socks with holes in the toes. In another part of Reclamation Level grapefruit rinds, coffee grounds, old tampons, and other garbage moulder peacefully into the soil. Around Zubeydeh on the grass lie children's books with gay, inviting covers and no last pages, spelling out a daydream-message Irene cannot (in her half-sleep) quite understand: *Yelena and Boris Lead the Revolution, Etsuko Wins the Race, Duc Does Acrobatics, Golda Tames a Dragon, Tomas Builds a Moon Rocket, Marie Transmutes Metals, Chinua Hybridizes Plants, Irene Goes Home, Premieress of Ka'abah Says Taxes Lowered: Crowds Cheer As New Dignitary Discards Veil....*

Asleep, Irene dreams. In her dream Zubeydeh is a grown woman and in her Ka'abite dress sits on a rocky promontory, a little above Irene, brooding behind her veil like the Spirit of the Abyss; Zubeydeh is waiting for something to happen. Far below the two of them Irene can see a desert valley and an old, dry watercourse where a river ran ages ago; the rock walls of the valley rise not into the sky but into a half-lit, interior greyness like the roof of a vast cavern; Irene knows that they are in the centermost vacancy of someone's mind, that they have found their way at last into the most secret place of Ka'abah. Farther out towards the surface there may be tumultuous winds, fiery conflagrations, and rains of blood, but here all is still, and in the grey, colorless half-light Irene can see that the floor of the valley below is thickly covered with bones. Innumerable skeletons are spread from wall to wall, and piled up immeasurably into the half-grey, half-lost rocky ceiling so far from any open love or light, are skeletons lying as they fell long ago in aeons-old attitudes of terror or flight, bones intermingled with bones, heaps of bones choking the dry watercourse and stretching back between the valley walls, a dry, silent carpeting as far as the eye can see.

Nothing has happened here for a long, long time.

It is so dry, so still, so movelessly grey that Irene knows at once whose soul it is—it is Aunt Dunya's soul—and she knows that it no longer makes any sense to ask whether Dunya is happy or unhappy, so changeless, so sterile, so truly mad is she, for no rain falls and no wind from Heaven blows upon these multitudes of the slain.

Quietly in Irene's ear comes a little, cooing sigh, *Shall these bones live?* but Irene knows the words are spoken by no living voice, indeed by no voice at all; they are spoken by nothing; it's only the air that speaks, a vagrant eddy here or there, air forming and re-forming itself, by chance, into the memory of words.

And Irene must answer with all her heart, *It is impossible*, for even the old sorcerers and wizards could not make something out of nothing; for an ocean there must be a drop of water, for a human being the paring of a nail, for a forest a blade of grass. But here there is nothing.

And the whisper comes again, but louder this time— *Shall these bones live!*—and it stirs the edge of Zubeydeh's veil where she sits brooding over the abyss. And a little, errant breeze without the power of a fingernail goes down into the valley and breathes over the dry bones, a little breeze not even as alive as the real Aunt

Dunya's voice, which now passes from wall to wall over the dead watercourse and the barren rocks. It is nothing living but only the memory of another voice, the voice of Dunyazad, Shahrazad's sister, that mad, dead, haunted woman who could not tell stories, who could not save herself. It is the voicelessness of Dunyazad that passes like a sigh from wall to wall of the valley of dry bones and shivers faintly over the multitude of the dead. It has no Word. It has nothing to say. It whispers its crazy nonsense thoughtlessly and hopelessly to nothing at all, but where it passes, throughout the length of that still, grey place, there is the barest shiver, the faintest stir, the dimmest, most imperceptible rustling. You can barely see it. You can barely hear it. From autumn leaf to autumn leaf goes the message: something, nothing, everything. Something is coming out of nothing. For the first time, something will be created out of nothing. There is not a drop of water, not a blade of grass, not a single word.

But they move.

And they rise.

BERKLEY'S FINEST SCIENCE FICTION!

Robert A. Heinlein

GLORY ROAD	(03783-5—$1.95)
I WILL FEAR NO EVIL	(03425-9—$2.25)
THE MOON IS A HARSH MISTRESS	(03850-5—$1.95)
THE PAST THROUGH TOMORROW	(03785-1—$2.95)
STARSHIP TROOPERS	(03787-8—$1.75)
STRANGER IN A STRANGE LAND	(03782-7—$2.25)
TIME ENOUGH FOR LOVE	(04373-8—$2.50)

* * * * * *

Robert Silverberg

HAWKSBILL STATION	(03679-0—$1.75)
THE MASKS OF TIME	(03871-8—$1.95)
TO LIVE AGAIN	(03774-6—$1.95)
TO OPEN THE SKY	(03810-6—$1.95)
UNFAMILIAR TERRITORY	(03882-3—$1.95)
A TIME OF CHANGES (With a new Introduction)	(04051-8—$1.95)

✓ 9/98 2x LT 9/98 18 x 3/13 LT 6/12
11/01 11 x 10/01 23 x 4/17 LT 3/17

CENTRAL-1

Macdonald, George, 1824–1905.
    The light princess. With pictures by Maurice
New York, Farrar, Straus and Giroux ₍1969₎

    110 p. illus. 20 cm. 3.95

    Because she is not invited to the christening of the pri
King's sister casts a spell depriving the child of gravity
ability to weep tears.
    "An Ariel book."

24 x 8/19 LT 8/18

₍1. Fairy tales₎   I. Sendak, Maurice, illus. II. Title.

                                    823′.8 [Fic]   6

₍5₎

THE LIGHT PRINCESS

THE LIGHT PRINCESS

by

GEORGE MACDONALD

With pictures by

MAURICE SENDAK

An Ariel Book

FARRAR, STRAUS AND GIROUX

New York

For Michael di Capua

M. S.

What! No Children?

Once upon a time, so long ago that I have quite forgotten the date, there lived a king and queen who had no children.

And the king said to himself, "All the queens of my acquaintance have children, some three, some seven, and some as many as twelve; and my queen has not one. I feel ill-used." So he made up his mind to be cross with his wife about it. But she bore it all like a good patient queen as she was. Then the king grew very cross indeed. But the queen pretended to take it all as a joke, and a very good one too.

"Why don't you have any daughters, at least?" said he. "I don't say *sons;* that might be too much to expect."

"I am sure, dear king, I am very sorry," said the queen.

"So you ought to be," retorted the king; "you are not going to make a virtue of *that*, surely."

But he was not an ill-tempered king, and in any matter of less moment would have let the queen have her own way with all his heart. This, however, was an affair of state.

The queen smiled.

"You must have patience with a lady, you know, dear king," said she.

She was, indeed, a very nice queen, and heartily sorry that she could not oblige the king immediately.

Won't I, Just?

The king tried to have patience, but he succeeded very badly. It was more than he deserved, therefore, when, at last, the queen gave him a daughter —as lovely a little princess as ever cried.

The day drew near when the infant must be christened. The king wrote all the invitations with his own hand. Of course somebody was forgotten.

Now it does not generally matter if somebody *is* forgotten, only you must mind who. Unfortunately, the king forgot without intending to forget; and so the chance fell upon the Princess Makemnoit, which was awkward. For the princess was the king's own sister; and he ought not to have forgotten her. But she had made herself so disagreeable to the old king, their father, that he had forgotten her in making his will; and so it was no wonder that her brother forgot her in writing his invitations. But poor relations don't do anything to keep you in mind of them. Why don't they? The king could not see into the garret she lived in, could he?

She was a sour, spiteful creature. The wrinkles of contempt crossed the wrinkles of peevishness, and made her face as full of wrinkles as a pat of butter. If ever a king could be justified in forgetting anybody, this king was justified in forgetting his sister, even at a christening. She looked very odd, too. Her forehead was as large as all the rest of her face, and projected over it like a precipice. When she was angry, her little eyes flashed blue. When she hated anybody, they shone yellow and green. What they looked like when she loved anybody, I do not know; for I never heard of her loving anybody but herself, and I do not think she could have managed that if she had not somehow got used to herself. But what made it highly imprudent in the

4

king to forget her was—that she was awfully clever. In fact, she was a witch; and when she bewitched anybody, he very soon had enough of it; for she beat all the wicked fairies in wickedness, and all the clever ones in cleverness. She despised all the modes we read of in history, in which offended fairies and witches have taken their revenges; and therefore, after waiting and waiting in vain for an invitation, she made up her mind at last to go without one, and make the whole family miserable, like a princess as she was.

So she put on her best gown, went to the palace, was kindly received by the happy monarch, who forgot that he had forgotten her, and took her place in the procession to the royal chapel. When they were all gathered about the font, she contrived to get next to it, and throw something into the water; after which she maintained a very respectful demeanour till the water was applied to the child's face. But at that moment she turned round in her place three times, and muttered the following words, loud enough for those beside her to hear:—

>   *"Light of spirit, by my charms,*
>   *Light of body, every part,*
>   *Never weary human arms—*
>   *Only crush thy parents' heart!"*

They all thought she had lost her wits, and was repeating some foolish nursery rhyme; but a shudder went through the whole of them notwithstanding. The baby, on the contrary, began to laugh and crow; while the nurse gave a start and a smothered cry, for she thought she was struck with paralysis: she could not feel the baby in her arms. But she clasped it tight and said nothing.

The mischief was done.

· *3* ·

She Can't Be Ours.

Her atrocious aunt had deprived the child of all her gravity. If you ask me how this was effected,

I answer, "In the easiest way in the world. She had only to destroy gravitation." For the princess was a philosopher, and knew all the *ins* and *outs* of the laws of gravitation as well as the *ins* and *outs* of her boot-lace. And being a witch as well, she could abrogate those laws in a moment; or at least so clog their wheels and rust their bearings, that they would not work at all. But we have more to do with what followed than with how it was done.

The first awkwardness that resulted from this unhappy privation was, that the moment the nurse began to float the baby up and down, she flew from her arms towards the ceiling. Happily, the resistance of the air brought her ascending career to a close within a foot of it. There she remained, horizontal as when she left her nurse's arms, kicking and laughing amazingly. The nurse in terror flew to the bell, and begged the footman, who answered it, to bring up the house-steps directly. Trembling in every limb, she climbed upon the steps, and had to stand upon the very top, and reach up, before she could catch the floating tail of the baby's long clothes.

When the strange fact came to be known, there was a terrible commotion in the palace. The occasion of its discovery by the king was naturally a repetition of the nurse's experience. Astonished that he felt no weight when the child was laid in his arms, he began to wave her up and—not down, for she slowly ascended to the ceiling as before, and there remained floating in perfect comfort and satisfaction, as was testified by her peals of tiny laughter. The king stood staring up in speechless amazement, and trembled so that his beard shook like grass in the wind. At last, turning to the queen, who was just as horror-struck as himself, he said, gasping, staring, and stammering,—

"She *can't* be ours, queen!"

Now the queen was much cleverer than the king, and had begun already to suspect that "this effect defective came by cause."

"I am sure she is ours," answered she. "But we ought to have taken better care of her at the christening. People who were never invited ought not to have been present."

"Oh, ho!" said the king, tapping his forehead with his forefinger, "I have it all. I've found her out. Don't you see it, queen? Princess Makemnoit has bewitched her."

"That's just what I say," answered the queen.

"I beg your pardon, my love; I did not hear you.—John! bring the steps I get on my throne with."

For he was a little king with a great throne, like many other kings.

The throne-steps were brought, and set upon the dining-table, and John got upon the top of them. But he could not reach the little princess, who lay like a baby-laughter-cloud in the air, exploding continuously.

"Take the tongs, John," said his Majesty; and getting up on the table, he handed them to him.

John could reach the baby now, and the little princess was handed down by the tongs.

· 4 ·

Where Is She?

One fine summer day, a month after these her first adventures, during which time she had been very carefully watched, the princess was lying on the bed in the queen's own chamber, fast asleep. One of the windows was open, for it was noon, and the day was so sultry that the little girl was wrapped in nothing less ethereal than slumber itself. The queen came into the room, and not observing that the baby was on the bed, opened another window. A frolicsome fairy wind, which had been watching for a chance of mischief, rushed in at the one window, and taking its way over the bed where the child was lying, caught her up, and rolling and floating her along like a piece of flue, or a dandelion seed, carried her with it through the opposite window, and away. The queen went down-stairs, quite ignorant of the loss she had herself occasioned.

When the nurse returned, she supposed that her Majesty had carried her off, and, dreading a scolding, delayed making inquiry about her. But hearing nothing, she grew uneasy, and went at length to the queen's boudoir, where she found her Majesty.

"Please, your Majesty, shall I take the baby?" said she.

"Where is she?" asked the queen.

"Please forgive me. I know it was wrong."

"What do you mean?" said the queen, looking grave.

"Oh! don't frighten me, your Majesty!" exclaimed the nurse, clasping her hands.

The queen saw that something was amiss, and fell down in a faint. The nurse rushed about the palace, screaming, "My baby! my baby!"

Every one ran to the queen's room. But the

queen could give no orders. They soon found out,
however, that the princess was missing, and in a
moment the palace was like a beehive in a garden;
and in one minute more the queen was brought to
herself by a great shout and a clapping of hands.
They had found the princess fast asleep under a
rose-bush, to which the elvish little wind-puff had
carried her, finishing its mischief by shaking a
shower of red rose-leaves all over the little white
sleeper. Startled by the noise the servants made,
she woke, and, furious with glee, scattered the rose-
leaves in all directions, like a shower of spray in
the sunset.

She was watched more carefully after this, no
doubt; yet it would be endless to relate all the odd
incidents resulting from this peculiarity of the
young princess. But there never was a baby in a
house, not to say a palace, that kept the household
in such constant good humour, at least below-
stairs. If it was not easy for her nurses to hold her,
at least she made neither their arms nor their

hearts ache. And she was so nice to play at ball with! There was positively no danger of letting her fall. They might throw her down, or knock her down, or push her down, but couldn't *let* her down. It is true, they might let her fly into the fire or the coal-hole, or through the window; but none of these accidents had happened as yet. If you heard peals of laughter resounding from some unknown region, you might be sure enough of the cause. Going down into the kitchen, or *the room*, you would find Jane and Thomas, and Robert and Susan, all and sum, playing at ball with the little princess. She was the ball herself, and did not enjoy it the less for that. Away she went, flying from one to another, screeching with laughter. And the servants loved the ball itself better even than the game. But they had to take some care how they threw her, for if she received an upward direction, she would never come down again without being fetched.

· 5 ·

What Is to Be Done?

But above-stairs it was different. One day, for instance, after breakfast, the king went into his counting-house, and counted out his money.

The operation gave him no pleasure.

"To think," said he to himself, "that every one of these gold sovereigns weighs a quarter of an ounce, and my real, live, flesh-and-blood princess weighs nothing at all!"

And he hated his gold sovereigns, as they lay with a broad smile of self-satisfaction all over their yellow faces.

The queen was in the parlour, eating bread and honey. But at the second mouthful she burst out crying, and could not swallow it.

The king heard her sobbing. Glad of anybody, but especially of his queen, to quarrel with, he clashed his gold sovereigns into his money-box, clapped his crown on his head, and rushed into the parlour.

"What is all this about?" exclaimed he. "What are you crying for, queen?"

"I can't eat it," said the queen, looking ruefully at the honey-pot.

"No wonder!" retorted the king. "You've just eaten your breakfast—two turkey eggs, and three anchovies."

"Oh, that's not it!" sobbed her Majesty. "It's my child, my child!"

"Well, what's the matter with your child? She's neither up the chimney nor down the draw-well. Just hear her laughing."

Yet the king could not help a sigh, which he tried to turn into a cough, saying—

"It is a good thing to be light-hearted, I am sure, whether she be ours or not."

"It is a bad thing to be light-headed," answered the queen, looking with prophetic soul far into the future.

" 'Tis a good thing to be light-handed," said the king.

" 'Tis a bad thing to be light-fingered," answered the queen.

" 'Tis a good thing to be light-footed," said the king.

" 'Tis a bad thing—" began the queen; but the king interrupted her.

"In fact," said he, with the tone of one who concludes an argument in which he has had only imaginary opponents, and in which, therefore, he has come off triumphant—"in fact, it is a good thing altogether to be light-bodied."

"But it is a bad thing altogether to be light-minded," retorted the queen, who was beginning to lose her temper.

This last answer quite discomfited his Majesty, who turned on his heel, and betook himself to his counting-house again. But he was not half-way towards it, when the voice of his queen overtook him.

"And it's a bad thing to be light-haired," screamed she, determined to have more last words, now that her spirit was roused.

The queen's hair was black as night; and the king's had been, and his daughter's was, golden as morning. But it was not this reflection on his hair that arrested him; it was the double use of the word *light*. For the king hated all witticisms, and punning especially. And besides, he could not tell whether the queen meant light-*haired* or light-*heired;* for why might she not aspirate her vowels when she was ex-asperated herself?

He turned upon his other heel, and rejoined her. She looked angry still, because she knew that she was guilty, or, what was much the same, knew that he thought so.

"My dear queen," said he, "duplicity of any sort is exceedingly objectionable between married people of any rank, not to say kings and queens; and the most objectionable form duplicity can assume is that of punning."

"There!" said the queen, "I never made a jest, but I broke it in the making. I am the most unfortunate woman in the world!"

She looked so rueful, that the king took her in his arms; and they sat down to consult.

"Can you bear this?" said the king.

"No, I can't," said the queen.

"Well, what's to be done?" said the king.

"I'm sure I don't know," said the queen. "But might you not try an apology?"

"To my old sister, I suppose you mean?" said the king.

"Yes," said the queen.

"Well, I don't mind," said the king.

So he went the next morning to the house of the princess, and, making a very humble apology, begged her to undo the spell. But the princess declared, with a grave face, that she knew nothing at all about it. Her eyes, however, shone pink, which was a sign that she was happy. She advised the king and queen to have patience, and to mend their ways. The king returned disconsolate. The queen tried to comfort him.

"We will wait till she is older. She may then be able to suggest something herself. She will know at least how she feels, and explain things to us."

"But what if she should marry?" exclaimed the king, in sudden consternation at the idea.

"Well, what of that?" rejoined the queen.

"Just think! If she were to have children! In the course of a hundred years the air might be as full of floating children as of gossamers in autumn."

"That is no business of ours," replied the queen. "Besides, by that time they will have learned to take care of themselves."

A sigh was the king's only answer.

He would have consulted the court physicians; but he was afraid they would try experiments upon her.

· 6 ·

She Laughs Too Much.

Meantime, notwithstanding awkward occurrences, and griefs that she brought upon her parents, the little princess laughed and grew—not fat, but plump and tall. She reached the age of seventeen, without having fallen into any worse scrape than a chimney; by rescuing her from which, a little bird-nesting urchin got fame and a black face. Nor, thoughtless as she was, had she committed anything worse than laughter at everybody and everything that came in her way. When she was told, for the sake of experiment, that General Clanrunfort was cut to pieces with all his troops, she laughed; when she heard that the enemy was on his way to besiege her papa's capital, she laughed hugely; but when she was told that the city would certainly be abandoned to the mercy of the enemy's soldiery—why, then she laughed immoderately. She never could be brought to see the serious side of anything. When her mother cried, she said,—

"What queer faces mamma makes! And she squeezes water out of her cheeks? Funny mamma!"

And when her papa stormed at her, she laughed, and danced round and round him, clapping her hands, and crying—

"Do it again, papa. Do it again! It's such fun! Dear, funny papa!"

And if he tried to catch her, she glided from him in an instant, not in the least afraid of him, but thinking it part of the game not to be caught. With one push of her foot, she would be floating in the air above his head; or she would go dancing backwards and forwards and sideways, like a great butterfly. It happened several times, when her father and mother were holding a consultation about her in private, that they were interrupted by vainly repressed outbursts of laughter over their heads; and looking up with indignation, saw her floating at full length in the air above them, whence she regarded them with the most comical appreciation of the position.

One day an awkward accident happened. The princess had come out upon the lawn with one of her attendants, who held her by the hand. Spying her father at the other side of the lawn, she snatched her hand from the maid's, and sped across to him. Now when she wanted to run alone, her custom was to catch up a stone in each hand, so that she might come down again after a bound. Whatever she wore as part of her attire had no effect in this way: even gold, when it thus became as it were a part of herself, lost all its weight for the time. But whatever she only held in her hands retained its downward tendency. On this occasion she could see nothing to catch up but a huge toad, that was walking across the lawn as if he had a hundred years to do it in. Not knowing what disgust meant, for this was one of her peculiarities, she snatched up the toad and bounded away. She

had almost reached her father, and he was holding out his arms to receive her, and take from her lips the kiss which hovered on them like a butterfly on a rosebud, when a puff of wind blew her aside into the arms of a young page, who had just been receiving a message from his Majesty. Now it was no great peculiarity in the princess that, once she was set agoing, it always cost her time and trouble to check herself. On this occasion there was no time. She *must* kiss—and she kissed the page. She did not mind it much; for she had no shyness in her composition; and she knew, besides, that she could not help it. So she only laughed, like a musical box. The poor page fared the worst. For the princess, trying to correct the unfortunate tendency of the kiss, put out her hands to keep her off the page; so that, along with the kiss, he received, on the other cheek, a slap with the huge black toad, which she poked right into his eye. He tried to laugh, too, but the attempt resulted in such an odd contortion of countenance, as showed that there was no danger of his pluming himself on the kiss. As for the king, his dignity was greatly hurt, and he did not speak to the page for a whole month.

I may here remark that it was very amusing to see her run, if her mode of progression could properly be called running. For first she would make a bound; then, having alighted, she would run a few steps, and make another bound. Sometimes she would fancy she had reached the ground before she actually had, and her feet would go backwards and forwards, running upon nothing at all, like those of a chicken on its back. Then she would laugh like the very spirit of fun; only in her laugh there was something missing. What it was, I find myself unable to describe. I think it was a certain tone, depending upon the possibility of sorrow— *morbidezza*, perhaps. She never smiled.

· 7 ·

Try Metaphysics.

After a long avoidance of the painful subject, the king and queen resolved to hold a council of three upon it; and so they sent for the princess. In she came, sliding and flitting and gliding from one piece of furniture to another, and put herself at last in an armchair, in a sitting posture. Whether she could be said *to sit*, seeing she received no support from the seat of the chair, I do not pretend to determine.

"My dear child," said the king, "you must be aware by this time that you are not exactly like other people."

"Oh, you dear funny papa! I have got a nose, and two eyes, and all the rest. So have you. So has mamma."

"Now be serious, my dear, for once," said the queen.

"No, thank you, mamma; I had rather not."

"Would you not like to be able to walk like other people?" said the king.

"No indeed, I should think not. You only crawl. You are such slow coaches!"

"How do you feel, my child?" he resumed, after a pause of discomfiture.

"Quite well, thank you."

"I mean, what do you feel like?"

"Like nothing at all, that I know of."

"You must feel like something."

"I feel like a princess with such a funny papa, and such a dear pet of a queen-mamma!"

"Now really!" began the queen; but the princess interrupted her.

"Oh yes," she added, "I remember. I have a curious feeling sometimes, as if I were the only person that had any sense in the whole world."

She had been trying to behave herself with dignity; but now she burst into a violent fit of laughter, threw herself backwards over the chair, and went rolling about the floor in an ecstasy of enjoyment. The king picked her up easier than one does a down quilt, and replaced her in her former relation to the chair. The exact preposition expressing this relation I do not happen to know.

"Is there nothing you wish for?" resumed the king, who had learned by this time that it was useless to be angry with her.

"Oh, you dear papa!—yes," answered she.

"What is it, my darling?"

"I have been longing for it—oh, such a time!—ever since last night."

"Tell me what it is."

"Will you promise to let me have it?"

The king was on the point of saying *Yes*, but the wiser queen checked him with a single motion of her head.

"Tell me what it is first," said he.

"No no. Promise first."

"I dare not. What is it?"

"Mind, I hold you to your promise.—It is—to

be tied to the end of a string—a very long string indeed, and be flown like a kite. Oh, such fun! I would rain rose-water, and hail sugar-plums, and snow whipped-cream, and—and—and—"

A fit of laughing checked her; and she would have been off again over the floor, had not the king started up and caught her just in time. Seeing nothing but talk could be got out of her, he rang the bell, and sent her away with two of her ladies-in-waiting.

"Now, queen," he said, turning to her Majesty, "what *is* to be done?"

"There is but one thing left," answered she. "Let us consult the college of Metaphysicians."

"Bravo!" cried the king; "we will."

Now at the head of this college were two very wise Chinese philosophers—by name Hum-Drum, and Kopy-Keck. For them the king sent; and straightway they came. In a long speech he communicated to them what they knew very well already—as who did not?—namely, the peculiar condition of his daughter in relation to the globe on which she dwelt; and requested them to consult together as to what might be the cause and probable cure of her *infirmity*. The king laid stress upon the word, but failed to discover his own pun. The queen laughed; but Hum-Drum and Kopy-Keck heard with humility and retired in silence.

The consultation consisted chiefly in propounding and supporting, for the thousandth time, each his favourite theories. For the condition of the princess afforded delightful scope for the discussion of every question arising from the division of thought—in fact, of all the Metaphysics of the Chinese Empire. But it is only justice to say that they did not altogether neglect the discussion of the practical question, *what was to be done.*

Hum-Drum was a Materialist, and Kopy-Keck was a Spiritualist. The former was slow and sententious; the latter was quick and flighty: the latter had generally the first word; the former the last.

"I reassert my former assertion," began Kopy-

Keck, with a plunge. "There is not a fault in the princess, body or soul; only they are wrong put together. Listen to me now, Hum-Drum, and I will tell you in brief what I think. Don't speak. Don't answer me. I *won't* hear you till I have done. —At that decisive moment, when souls seek their appointed habitations, two eager souls met, struck, rebounded, lost their way, and arrived each at the wrong place. The soul of the princess was one of those, and she went far astray. She does not belong by rights to this world at all, but to some other planet, probably Mercury. Her proclivity to her true sphere destroys all the natural influence which this orb would otherwise possess over her corporeal frame. She cares for nothing here. There is no relation between her and this world.

"She must therefore be taught, by the sternest compulsion, to take an interest in the earth as the earth. She must study every department of its history—its animal history; its vegetable history; its mineral history; its social history; its moral history; its political history; its scientific history; its literary history; its musical history; its artistical history; above all, its metaphysical history. She must begin with the Chinese dynasty and end with Japan. But first of all she must study geology, and especially the history of the extinct races of animals—their natures, their habits, their loves, their hates, their revenges. She must——"

"Hold, h-o-o-old!" roared Hum-Drum. "It is certainly my turn now. My rooted and insubvertible conviction is, that the causes of the anomalies evident in the princess's condition are strictly and solely physical. But that is only tantamount to acknowledging that they exist. Hear my opinion.—From some cause or other, of no importance to our inquiry, the motion of her heart has been reversed. That remarkable combination of the suction and the force-pump works the wrong way—I mean in the case of the unfortunate princess: it draws in where it should force out, and forces out where it should draw in. The offices of the auricles and the ventricles are subverted. The blood is sent forth by the veins, and returns by the arteries. Consequently it is running the wrong way through all her corporeal organism—lungs and all. Is it then at all mysterious, seeing that such is the case, that on the other particular of gravitation as well, she should differ from normal humanity? My proposal for the cure is this:—

"Phlebotomize until she is reduced to the last point of safety. Let it be effected, if necessary, in a warm bath. When she is reduced to a state of perfect asphyxy, apply a ligature to the left ankle, drawing it as tight as the bone will bear. Apply, at the same moment, another of equal tension around the right wrist. By means of plates constructed for the purpose, place the other foot and hand under the receivers of two air-pumps. Exhaust the receivers. Exhibit a pint of French brandy, and await the result."

"Which would presently arrive in the form of grim Death," said Kopy-Keck.

"If it should, she would yet die in doing our duty," retorted Hum-Drum.

But their Majesties had too much tenderness for their volatile offspring to subject her to either of the schemes of the equally unscrupulous philosophers. Indeed, the most complete knowledge of the laws of nature would have been unserviceable in her case; for it was impossible to classify her. She was a fifth imponderable body, sharing all the other properties of the ponderable.

· 8 ·

Try a Drop of Water.

Perhaps the best thing for the princess would have been to fall in love. But how a princess who had no gravity could fall into anything is a difficulty—perhaps *the* difficulty.

As for her own feelings on the subject, she did not even know that there was such a beehive of honey and stings to be fallen into. But now I come to mention another curious fact about her.

The palace was built on the shores of the loveliest lake in the world; and the princess loved this lake more than father or mother. The root of this preference no doubt, although the princess did not recognise it as such, was, that the moment she got into it, she recovered the natural right of which she had been so wickedly deprived—namely, gravity. Whether this was owing to the fact that water had been employed as the means of conveying the injury, I do not know. But it is certain that she could swim and dive like the duck that her old nurse said she was. The manner in which this alleviation of her misfortune was discovered was as follows.

One summer evening, during the carnival of the country, she had been taken upon the lake by the king and queen, in the royal barge. They were accompanied by many of the courtiers in a fleet of little boats. In the middle of the lake she wanted to get into the lord chancellor's barge, for his daughter, who was a great favourite with her, was in it with her father. Now though the old king rarely condescended to make light of his misfortune, yet, happening on this occasion to be in a particularly good humour, as the barges approached each other, he caught up the princess to throw her into the chancellor's barge. He lost his balance, however, and, dropping into the bottom of the barge, lost his hold of his daughter; not, however, before imparting to her the downward tendency of his own person, though in a somewhat different direction; for, as the king fell into the boat, she fell into the water. With a burst of delighted laughter she disappeared in the lake. A cry of horror ascended from the boats. They had never seen the princess go down before. Half the men were under water in a moment; but they had all, one after another, come up to the surface again for breath, when—tinkle, tinkle, babble, and gush! came the princess's laugh over the water from far away. There she was, swimming like a swan. Nor would she come out for king or queen, chancellor or daughter. She was perfectly obstinate.

But at the same time she seemed more sedate than usual. Perhaps that was because a great pleasure spoils laughing. At all events, after this, the passion of her life was to get into the water, and she was always the better behaved and the more beautiful the more she had of it. Summer and winter it was quite the same; only she could not stay so long in the water when they had to break the ice to let her in. Any day, from morning till evening in summer, she might be descried—a streak of white in the blue water—lying as still as the shadow of a cloud, or shooting along like a dolphin; disappearing, and coming up again far off, just where one did not expect her. She would have been in the lake of a night, too, if she could have had her way; for the balcony of her window overhung a deep pool in it; and through a shallow reedy passage she could have swum out into the wide wet water, and no one would have been any

the wiser. Indeed, when she happened to wake in the moonlight she could hardly resist the temptation. But there was the sad difficulty of getting into it. She had as great a dread of the air as some children have of the water. For the slightest gust of wind would blow her away; and a gust might arise in the stillest moment. And if she gave herself a push towards the water and just failed of reaching it, her situation would be dreadfully awkward, irrespective of the wind; for at best there she would have to remain, suspended in her nightgown, till she was seen and angled for by someone from the window.

"Oh! if I had my gravity," thought she, contemplating the water, "I would flash off this balcony like a long white sea-bird, headlong into the darling wetness. Heigh-ho!"

This was the only consideration that made her wish to be like other people.

Another reason for her being fond of the water was that in it alone she enjoyed any freedom. For she could not walk out without a *cortége*, consisting in part of a troop of light horse, for fear of the liberties which the wind might take with her. And the king grew more apprehensive with increasing years, till at last he would not allow her to walk abroad at all without some twenty silken cords fastened to as many parts of her dress, and held by twenty noblemen. Of course horseback was out of the question. But she bade good-by to all this ceremony when she got into the water.

And so remarkable were its effects upon her, especially in restoring her for the time to the ordinary human gravity, that Hum-Drum and Kopy-Keck agreed in recommending the king to bury her alive for three years; in the hope that, as the water did her so much good, the earth would do her yet more. But the king had some vulgar prejudices against the experiment, and would not give his consent. Foiled in this, they yet agreed in another recommendation; which, seeing that one imported his opinions from China and the other from Thibet, was very remarkable indeed. They argued that, if water of external origin and application could be so efficacious, water from a deeper source might work a perfect cure; in short, that if the poor afflicted princess could by any means be made to cry, she might recover her lost gravity.

But how was this to be brought about? Therein lay all the difficulty—to meet which the philosophers were not wise enough. To make the princess cry was as impossible as to make her weigh. They sent for a professional beggar; commanded him to prepare his most touching oracle of woe; helped him out of the court charade box, to whatever he wanted for dressing up, and promised great rewards in the event of his success. But it was all in vain. She listened to the mendicant artist's story, and gazed at his marvellous make up, till she could contain herself no longer, and went into the most undignified contortions for relief, shrieking, positively screeching with laughter.

When she had a little recovered herself, she

ordered her attendants to drive him away, and not give him a single copper; whereupon his look of mortified discomfiture wrought her punishment and his revenge, for it sent her into violent hysterics, from which she was with difficulty recovered.

But so anxious was the king that the suggestion should have a fair trial, that he put himself in a rage one day, and, rushing up to her room, gave her an awful whipping. Yet not a tear would flow. She looked grave, and her laughing sounded uncommonly like screaming—that was all. The good old tyrant, though he put on his best gold spectacles to look, could not discover the smallest cloud in the serene blue of her eyes.

· 9 ·

Put Me in Again.

It must have been about this time that the son of a king, who lived a thousand miles from Lagobel, set out to look for the daughter of a queen. He

48

travelled far and wide, but as sure as he found a princess, he found some fault in her. Of course he could not marry a mere woman, however beautiful; and there was no princess to be found worthy of him. Whether the prince was so near perfection that he had a right to demand perfection itself, I cannot pretend to say. All I know is, that he was a fine, handsome, brave, generous, well-bred, and well-behaved youth, as all princes are.

In his wanderings he had come across some reports about our princess; but as everybody said she was bewitched, he never dreamed that she could bewitch him. For what indeed could a prince do with a princess that had lost her gravity? Who could tell what she might not lose next? She might lose her visibility, or her tangibility; or, in short, the power of making impressions upon the radical sensorium; so that he should never be able to tell whether she was dead or alive. Of course he made no further inquiries about her.

One day he lost sight of his retinue in a great

forest. These forests are very useful in delivering princes from their courtiers, like a sieve that keeps back the bran. Then the princes get away to follow their fortunes. In this way they have the advantage of the princesses, who are forced to marry before they have had a bit of fun. I wish our princesses got lost in a forest sometimes.

One lovely evening, after wandering about for many days, he found that he was approaching the outskirts of this forest; for the trees had got so thin that he could see the sunset through them; and he soon came upon a kind of heath. Next he came upon signs of human neighbourhood; but by this time it was getting late, and there was nobody in the fields to direct him.

After travelling for another hour, his horse, quite worn out with long labour and lack of food, fell, and was unable to rise again. So he continued his journey on foot. At length he entered another wood—not a wild forest, but a civilized wood, through which a footpath led him to the side of a lake. Along this path the prince pursued his way through the gathering darkness. Suddenly he paused, and listened. Strange sounds came across the water. It was, in fact, the princess laughing. Now there was something odd in her laugh, as I have already hinted; for the hatching of a real hearty laugh requires the incubation of gravity; and perhaps this was how the prince mistook the laughter for screaming. Looking over the lake, he saw something white in the water; and, in an instant, he had torn off his tunic, kicked off his sandals, and plunged in. He soon reached the white object, and found that it was a woman. There was not light enough to show that she was a princess, but quite enough to show that she was a lady, for it does not want much light to see that.

Now I cannot tell how it came about,—whether she pretended to be drowning, or whether he frightened her, or caught her so as to embarrass her,—but certainly he brought her to shore in a fashion ignominious to a swimmer, and more nearly drowned than she had ever expected to be; for the water had got into her throat as often as she had tried to speak.

At the place to which he bore her, the bank was only a foot or two above the water; so he gave her a strong lift out of the water, to lay her on the bank. But, her gravitation ceasing the moment she left the water, away she went up into the air, scolding and screaming.

"You naughty, *naughty*, NAUGHTY, NAUGHTY man!" she cried.

No one had ever succeeded in putting her into a passion before.—When the prince saw her ascend, he thought he must have been bewitched, and have mistaken a great swan for a lady. But the princess caught hold of the topmost cone upon a lofty fir. This came off; but she caught at another; and, in fact, stopped herself by gathering cones, dropping them as the stalks gave way. The prince, meantime, stood in the water, staring, and forgetting to get out. But the princess disappearing, he scrambled on shore, and went in the direction of the tree. There he found her climbing down one of the branches towards the stem. But in the darkness of the wood, the prince continued in some bewilderment as to what the phenomenon could be; until, reaching the ground, and seeing him standing there, she caught hold of him, and said,—

"I'll tell papa."

"Oh no, you won't!" returned the prince.

"Yes, I will," she persisted. "What business had you to pull me down out of the water, and throw me to the bottom of the air? I never did you any harm."

"Pardon me. I did not mean to hurt you."

"I don't believe you have any brains; and that is a worse loss than your wretched gravity. I pity you."

The prince now saw that he had come upon the bewitched princess, and had already offended her. But before he could think what to say next, she burst out angrily, giving a stamp with her foot that would have sent her aloft again but for the hold she had of his arm,—

"Put me up directly."

"Put you up where, you beauty?" asked the prince.

He had fallen in love with her almost, already; for her anger made her more charming than any one else had ever beheld her; and, as far as he could see, which certainly was not far, she had not a single fault about her, except, of course, that she had not any gravity. No prince, however, would judge of a princess by weight. The loveliness of her foot he would hardly estimate by the depth of the impression it could make in mud.

"Put you up where, you beauty?" asked the prince.

"In the water, you stupid!" answered the princess.

"Come, then," said the prince.

The condition of her dress, increasing her usual difficulty in walking, compelled her to cling to him; and he could hardly persuade himself that he was not in a delightful dream, notwithstanding the torrent of musical abuse with which she overwhelmed him. The prince being therefore in no hurry, they came upon the lake at quite another part, where the bank was twenty-five feet high at least; and when they had reached the edge, he turned towards the princess, and said,—

"How am I to put you in?"

"That is your business," she answered, quite snappishly. "You took me out—put me in again."

"Very well," said the prince; and, catching her up in his arms, he sprang with her from the rock. The princess had just time to give one delighted shriek of laughter before the water closed over them. When they came to the surface, she found that, for a moment or two, she could not even laugh, for she had gone down with such a rush, that it was with difficulty she recovered her breath. The instant they reached the surface—

"How do you like falling in?" said the prince.

After some effort the princess panted out,—

"Is that what you call *falling in?*"

"Yes," answered the prince, "I should think it a very tolerable specimen."

"It seemed to me like going up," rejoined she.

"My feeling was certainly one of elevation too," the prince conceded.

The princess did not appear to understand him, for she retorted his question:—

"How do *you* like falling in?" said the princess.

"Beyond everything," answered he; "for I have fallen in with the only perfect creature I ever saw."

"No more of that: I am tired of it," said the princess.

Perhaps she shared her father's aversion to punning.

"Don't you like falling in then?" said the prince.

"It is the most delightful fun I ever had in my life," answered she. "I never fell before. I wish I could learn. To think I am the only person in my father's kingdom that can't fall!"

Here the poor princess looked almost sad.

"I shall be most happy to fall in with you any time you like," said the prince, devotedly.

"Thank you. I don't know. Perhaps it would not be proper. But I don't care. At all events, as we have fallen in, let us have a swim together."

"With all my heart," responded the prince.

And away they went, swimming, and diving, and floating, until at last they heard cries along the shore, and saw lights glancing in all directions. It was now quite late, and there was no moon.

"I must go home," said the princess. "I am very sorry, for this is delightful."

"So am I," returned the prince. "But I am glad I haven't a home to go to—at least, I don't exactly know where it is."

"I wish I hadn't one either," rejoined the princess; "it is so stupid! I have a great mind," she continued, "to play them all a trick. Why couldn't they leave me alone? They won't trust me in the lake for a single night!—You see where that green light is burning? That is the window of my room. Now if you would just swim there with me very quietly, and when we are all but under the balcony, give me such a push—*up* you call it—as you did a little while ago, I should be able to catch hold of the balcony, and get in at the window; and then they may look for me till to-morrow morning!"

"With more obedience than pleasure," said the prince, gallantly; and away they swam, very gently.

"Will you be in the lake to-morrow night?" the prince ventured to ask.

"To be sure I will. I don't think so. Perhaps," was the princess's somewhat strange answer.

But the prince was intelligent enough not to press her further; and merely whispered, as he gave her the parting lift, "Don't tell." The only answer the princess returned was a roguish look. She was already a yard above his head. The look seemed to say, "Never fear. It is too good fun to spoil that way."

So perfectly like other people had she been in the water, that even yet the prince could scarcely believe his eyes when he saw her ascend slowly, grasp the balcony, and disappear through the window. He turned, almost expecting to see her still by his side. But he was alone in the water. So he swam away quietly, and watched the lights roving about the shore for hours after the princess was safe in her chamber. As soon as they disappeared, he landed in search of his tunic and sword, and, after some trouble, found them again. Then he made the best of his way round the lake to the other side. There the wood was wilder, and the shore steeper—rising more immediately towards the mountains which surrounded the lake on all sides, and kept sending it messages of silvery streams from morning to night, and all night long. He soon found a spot whence he could see the green light in the princess's room, and where, even in the broad daylight, he would be in no danger of being discovered from the opposite shore. It was a sort of cave in the rock, where he provided himself a bed of withered leaves, and lay down too tired for hunger to keep him awake. All night long he dreamed that he was swimming with the princess.

• 10 •

Look at the Moon.

Early the next morning the prince set out to look for something to eat, which he soon found at a forester's hut, where for many following days he was supplied with all that a brave prince could consider necessary. And having plenty to keep him alive for the present, he would not think of wants not yet in existence. Whenever Care intruded, this prince always bowed him out in the most princely manner.

When he returned from his breakfast to his watch-cave, he saw the princess already floating about in the lake, attended by the king and queen —whom he knew by their crowns—and a great company in lovely little boats, with canopies of all the colours of the rainbow, and flags and streamers of a great many more. It was a very bright day, and soon the prince, burned up with the heat, began to long for the cold water and the cool princess. But he had to endure till twilight; for the boats had provisions on board, and it was not till the sun went down that the gay party began to vanish. Boat after boat drew away to the shore, following that of the king and queen, till only one, apparently the princess's own boat, remained. But she did not want to go home even yet, and the prince thought he saw her order the boat to the shore without her. At all events, it rowed away; and now, of all the radiant company, only one white speck remained. Then the prince began to sing.

And this is what he sung:—

> "*Lady fair,*
> *Swan-white,*

Lift thine eyes,
Banish night
By the might
Of thine eyes.

Snowy arms,
Oars of snow,
Oar her hither,
Plashing low.
Soft and slow,
Oar her hither.

Stream behind her
O'er the lake,
Radiant whiteness!
In her wake
Following, following for her sake
Radiant whiteness!

Cling about her,
Waters blue;
Part not from her,

But renew
Cold and true
Kisses round her.

Lap me round,
Waters sad
That have left her
Make me glad,
For ye had
Kissed her ere ye left her."

Before he had finished his song, the princess was just under the place where he sat, and looking up to find him. Her ears had led her truly.

"Would you like a fall, princess?" said the prince, looking down.

"Ah! there you are! Yes, if you please, prince," said the princess, looking up.

"How do you know I am a prince, princess?" said the prince.

"Because you are a very nice young man, prince," said the princess.

"Come up then, princess."

"Fetch me, prince."

The prince took off his scarf, then his sword-belt, then his tunic, and tied them all together, and let them down. But the line was far too short. He unwound his turban, and added it to the rest, when it was all but long enough; and his purse completed it. The princess just managed to lay hold of the knot of money, and was beside him in a moment. This rock was much higher than the other, and the splash and the dive were tremendous. The princess was in ecstasies of delight, and their swim was delicious.

Night after night they met, and swam about in the dark clear lake; where such was the prince's gladness, that (whether the princess's way of looking at things infected him, or he was actually getting light-headed) he often fancied that he was swimming in the sky instead of the lake. But when he talked about being in heaven, the princess laughed at him dreadfully.

When the moon came, she brought them fresh pleasure. Everything looked strange and new in her light, with an old, withered, yet unfading newness. When the moon was nearly full, one of their great delights was, to dive deep in the water, and then, turning round, look up through it at the great blot of light close above them, shimmering and trembling and wavering, spreading and contracting, seeming to melt away, and again grow solid. Then they would shoot up through the blot; and lo! there was the moon, far off, clear and steady and cold, and very lovely, at the bottom of a deeper and bluer lake than theirs, as the princess said.

The prince soon found out that while in the water the princess was very like other people. And besides this, she was not so forward in her questions or pert in her replies at sea as on shore. Neither did she laugh so much; and when she did laugh, it was more gently. She seemed altogether more modest and maidenly in the water than out of it.

But when the prince, who had really fallen in love when he fell in the lake, began to talk to her about love, she always turned her head towards him and laughed. After a while she began to look puzzled, as if she were trying to understand what he meant, but could not—revealing a notion that he meant something. But as soon as ever she left the lake, she was so altered, that the prince said to himself, "If I marry her, I see no help for it: we must turn merman and mermaid, and go out to sea at once."

· *II* ·

Hiss!

The princess's pleasure in the lake had grown to a passion, and she could scarcely bear to be out of it for an hour. Imagine then her consternation, when, diving with the prince one night, a sudden suspicion seized her that the lake was not so deep as it used to be. The prince could not imagine what had happened. She shot to the surface, and, without a word, swam at full speed towards the higher side of the lake. He followed, begging to know if she was ill, or what was the matter. She never turned her head, or took the smallest notice of his question. Arrived at the shore, she coasted the rocks with minute inspection. But she was not able to come to a conclusion, for the moon was very small, and so she could not see well. She turned therefore and swam home, without saying a word to explain her conduct to the prince, of whose presence she seemed no longer conscious. He withdrew to his cave, in great perplexity and distress.

Next day she made many observations, which, alas! strengthened her fears. She saw that the banks were too dry; and that the grass on the shore, and the trailing plants on the rocks, were withering away. She caused marks to be made along the borders, and examined them, day after day, in all directions of the wind; till at last the horrible idea became a certain fact—that the surface of the lake was slowly sinking.

The poor princess nearly went out of the little mind she had. It was awful to her to see the lake, which she loved more than any living thing, lie dying before her eyes. It sank away, slowly vanishing. The tops of rocks that had never been seen till now, began to appear far down in the clear water. Before long they were dry in the sun. It was fearful to think of the mud that would soon lie there baking and festering, full of lovely creatures dying, and ugly creatures coming to life, like the unmaking of a world. And how hot the sun would be without any lake! She could not bear to swim in it any more, and began to pine away. Her life seemed bound up with it; and ever as the lake sank, she pined. People said she would not live an hour after the lake was gone.

But she never cried.

Proclamation was made to all the kingdom, that whosoever should discover the cause of the lake's decrease, would be rewarded after a princely fashion. Hum-Drum and Kopy-Keck applied themselves to their physics and metaphysics; but in vain. Not even they could suggest a cause.

Now the fact was that the old princess was at the root of the mischief. When she heard that her niece found more pleasure in the water than any one else out of it, she went into a rage, and cursed herself for her want of foresight.

"But," said she, "I will soon set all right. The king and the people shall die of thirst; their brains shall boil and frizzle in their skulls before I will lose my revenge."

And she laughed a ferocious laugh, that made the hairs on the back of her black cat stand erect with terror.

Then she went to an old chest in the room, and opening it, took out what looked like a piece of dried seaweed. This she threw into a tub of water. Then she threw some powder into the water, and stirred it with her bare arm, muttering over it words of hideous sound, and yet more hideous import. Then she set the tub aside, and took from the chest a huge bunch of a hundred rusty keys, that clattered in her shaking hands. Then she sat down and proceeded to oil them all. Before she had finished, out from the tub, the water of which had kept on a slow motion ever since she had ceased stirring it, came the head and half the body of a huge gray snake. But the witch did not look round. It grew out of the tub, waving itself backwards and forwards with a slow horizontal motion, till it reached the princess, when it laid its head upon her shoulder, and gave a low hiss in her ear. She started—but with joy; and seeing the head resting on her shoulder, drew it towards her and kissed it. Then she drew it all out of the tub, and wound it round her body. It was one of those dreadful creatures which few have ever beheld— the White Snakes of Darkness.

Then she took the keys and went down to her cellar; and as she unlocked the door she said to herself,—

"This *is* worth living for!"

Locking the door behind her, she descended a few steps into the cellar, and crossing it, unlocked another door into a dark, narrow passage. She locked this also behind her, and descended a few more steps. If any one had followed the witch-princess, he would have heard her unlock exactly one hundred doors, and descend a few steps after unlocking each. When she had unlocked the last, she entered a vast cave, the roof of which was supported by huge natural pillars of rock. Now this roof was the under side of the bottom of the lake.

She then untwined the snake from her body, and held it by the tail high above her. The hideous creature stretched up its head towards the roof of the cavern, which it was just able to reach. It then began to move its head backwards and forwards, with a slow oscillating motion, as if looking for something. At the same moment the witch began to walk round and round the cavern, coming nearer to the centre every circuit; while the head

of the snake described the same path over the roof
that she did over the floor, for she kept holding it
up. And still it kept slowly oscillating. Round and
round the cavern they went, ever lessening the
circuit, till at last the snake made a sudden dart,
and clung to the roof with its mouth.

"That's right, my beauty!" cried the princess;
"drain it dry."

She let it go, left it hanging, and sat down on a
great stone, with her black cat, which had followed
her all round the cave, by her side. Then she began
to knit and mutter awful words. The snake hung
like a huge leech, sucking at the stone; the cat
stood with his back arched, and his tail like a piece
of cable, looking up at the snake; and the old
woman sat and knitted and muttered. Seven days
and seven nights they remained thus; when suddenly the serpent dropped from the roof as if
exhausted, and shrivelled up till it was again like
a piece of dried seaweed. The witch started to her
feet, picked it up, put it in her pocket, and looked

up at the roof. One drop of water was trembling on the spot where the snake had been sucking. As soon as she saw that, she turned and fled, followed by her cat. Shutting the door in a terrible hurry, she locked it, and having muttered some frightful words, sped to the next, which also she locked and muttered over; and so with all the hundred doors, till she arrived in her own cellar. Then she sat down on the floor ready to faint, but listening with malicious delight to the rushing of the water, which she could hear distinctly through all the hundred doors.

But this was not enough. Now that she had tasted revenge, she lost her patience. Without further measures, the lake would be too long in disappearing. So the next night, with the last shred of the dying old moon rising, she took some of the water in which she had revived the snake, put it in a bottle, and set out, accompanied by her cat. Before morning she had made the entire circuit of the lake, muttering fearful words as she crossed every stream, and casting into it some of the water out of her bottle. When she had finished the circuit she muttered yet again, and flung a handful of water towards the moon. Thereupon every spring in the country ceased to throb and bubble, dying away like the pulse of a dying man. The next day there was no sound of falling water to be heard along the borders of the lake. The very courses were dry; and the mountains showed no silvery streaks down their dark sides. And not alone had the fountains of mother Earth ceased to flow; for all the babies throughout the country were crying dreadfully—only without tears.

· *12* ·

Where Is the Prince?

Never since the night when the princess left him so abruptly had the prince had a single interview with her. He had seen her once or twice in the lake; but as far as he could discover, she had not been in it any more at night. He had sat and sung, and looked in vain for his Nereid; while she, like a true Nereid, was wasting away with her lake, sinking as it sank, withering as it dried. When at length he discovered the change that was taking place in the level of the water, he was in great alarm and perplexity. He could not tell whether the lake was dying because the lady had forsaken it; or whether the lady would not come because the lake had begun to sink. But he resolved to know so much at least.

He disguised himself, and, going to the palace, requested to see the lord chamberlain. His appearance at once gained his request; and the lord chamberlain, being a man of some insight, perceived that there was more in the prince's solicitation than met the ear. He felt likewise that no one could tell whence a solution of the present difficulties might arise. So he granted the prince's prayer to be made shoeblack to the princess. It was rather cunning in the prince to request such an easy post, for the princess could not possibly soil as many shoes as other princesses.

He soon learned all that could be told about the princess. He went nearly distracted; but after roaming about the lake for days, and diving in every depth that remained, all that he could do was to put an extra polish on the dainty pair of boots that was never called for.

For the princess kept her room, with the curtains drawn to shut out the dying lake. But she could not shut it out of her mind for a moment. It haunted her imagination so that she felt as if the lake were her soul, drying up within her, first to mud, then to madness and death. She thus brooded over the change, with all its dreadful accompaniments, till she was nearly distracted. As for the prince, she had forgotten him. However much she had enjoyed his company in the water, she did not care for him without it. But she seemed to have forgotten her father and mother too.

The lake went on sinking. Small slimy spots

began to appear, which glittered steadily amidst the changeful shine of the water. These grew to broad patches of mud, which widened and spread, with rocks here and there, and floundering fishes and crawling eels swarming. The people went everywhere catching these, and looking for anything that might have dropped from the royal boats.

At length the lake was all but gone, only a few of the deepest pools remaining unexhausted.

It happened one day that a party of youngsters found themselves on the brink of one of these pools in the very centre of the lake. It was a rocky basin of considerable depth. Looking in, they saw at the bottom something that shone yellow in the sun. A little boy jumped in and dived for it. It was a plate of gold covered with writing. They carried it to the king. On one side of it stood these words:—

"Death alone from death can save.
Love is death, and so is brave—

Love can fill the deepest grave.
Love loves on beneath the wave.''

Now this was enigmatical enough to the king and courtiers. But the reverse of the plate explained it a little. Its writing amounted to this:—

''If the lake should disappear, they must find the hole through which the water ran. But it would be useless to try to stop it by any ordinary means. There was but one effectual mode.—The body of a living man could alone stanch the flow. The man must give himself of his own will; and the lake must take his life as it filled. Otherwise the offering would be of no avail. If the nation could not provide one hero, it was time it should perish.''

· *13* ·

Here I Am.

This was a very disheartening revelation to the king—not that he was unwilling to sacrifice a subject, but that he was hopeless of finding a man willing to sacrifice himself. No time was to be lost, however, for the princess was lying motionless on her bed, and taking no nourishment but lake-water, which was now none of the best. Therefore the king caused the contents of the wonderful plate of gold to be published throughout the country.

No one, however, came forward.

The prince, having gone several days' journey into the forest, to consult a hermit whom he had met there on his way to Lagobel, knew nothing of the oracle till his return.

When he had acquainted himself with all the particulars, he sat down and thought,—

"She will die if I don't do it, and life would be nothing to me without her; so I shall lose nothing by doing it. And life will be as pleasant to her as ever, for she will soon forget me. And there will be so much more beauty and happiness in the world! —To be sure, I shall not see it." (Here the poor prince gave a sigh.) "How lovely the lake will be in the moonlight, with that glorious creature sporting in it like a wild goddess!—It is rather hard to be drowned by inches, though. Let me see—that will be seventy inches of me to drown." (Here he tried to laugh, but could not.) "The longer the better, however," he resumed: "for can I not bargain that the princess shall be beside me all the time? So I shall see her once more, kiss her perhaps, —who knows? and die looking in her eyes. It will be no death. At least, I shall not feel it. And to see the lake filling for the beauty again!—All right! I am ready."

He kissed the princess's boot, laid it down, and hurried to the king's apartment. But feeling, as he went, that anything sentimental would be disagreeable, he resolved to carry off the whole affair with nonchalance. So he knocked at the door of the king's counting-house, where it was all but a capital crime to disturb him.

When the king heard the knock he started up, and opened the door in a rage. Seeing only the shoeblack, he drew his sword. This, I am sorry to say, was his usual mode of asserting his regality when he thought his dignity was in danger. But the prince was not in the least alarmed.

"Please your Majesty, I'm your butler," said he.

"My butler! you lying rascal! What do you mean?"

"I mean, I will cork your big bottle."

"Is the fellow mad?" bawled the king, raising the point of his sword.

"I will put a stopper—plug—what you call it, in your leaky lake, grand monarch," said the prince.

The king was in such a rage that before he could speak he had time to cool, and to reflect that it would be great waste to kill the only man who was willing to be useful in the present emergency, seeing that in the end the insolent fellow would be as dead as if he had died by his Majesty's own hand.

"Oh!" said he at last, putting up his sword with

difficulty, it was so long; "I am obliged to you, you young fool! Take a glass of wine?"

"No, thank you," replied the prince.

"Very well," said the king. "Would you like to run and see your parents before you make your experiment?"

"No, thank you," said the prince.

"Then we will go and look for the hole at once," said his Majesty, and proceeded to call some attendants.

"Stop, please your Majesty; I have a condition to make," interposed the prince.

"What!" exclaimed the king, "a condition! and with me! How dare you?"

"As you please," returned the prince, coolly. "I wish your Majesty a good morning."

"You wretch! I will have you put in a sack, and stuck in the hole."

"Very well, your Majesty," replied the prince, becoming a little more respectful, lest the wrath of the king should deprive him of the pleasure of

dying for the princess. "But what good will that do your Majesty? Please to remember that the oracle says the victim must offer himself."

"Well, you *have* offered yourself," retorted the king.

"Yes, upon one condition."

"Condition again!" roared the king, once more drawing his sword. "Begone! Somebody else will be glad enough to take the honour off your shoulders."

"Your Majesty knows it will not be easy to get another to take my place."

"Well, what is your condition?" growled the king, feeling that the prince was right.

"Only this," replied the prince: "that, as I must on no account die before I am fairly drowned, and the waiting will be rather wearisome, the princess, your daughter, shall go with me, feed me with her own hands, and look at me now and then to comfort me; for you must confess it *is* rather hard. As soon as the water is up to my eyes, she may go and be happy, and forget her poor shoeblack."

Here the prince's voice faltered, and he very nearly grew sentimental, in spite of his resolution.

"Why didn't you tell me before what your condition was? Such a fuss about nothing!" exclaimed the king.

"Do you grant it?" persisted the prince.

"Of course I do," replied the king.

"Very well. I am ready."

"Go and have some dinner, then, while I set my people to find the place."

The king ordered out his guards, and gave directions to the officers to find the hole in the lake at once. So the bed of the lake was marked out in divisions and thoroughly examined, and in an hour or so the hole was discovered. It was in the middle of a stone, near the centre of the lake, in the very pool where the golden plate had been found. It was a three-cornered hole of no great size. There was water all round the stone, but very little was flowing through the hole.

This Is Very Kind of You.

The prince went to dress for the occasion, for he was resolved to die like a prince.

When the princess heard that a man had offered to die for her, she was so transported that she jumped off the bed, feeble as she was, and danced about the room for joy. She did not care who the man was; that was nothing to her. The hole wanted stopping; and if only a man would do, why, take one. In an hour or two more everything was ready. Her maid dressed her in haste, and they carried her to the side of the lake. When she saw it she shrieked, and covered her face with her hands. They bore her across to the stone where they had already placed a little boat for her.

The water was not deep enough to float it, but they hoped it would be, before long. They laid her on cushions, placed in the boat wines and fruits and other nice things, and stretched a canopy over all.

In a few minutes the prince appeared. The princess recognized him at once, but did not think it worth while to acknowledge him.

"Here I am," said the prince. "Put me in."

"They told me it was a shoeblack," said the princess.

"So I am," said the prince. "I blacked your little boots three times a day, because they were all I could get of you. Put me in."

The courtiers did not resent his bluntness, except by saying to each other that he was taking it out in impudence.

But how was he to be put in? The golden plate contained no instructions on this point. The prince looked at the hole, and saw but one way. He put both his legs into it, sitting on the stone, and, stooping forward, covered the corner that remained open with his two hands. In this uncomfortable position he resolved to abide his fate, and turning to the people, said,—

"Now you can go."

The king had already gone home to dinner.

"Now you can go," repeated the princess after him, like a parrot.

The people obeyed her and went.

Presently a little wave flowed over the stone, and wetted one of the prince's knees. But he did not mind it much. He began to sing, and the song he sang was this:—

> "*As a world that has no well,*
> *Darkly bright in forest dell;*
> *As a world without the gleam*
> *Of the downward-going stream;*
> *As a world without the glance*
> *Of the ocean's fair expanse;*
> *As a world where never rain*
> *Glittered on the sunny plain;—*
> *Such, my heart, thy world would be,*
> *If no love did flow in thee.*

As a world without the sound
Of the rivulets underground;
Or the bubbling of the spring
Out of darkness wandering;
Or the mighty rush and flowing
Of the river's downward going;
Or the music-showers that drop
On the outspread beech's top;
Or the ocean's mighty voice,
When his lifted waves rejoice;—
Such, my soul, thy world would be,
If no love did sing in thee.

Lady, keep thy world's delight;
Keep the waters in thy sight.
Love hath made me strong to go,
For thy sake, to realms below,
Where the water's shine and hum
Through the darkness never come;
Let, I pray, one thought of me
Spring, a little well, in thee;

Lest thy loveless soul be found
Like a dry and thirsty ground."

"Sing again, prince. It makes it less tedious," said the princess.

But the prince was too much overcome to sing any more, and a long pause followed.

"This is very kind of you, prince," said the princess at last, quite coolly, as she lay in the boat with her eyes shut.

"I am sorry I can't return the compliment," thought the prince; "but you are worth dying for, after all."

Again a wavelet, and another, and another flowed over the stone, and wetted both the prince's knees; but he did not speak or move. Two—three —four hours passed in this way, the princess apparently asleep, and the prince very patient. But he was much disappointed in his position, for he had none of the consolation he had hoped for.

At last he could bear it no longer.

"Princess!" said he.

But at the moment up started the princess, crying,—

"I'm afloat! I'm afloat!"

And the little boat bumped against the stone.

"Princess!" repeated the prince, encouraged by seeing her wide awake and looking eagerly at the water.

"Well?" said she, without looking round.

"Your papa promised that you should look at me, and you haven't looked at me once."

"Did he? Then I suppose I must. But I am so sleepy!"

"Sleep then, darling, and don't mind me," said the poor prince.

"Really, you are very good," replied the princess. "I think I will go to sleep again."

"Just give me a glass of wine and a biscuit first," said the prince, very humbly.

"With all my heart," said the princess, and gaped as she said it.

She got the wine and the biscuit, however, and leaning over the side of the boat towards him, was compelled to look at him.

"Why, prince," she said, "you don't look well! Are you sure you don't mind it?"

"Not a bit," answered he, feeling very faint indeed. "Only I shall die before it is of any use to you, unless I have something to eat."

"There, then," said she, holding out the wine to him.

"Ah! you must feed me. I dare not move my hands. The water would run away directly."

"Good gracious!" said the princess; and she began at once to feed him with bits of biscuit and sips of wine.

As she fed him, he contrived to kiss the tips of her fingers now and then. She did not seem to mind it, one way or the other. But the prince felt better.

"Now for your own sake, princess," said he, "I cannot let you go to sleep. You must sit and look at me, else I shall not be able to keep up."

"Well, I will do anything I can to oblige you," answered she, with condescension; and, sitting down, she did look at him, and kept looking at him with wonderful steadiness, considering all things.

The sun went down, and the moon rose, and, gush after gush, the waters were rising up the prince's body. They were up to his waist now.

"Why can't we go and have a swim?" said the princess. "There seems to be water enough just about here."

"I shall never swim more," said the prince.

"Oh, I forgot," said the princess, and was silent.

So the water grew and grew, and rose up and up on the prince. And the princess sat and looked at him. She fed him now and then. The night wore on. The waters rose and rose. The moon rose likewise higher and higher, and shone full on the face of the dying prince. The water was up to his neck.

"Will you kiss me, princess?" said he, feebly.

The nonchalance was all gone now.

"Yes, I will," answered the princess, and kissed him with a long, sweet, cold kiss.

"Now," said he, with a sigh of content, "I die happy."

He did not speak again. The princess gave him some wine for the last time: he was past eating. Then she sat down again, and looked at him. The water rose and rose. It touched his chin. It touched his lower lip. It touched between his lips. He shut them hard to keep it out. The princess began to feel strange. It touched his upper lip. He breathed through his nostrils. The princess looked wild. It covered his nostrils. Her eyes looked scared, and shone strange in the moonlight. His head fell back; the water closed over it, and the bubbles of his last breath bubbled up through the water. The princess gave a shriek, and sprang into the lake.

She laid hold first of one leg, and then of the other, and pulled and tugged, but she could not move either. She stopped to take breath, and that made her think that he could not get any breath. She was frantic. She got hold of him, and held his head above the water, which was possible now his hands were no longer on the hole. But it was of no use, for he was past breathing.

Love and water brought back all her strength. She got under the water, and pulled and pulled with her whole might, till at last she got one leg out. The other easily followed. How she got him into the boat she never could tell; but when she did, she fainted away. Coming to herself, she seized the oars, kept herself steady as best she could, and rowed and rowed, though she had never rowed before. Round rocks, and over shallows, and through mud she rowed, till she got to the landing-stairs of the palace. By this time her people were on the shore, for they had heard her shriek. She made them carry the prince to her own room, and lay him in her bed, and light a fire, and send for the doctors.

"But the lake, your Highness!" said the chamberlain, who, roused by the noise, came in, in his nightcap.

"Go and drown yourself in it!" she said.

This was the last rudeness of which the princess was ever guilty; and one must allow that she had good cause to feel provoked with the lord chamberlain.

Had it been the king himself, he would have fared no better. But both he and the queen were fast asleep. And the chamberlain went back to his bed. Somehow, the doctors never came. So the princess and her old nurse were left with the prince. But the old nurse was a wise woman, and knew what to do.

They tried everything for a long time without success. The princess was nearly distracted between hope and fear, but she tried on and on, one thing after another, and everything over and over again.

At last, when they had all but given it up, just as the sun rose, the prince opened his eyes.

· *15* ·

Look at the Rain!

The princess burst into a passion of tears, and *fell* on the floor. There she lay for an hour, and her tears never ceased. All the pent-up crying of her life was spent now. And a rain came on, such as had never been seen in that country. The sun shone all the time, and the great drops, which fell straight to the earth, shone likewise. The palace was in the heart of a rainbow. It was a rain of rubies, and sapphires, and emeralds, and topazes. The torrents poured from the mountains like molten gold; and if it had not been for its subterraneous outlet, the lake would have overflowed and inundated the country. It was full from shore to shore.

But the princess did not heed the lake. She lay on the floor and wept, and this rain within doors was far more wonderful than the rain out of doors.

For when it abated a little, and she proceeded to rise, she found, to her astonishment, that she could not. At length, after many efforts, she succeeded in getting upon her feet. But she tumbled down again directly. Hearing her fall, her old nurse uttered a yell of delight, and ran to her, screaming,—

"My darling child! she's found her gravity!"

"Oh, that's it! is it?" said the princess, rubbing her shoulder and her knee alternately. "I consider it very unpleasant. I feel as if I should be crushed to pieces."

"Hurrah!" cried the prince from the bed. "If you've come round, princess, so have I. How's the lake?"

"Brimful," answered the nurse.

"Then we're all happy."

"That we are indeed!" answered the princess, sobbing.

And there was rejoicing all over the country that rainy day. Even the babies forgot their past troubles, and danced and crowed amazingly. And the king told stories, and the queen listened to them. And he divided the money in his box, and she the honey in her pot, among all the children. And there was such jubilation as was never heard of before.

Of course the prince and princess were betrothed at once. But the princess had to learn to walk, before they could be married with any propriety. And this was not so easy at her time of life, for she could walk no more than a baby. She was always falling down and hurting herself.

"Is this the gravity you used to make so much of?" said she one day to the prince, as he raised her from the floor. "For my part, I was a great deal more comfortable without it."

"No, no, that's not it. This is it," replied the prince, as he took her up, and carried her about like a baby, kissing her all the time. "This is gravity."

"That's better," said she. "I don't mind that so much."

And she smiled the sweetest, loveliest smile in the prince's face. And she gave him one little kiss in return for all his; and he thought them overpaid, for he was beside himself with delight. I fear she complained of her gravity more than once after this, notwithstanding.

It was a long time before she got reconciled to walking. But the pain of learning it was quite counterbalanced by two things, either of which would have been sufficient consolation. The first was, that the prince himself was her teacher; and the second, that she could tumble into the lake as often as she pleased. Still, she preferred to have the prince jump in with her; and the splash they made before was nothing to the splash they made now.

The lake never sank again. In process of time, it wore the roof of the cavern quite through, and was twice as deep as before.

The only revenge the princess took upon her aunt was to tread pretty hard on her gouty toe the next time she saw her. But she was sorry for it the very next day, when she heard that the water had undermined her house, and that it had fallen in the night, burying her in its ruins; whence no one ever ventured to dig up her body. There she lies to this day.

So the prince and princess lived and were happy; and had crowns of gold, and clothes of cloth, and shoes of leather, and children of boys and girls, not one of whom was ever known, on the most critical occasion, to lose the smallest atom of his or her due proportion of gravity.